"I've never pitied you…"

Cody's eyes softened. "Yeah, I know." He took a step. "Willow."

"You'd better go." Willow's voice shook. "I'm glad your sentence was shortened. I hope that's behind you now. I wish you all the best—"

"Wow. That's like a Dear John letter. Is that how you really want it, Willow?"

"Yes," she said.

"You…love him?" For a long moment Cody didn't speak again, then with his voice barely above a whisper, he said, "Do you love him as much as you said you loved me?"

What she needed to say, what he needed to hear, was yes, but the word stuck in her throat. Her lips pressed tight, she could only nod.

She'd never imagined seeing Cody up close again, hearing his voice flow over her like water or smelling the clean, fresh masculine scent of his skin. Feeling like this.

"Go." Then she forced herself to say, "For your own good, Cody. Don't come back."

Dear Reader,

Mistletoe Cowboy is the latest in my Kansas Cowboys series, but I've "known" Cody Jones since he first came on the scene in *Last Chance Cowboy*. Cody was a bad boy even then and reappeared in *Twins Under the Tree*. Now he's back—having gone from bad to worse. An ex-con, he's determined to really turn his life around this time. Oh, and to win Willow Bodine's love forever. Too bad she's engaged to someone else.

Why did I choose to write about this bad boy? I fell for Cody right away, and so did readers, who asked me to please give him a book of his own. He's made mistakes, yet he's sweet and has a good heart. And as a bonus, there's the other love of Cody's life, a mustang mare he calls Diva.

By the way, she's loosely modeled after a noble horse my husband and I once owned. Like Diva, Windsor Castle had quite the life. For a time, as a member of the mounted police force in New Haven, he even became a local celebrity. On his regular patrols downtown, he always stopped at one of the museums to wait until a staff member came out with his daily apple. Still miss you, buddy.

I hope you all enjoy the ups and downs Diva, Cody and Willow go through in *Mistletoe Cowboy* while seeking their happy ending!

All my best,

Leigh

HEARTWARMING

Mistletoe Cowboy

Leigh Riker

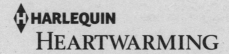

HARLEQUIN
HEARTWARMING

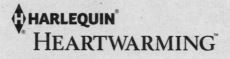

ISBN-13: 978-1-335-88996-6

Mistletoe Cowboy

Copyright © 2020 by Leigh Riker

Recycling programs for this product may not exist in your area.

This edition published by arrangement with Harlequin Books S.A.

For questions and comments about the quality of this book, please contact us at CustomerService@Harlequin.com.

Harlequin Enterprises ULC
22 Adelaide St. West, 40th Floor
Toronto, Ontario M5H 4E3, Canada
www.Harlequin.com

Printed in U.S.A.

Leigh Riker, like so many dedicated readers, grew up with her nose in a book, and weekly trips to the local library for a new stack of stories were a favorite thing to do. This award-winning *USA TODAY* bestselling author still can't imagine a better way to spend her time than to curl up with a good romance novel—unless it is to write one! She is a member of the Authors Guild, Novelists, Inc. and Romance Writers of America. When not at the computer, she's out on the patio tending flowers, watching hummingbirds, spending time with family and friends, or, perhaps, traveling (for research purposes, of course). She loves to hear from readers. You can find Leigh on her website, leighriker.com, on Facebook at leighrikerauthor and on Twitter, @lbrwriter.

Books by Leigh Riker

Harlequin Heartwarming

Kansas Cowboys

The Reluctant Rancher
Last Chance Cowboy
Cowboy on Call
Her Cowboy Sheriff
The Rancher's Second Chance
Twins Under the Tree
The Cowboy's Secret Baby

A Heartwarming Thanksgiving
"Her Thanksgiving Soldier"
Lost and Found Family
Man of the Family
If I Loved YouTitle

Visit the Author Profile page at Harlequin.com for more titles.

For Oliver

Welcome to this beautiful world, sweet boy.

You already have my heart.

CHAPTER ONE

"HE'S GETTING OUT."

Her brother's grim statement took Willow Bodine by surprise. Those few words shocked her, really, from the base of her blond ponytail to her polished boots. The hard tone of his voice, though, wasn't the reason her heart skipped a beat. She turned from the dapple-gray horse she'd been grooming in the July morning sun outside the barn, one hand resting on Silver's warm sleek neck, then schooled her expression to resemble what she hoped was a blank slate. Her brother was testing her. "Am I supposed to react to that?"

Zach's mouth hardened, which seemed to be his default mode these days. Ever since their father's death, he'd looked mostly serious and determined—Willow knew a lot of that was her fault. Zach, who'd inherited the responsibility for the WB Ranch, wore the mantle well on his broad shoulders and had taken up the family cause—initially their dad's cause—about Cody Jones. "Just a warning," Zach told her now.

She tried a shrug. "Cody and I are done. We were finished before he left Barren."

Willow loved her brother. They'd been close until a few years ago when she'd practically destroyed their family because of her relationship with Cody. Since last December when their dad had died, she and Zach had been giving each other even more space.

He ran a hand through his hair, the color of dark honey. "Done? Left for a Kansas state prison, you mean. It's not as if Jones went on vacation to Hawaii."

Willow couldn't imagine Cody taking a fancy trip like that. Her brother might sometimes tease, calling her the Bodine princess, but Cody had come from nothing. Worse than that, even. She'd never pitied him—Cody wouldn't stand for that—but she'd always ached for him in her heart.

The prison was no beach resort—she'd seen that for herself. Without Zach's knowledge, she'd visited Cody soon after his sentence had been handed down last fall, and she would never forget the sight of him in those ugly prison scrubs across a table from her with a barrier between them. When he'd edged his hand through the small gap under the window, the guard nearby had frowned. Willow had quickly pulled back. If Cody had touched her, he'd be in even deeper trouble, and she would have been lost again in the dark pools of his eyes. Instead, she'd jumped up from her chair, said a choked goodbye over her shoulder, then run to her car.

"I thought his sentence was eleven months," she said at last, the maximum for the crime he'd committed. Why had he done such a foolish thing in the first place?

"Time off, I hear," Zach said, "for 'good behavior.'" His tone said that wasn't possible.

Willow stopped stroking her horse's neck. In her mind's eye, she could see Cody, who stood over six feet, his hair the shade of summer wheat, those dark eyes with a hint of humor, even mischief. "Then he's coming… home?" Not the wisest word she might have chosen.

A muscle ticked in Zach's jaw. His hazel eyes flickered. "If Cody Jones shows up in Barren…" His grip tightened on his belt as if he were wearing a holster with a sidearm. "If he tries to see you…"

"Zach, I make my own decisions." Cody was the worst of them in her brother's opinion. And perhaps he was right.

He said, "Jones steps one foot on this property, I'll—"

She threw up her hands. "What? End up in a holding cell at the sheriff's office?"

"It would be worth it," he said. "And talk about bad timing."

Zach was right about that. In the months Cody had been gone, Willow had finally begun to date someone else, and recently their relationship had turned serious, more so at first on his part than Willow had been prepared to deal with. But then a few nights ago, she had made a choice—one that eliminated Cody from any further consideration. It was so new she couldn't quite believe it was true.

"Jones broke your heart," Zach reminded her and her chin went up.

"Maybe I broke his, too."

He let out a harsh breath. "He's a loser, Willow. A lot of sweet talk, no substance. What has he ever done except herd cattle? Well… and steal a few head, then set that barn on fire. Not exactly the kind of man you should have brought home to Mom. Didn't Dad try to tell you about him?"

"Many times." Willow leaned her head against her horse's side. The mention of her father always made her eyes fill. During her worst times—after she and Cody broke up and he was arrested, then when her dad suffered a fatal heart attack for which she felt responsible—it was Silver that had listened to the hopelessness in Willow's voice as she tried to make sense of things. To somehow absolve herself of guilt. A lot of what Zach said about Cody was true. "You may be my big brother, but you don't need to worry about me."

"Yes, I do." That muscle jerked again. "I promised Dad I'd see to you and Mom." He choked up. "That was the last thing I said to him, and I keep my promises. He'd be rolling over in his grave if you took up with Jones again." He glanced at Willow's hand and the new ring she wore. "Especially now."

"Zach, lighten up. Why would I do that? Why are we having this discussion? Frankly, I feel insulted that you'd even mention him." She tried to change the subject. "Worry about yourself, why don't you—and the wife you still don't have."

He rubbed the back of his neck. This topic wasn't his favorite either. "If you meant why am I not seeing anyone special, when would I find the time? I have my hands full with this ranch—if it's the last thing I do, I'll preserve it for this family, you included."

Without another word, he disappeared into the barn, and Willow yearned for the simpler days when they'd been close. At least they weren't talking about Cody now.

She had to hope he wouldn't come anywhere near her.

PRISON HAD MADE a new man of him. A different one, anyway.

Cody Jones stepped out of Navarro Correctional Facility and took his first breath of free air in the better part of a year.

He gazed around, adjusting to the idea that he could do whatever he wanted now. Well, as long as he stayed in touch with his parole officer. He didn't dare blow that off or he'd be making a return trip through these gates to finish his full sentence—if he messed up again, more time might be added. He was starting the long walk down the driveway to the road where he'd hitch a ride when he noticed a familiar speed-yellow truck parked in one of the visitors' spots. The driver gave him a one-finger salute, which Cody hesitated to return. Having just gotten out, he shouldn't take up again with the wrong people.

But then, he'd been one of them. And his former partner in crime—their ringleader—had reportedly reformed. Cody was still a work in progress.

"Derek Moran." He strolled over to the pickup.

For a moment Cody considered the trouble he'd first gotten into with Derek and another guy, swiping cows from Wilson Cattle. Talk about dumb moves. They'd all avoided doing time for that after the ranch owner—Cody's boss then—refused to press charges. But Cody had been fired, and he'd made matters worse in a stupid attempt at revenge. After first running away, he'd returned long enough to torch Grey Wilson's barn and get himself sent up for arson. He had a lot to make up for now, a ton of apologies that needed to be said. "What're you doing here, Moran?"

Dark haired with pale blue eyes, Derek

jerked a thumb toward the prison. "Telling myself how lucky I was not to end up in that place."

"Yep. You were," Cody agreed. "Can't complain, though."

He tried what he hoped was a jaunty expression. "Three square meals a day, books to read, lots of exercise, no bills to pay..." But how much time would it really take before he saw himself as a free man, able to make his own choices again? To go anywhere he pleased?

Derek leaned an elbow on the open window. "How bad was it, really?"

"Bad at first," he admitted. "Thought I'd go crazy locked up in there."

Like Derek, Cody was used to being outdoors, having plenty of space to run, to ride, to just be. He flicked a glance toward the facility. He'd had plenty of company, though. The prison housed nearly two thousand men.

"I was lucky to be in minimum security. Even luckier to join their Wild Horse Program, training mustangs for adoption." One horse in particular, he meant, and his heart turned over. Cody was leaving a piece of himself behind.

Derek's eyes lit up. "Yeah? Horses? I'd rustle a few more head of cattle myself for that."

"No, you wouldn't. Trust me." Cody's gaze strayed again toward the farthest pasture, which he couldn't see from here. The mare would be there, head down in the tall grass, tail switching at flies. He would miss her. In fact, his heart was already bleeding. He'd been so close to getting her ready for someone to buy, all the while wishing he could adopt her, start his own business. Make something of himself.

He wondered if that could even work out—kind of like him and Willow Bodine.

"So." Derek shoved a hank of unruly hair off his face. "Need a ride?"

"Thanks." He had no other plans, no place to go. Cody rounded the truck to the passenger side. He could open this door, slide inside this cab, barrel down this drive with Derek. A man like other men. A man who needed to prove himself to the world somehow and not screw up this time. He climbed in.

He never had to see Navarro again. His pulse thudded in his throat. *I'm free*.

Prison did change a man, not for the worse.

He hoped. At least he would try his best to be a better person.

As they drove toward Barren, Cody half listened as Derek rattled on, catching him up on the local doings while Cody had been "away," as he called it. Derek was still playing the field, though he'd recently met a woman online he thought he'd like in person. Calvin Stern, their coconspirator with the cattle, was now living with his girlfriend. Of their old trouble-raising trio, Cody was the odd man out. For a moment he felt tempted to hop out at the nearest crossroads, head for parts unknown and make a totally new life for himself where people didn't know him. Except by the terms of his release, he had to stay in Stewart County. Still, he kept a hand on the door latch until all at once he really heard what Derek was saying. The last word stopped Cody's ruminations as his stomach bottomed out.

"…engaged." Derek slanted a look at Cody.

"Willow Bodine?" His blood stopped flowing. "She got engaged?"

"Just the other day. I wouldn't have known, but I ran into her brother—at Earl's Hardware—and he told me. Looked pleased as punch."

"I bet he did." Zachary Bodine had never

liked Cody, but he liked him even less near Willow, and he'd probably hoped Derek might pass on this message. An ache settled behind Cody's ribs. He'd made a lot of mistakes in his life—a straight streak through most of his twenties, especially here in Barren—that he needed to atone for, but he'd never thought Willow was one of them.

For a long moment, he entertained the fantasy of her, which had kept him sane during his time in prison. The mental image of her turned his knees weak. That silky blond hair to her waist, those cornflower blue eyes, her sassiness—at least with him. The lemon scent she always carried. There'd been a time when he thought Willow would find the courage to defy her father, leave home, choose Cody and become her own person, not the one other people thought they knew. His angel, he'd called her.

"You okay?" Derek glanced from the road. "Didn't mean to hit you with that."

"About Willow? Nah," he managed. "We split up around the time I got arrested and way before my trial." His throat ached. He tried to collect himself. Cody knew most of the eligible men in town, or he had before.

Maybe someone new had swept her off her feet. "Who's she planning to marry?"

"Thaddeus."

Cody sank deeper into the passenger seat. "Thad Nesbitt?"

"How many Thaddeuses do you know?"

Cody could have groaned aloud.

"He's had his eye on her for years, apparently," Derek said.

And Thad was quite a catch, already well-off through his family and his dad's profits from the oil fields up north. Before the old man had gone into politics, that is. A family of high achievers. Way out of Cody's league, and to make matters worse Thad had been a member of the prosecution's team at his trial.

"Did you hear Thad's father is the state's new attorney general?" Derek went on, the news getting more troubling with every word. "No wonder Zach couldn't be happier. His baby sister got herself a real prize."

What a pal, Derek. Thanks. Not that this didn't seem like a foregone conclusion. Cody should have seen it coming. The Bodines and Nesbitts were among the first families in the state.

A black depression threatened to swamp

Cody. Compared to Willow's fiancé, he was a complete nobody, the polar opposite of Thad Nesbitt. Not well educated, not rich, not employed even. And now Cody had a criminal record. Why would Willow give him the time of day again? And why was Derek rubbing salt in his wounds?

Never one to brood, Cody straightened, his steely gaze on the road ahead.

While he'd languished in prison, dreaming of her, Willow had sure been busy. Falling in love with someone else. Not that she didn't have a perfect right to do so.

"When's the wedding?"

Derek tapped one finger against the steering wheel. "I don't know, but the Bodines are putting on a big wingding of an engagement party soon."

Cody almost wished he could bypass Barren. Yet it seemed he had unfinished business with Willow still-Bodine. And, obviously, not much time. Once the wedding plans got rolling, there'd be no stopping that train.

"I think I'll have a talk with her anyway," he said.

Which didn't seem to surprise Derek.

CHAPTER TWO

JEAN BODINE WAS the strongest woman Willow had ever known. Her mother ran the WB ranch house with an iron fist wrapped in a velvet glove. But for a person with two names that humorously rhymed, she was certainly being serious today.

"Now, about this party." At the kitchen table Jean wrapped a strand of her still-blond hair around one finger, a nervous habit that had gotten worse since Willow's dad died.

"Party?" Willow repeated. She'd been in a fog since Zach had told her about Cody's early release from prison.

Her mother sighed. Her hazel eyes, like Zach's, met Willow's gaze. "You weren't listening, were you? Well, of course, we have to have a party to announce your engagement. Goodness, when I think of the guest list alone—friends and family, colleagues of Thad's father…"

"A houseful of important people," Willow murmured.

Her mom beamed. "I can imagine the event taking over this entire ranch."

Willow had never liked being on display, but shyness was not a valued Bodine trait. And for a time, she'd made up for that, feeling more comfortable with Cody, as if with him she'd been a different person. Even so, she'd always been happiest alone on the back of her horse, the wind in her face, the ground rushing past as she and Silver galloped across the fields. Her gaze strayed to the window. Thousands of acres of rich Kansas land spread out beyond the sparkling clean glass, and Willow wished she was out there now among the milling Herefords. Her morning ride, like her mood, had been short-circuited by the shocking news about Cody.

"The governor and his wife," Jean went on, ticking off the necessary guests. She was already wired about the party, but Willow felt edgy for a different reason, and hers had nothing to do with her new engagement. Her mom continued, "His staff, members of the state legislature, Barren's new mayor, the town council…"

With a flash of guilt, Willow stopped listening again. She twisted the ring on her third finger, left hand. She couldn't quite get used to it. When Thad had gone down on one knee beside their restaurant table the other night, then held out the yellow diamond as if he were offering her the world—which in a way he was—Willow had been numb with surprise. She should have expected it, though.

This was the next logical step in their courtship, even when she hadn't seen the proposal coming. But why not? She'd known Thad all her life, her family already adored him—and so did Willow. There'd been no reason to say no. But if only Thad had asked her in private without a dozen pairs of eyes watching...

Her mother bent her head to catch Willow's gaze, her own expression curious.

"You're right," Willow admitted. "My mind is elsewhere. Sorry."

"Willow, I understand you're not a party animal, for which I was grateful when you were in your teens, but this event is necessary. It will also be your official introduction to political society." As if Willow was still an eighteen-year-old debutante. Her mom said,

"Goodness, I think the whole house will need to be repainted. I'll talk to Zach tonight. And we'll need tents for the lawn… Oh," she said, as if a thought had just occurred to her, when Willow guessed she'd been making plans since she first saw the ring, "then there's the dinner menu…cocktails before that—"

Willow spun the ring on her finger again. Why didn't the idea of the party thrill her?

Her mother's gaze had followed Willow's to the diamond. "That is a showstopper, isn't it? Thad has wonderful taste, but he outdid himself." Her gaze blurred. "Tell me how he popped the question."

Willow rose from her chair. "Again, Mom?" She took a step toward the doorway, but her mother's voice stopped her.

"Baby, is there something wrong?"

Between you and Thad, she must mean, but there wasn't. Thad seemed nearly perfect—perfect for Willow. She loved him. He was handsome and smart, had a great smile and lots of confidence while Willow had a tendency to hold back except with people she felt closest to.

"Nothing's wrong," she murmured. "I just had some other news this morning. I'll help you later with the guest list." She already knew some of Thad's friends, the people in his family he'd want at the party.

"What news?"

"Cody," she admitted, hoping her voice didn't quaver.

Her mother's expression fell. "Oh, Willow. Zach mentioned that at breakfast." Jean had comforted Willow during her stormy relationship with Cody, after their breakup and then during his trial. "You're not going to see him, are you?"

"I doubt that." She remembered Zach's warning and mentally crossed her fingers.

She was engaged. There was no reason for her to see Cody again.

CODY SURVEYED THE small living room of the bungalow where the third member of their former trio, Calvin Stern, now lived with his girlfriend, Becca, one of Willow's pals. Derek had given him that lift from the prison, but after calling Calvin he'd dropped Cody off here. Derek had no room to share at Wilson Cattle, where he lived, but more likely he didn't want to endanger his job there. Cody couldn't blame him. His own recent address at Navarro said it all. And his sentence for arson was more serious than their cattle rustling. They hadn't also set fire to Grey Wilson's barn. "You sure this is okay?" he asked Calvin.

He shrugged. "If it wasn't okay for you to stay here, I would have said no."

Cody set his lone bag on the floor. "I won't be here long," he told Calvin, whose dark hair looked rumpled, as always.

Becca Carter kept staring at Cody. To him, she and Calvin seemed an odd pair, but they were obviously proud of their new digs and appeared happy in the life they were building together. Last December they'd had a baby boy, who was sleeping now in the nursery.

Becca was pretty enough, blonde like Willow, with blue eyes almost the same shade yet less vibrant. Maybe she hadn't been as willing to take Cody in, even for a night or two. That made things feel awkward, though, like he should just take his gear to wherever they said to sleep tonight, for one night only, then keep to himself with the door closed. "Don't worry about me. You won't even know I'm here."

Becca started toward the adjoining kitchen.

"I'll fix us something to eat. Is there anything you don't like, Cody?"

"I'd eat anything that's not off some cafeteria line." The prison's gray mystery meat, lumpy mashed potatoes and mushy peas were in his past now. He was never going back. He said, "And I would like to take a shower." To wash off the lingering stench of prison. The truth was, if he hadn't gotten into the Wild Horse Program, Cody feared he wouldn't have survived. Being locked up was like having his breath cut off.

"Let me show you the room," Calvin said, a hand on Cody's shoulder as if he understood how he felt.

"Thanks, Calvin."

Cody followed him along the short hall to the last room. Small but bright with lots of natural light, it held a twin bed covered with a heap of pillows and a paisley spread. Cody's eyes burned. "The lap of luxury," he said under his breath. "Lots better than trying to sleep on a hard cot with a scratchy blanket."

Calvin cleared his throat. "Baby's room is next door. Try not to wake him. Bathroom's straight across the hall. You'll have to share

with us so don't barge in if the door's shut.
The lock's broken."

"Thanks," he said again. "I appreciate this."

Calvin frowned a little. "What are you
going to do next, Cody?"

"Don't know. Haven't thought that far." He
still had no plans beyond finding a way to
see Willow.

Calvin said, "She's engaged," as if he'd
read Cody's mind.

"Yeah, I heard. Marrying..." He couldn't
say Thad's name. In court, he suspected Willow's fiancé had urged the judge to throw
the book at him. Thad had known, of course,
about Cody and Willow's past relationship.
"Guess Willow meant to let me know I'm history." Once she married Thad, Cody would
be like some fly fixed in amber. But did she
know Thad as well as he did?

"I wonder if Willow knows what she's
doing," Cody added.

"I wouldn't mess with the Bodines if I were
you."

You're not, but Cody didn't say that.

"I mean it," Calvin insisted. "Haven't you
had enough trouble?"

"From the day I was born," Cody agreed.

Especially after his folks died, when he'd begun to act out, and turned into a bad boy. A reputation he somehow needed to live down.

Calvin shifted his weight. "Me and Derek, we're doing okay now. Have you given any thought to a job? That is, if you mean to stick around awhile."

"I have to stay. I'm on parole, which means I need to be in Stewart County." Cody didn't meet his eyes. "Problem is, who would hire me?"

"I thought you liked working at the McMann ranch before."

Cody winced. After he'd torched the Wilsons' barn, he'd fled town again. Several years later, he'd come back to see Willow, gone to work under an assumed name at the McMann ranch—and finally gotten arrested there for his crime. "Yeah, the foreman told me once I got out, he'd let me have my old job back, but…" What if he'd changed his mind? The cockiness that had served Cody well from the time he could walk had deserted him in prison, where keeping a low profile, keeping quiet, could keep a man alive. By necessity, he'd grown up fast there, matured. He'd even—finally—learned a few things. "People have a way of forgetting their promises once you're an ex-con. I heard enough stories in Navarro from some of the reoffenders to know that's true."

Cody dumped his bag on the bed. He'd had enough of talking for now. A job could wait. First thing on his mind, right after that shower, would be to figure out how he could approach Willow.

"Think I'll get cleaned up before we eat. Something smells good," he said.

Calvin grinned. "Becca's a great cook."

"You're a lucky man."

"I am," Calvin agreed. "You can be, too, Cody."

"Maybe," he said. *I hope so.*

WILLOW STRODE INTO the barn the next morning, determined to take the ride that had been curtailed the day before by her conversation with Zach about Cody, but Silver wasn't in her stall. Zach poked his head out of the nearby tack room. "She's in the far pasture nibbling on lush grass. We've cleared the whole barn to re-stain the stall boards today. The horses are better out of the way. You can ride another time." The aisle in front of the tack room in which she kept her saddle was littered with paint cans, a tarp and other equipment, including several ladders and hay bales that barred her way.

Willow grabbed a lead rope from the hook by Silver's stall. She didn't need a saddle. "Bareback's fine with me." She started for the barn doors.

"Hold up. Don't cross that field trying to catch Silver with two dozen other horses milling around out there, some of 'em trouble without warning."

"Like I haven't done that a thousand times."

She throttled the rope in her hand. "Zach, I won't be wrapped in cotton. I know what you're afraid of, but I don't need your permission to ride."

"You're still my baby sister."

"You see, that's the problem here. I swear, I could live to be a hundred and you'd still see me that way." Willow stepped closer to him. "Please, Zach, give me some breathing room."

He half smiled, probably realizing she was right. "Can't help it. I'm my father's son." The smile faded as quickly as it had bloomed.

"There's no one else here to keep you safe, Willow."

She guessed he was thinking of Noah, their other brother, the eldest Bodine offspring. Zach rarely mentioned him, but Willow missed Noah. He'd come for their dad's funeral but was gone the next morning before she woke up. She imagined him still wearing his suit and tie then, thousands of dollars' worth of clothes from some designer label. His defection to New York was a sore subject with Zach, who, by default, had been handed the reins of the WB instead.

"He chose a different path," she murmured.

"Yeah, so much for us ranching together. It's all on me now." He touched her cheek. "He may have gone East, abandoned this place, but I never will. I've *had* to worry about you," he said, "especially since that bad fall you took in the show ring last year."

She almost groaned. *Here we go again.*

Willow had competed in dozens of shows at every level, almost from the time she could walk. Her ability to ride had never been in question until that spill, but lately this topic seemed to be always just under the surface of their every conversation.

"I quit competing after that, Zach. I understand your concerns, but I'm not going to stay in the house baking cookies or embroidering linens for my hope chest." Willow didn't have one.

Zach shook his head. "You can't imagine how I felt when Thad showed me that ring he planned to give you. He actually asked my permission for your hand in marriage. He's already tapped me to be best man for the wedding. I'll probably be godfather to your first baby. You marrying my best friend is like a dream come true."

"So, you don't really need to worry about me."

His mouth set. "I know Thad will take care of you, but..."

Willow rolled her eyes. "I don't need to be taken care of," she said as gently as she could. "I know how you cowboys can be, and Daddy was the worst of them, but I don't need your protection any more than I did his. I won't be happy unless I'm doing what I want to do, for me. You know I want to train horses, Zach. I think I'll be good at it—as a business, not a hobby."

"And risk breaking your neck again?"

He had a point. When she'd fallen, Willow had fractured several vertebrae. She'd spent the end of last year in rehab, healing and making plans to work with horses rather than compete in the show ring. "Zach, I know you mean well, but I've already made a start. I'm working with Olivia McCord and I've learned a lot from her."

He ignored that except to say, "You've done a fine job with Silver, but I only want what's best for you. Would you really take a chance on getting hurt again? What if you ended up in worse shape the next time?"

He didn't need to elaborate. She'd lived with pain for months after her fall, and Willow knew she'd been lucky to get all her normal function back. She also knew Zach tended to overreact where his *baby sister* was concerned. Zach loved her. So did Thad. Her mother, too. Even her oldest brother loved her, missing in action though he was from her life, and she loved them all. She didn't want to worry anyone.

"I won't get hurt," she said. "I don't want to quarrel with you, Zach, please."

After she and Cody broke up, and after her accident, her father's untimely death had changed everything again. She regretted the lost-forever possibility of making things right with him, too. Her rebellion with Cody might have been forgiven eventually. Instead, because of her, their father was gone.

She was still trying to find absolution from the rest of her family, and between the guilt that was her constant companion and the memory of the near-fatal fall she'd taken, she was a different person now.

Zach squeezed her shoulder. "We okay here?"

Willow wasn't quite sure what she would have said, maybe *I will be once I start training horses*, but Zach's gaze had shifted. His eyes narrowed as he looked behind her at the open barn doors. And Willow's heart almost stopped. Maybe she'd been waiting for this since yesterday—that would explain her lack of focus. She hadn't heard a car or truck pull in but, somehow, she knew the person her brother had already seen.

Zach said the name like an oath. "Cody Jones."

CHAPTER THREE

BEFORE WILLOW COULD react, Zach pushed her behind him. "I can't believe what I'm seeing." He took a step toward Cody, who stood outside the open doors, his wheat-colored hair struck through with summer sunlight, hands on his lean hips. He wore sneakers, jeans, a big belt buckle he'd won in some rodeo years ago and a navy blue T-shirt with writing on it. Willow couldn't make out what it said. But at her first sight of him since last fall at the prison shortly before her accident, her heart began to ache.

"Zach, I'll handle this," she said. The muscles in her brother's body were tensed for a fight. Hers had turned to water. "Cody, why are you here?"

His gaze on Zach, he muttered, "Didn't know any place better to find you, being the Bodine princess and all. Figured I'd have to visit your ivory tower."

"You're trespassing." His tone taut, Zach glanced toward the tack room, where a rack of rifles and shotguns had hung on the wall for decades, maybe a century. One of the first safety lessons Willow had learned as a toddler was to steer clear of them—though later on, she'd learned how to shoot like any self-respecting ranch kid. Zach was a crack shot. "Get off this property before I blow a hole through your worthless hide."

"Zach, please," she said.

He spun around to face her. His hazel eyes shot sparks. "Are you out of your mind? Oh yeah, I forgot. You lost that years ago with this...this *felon*. Then that wasn't enough. You had to take up with him again—until he ended up in jail." His fists knotted at his sides. "I swear, Willow—"

"He's on this ranch now. He might as well say whatever he's come to say."

Zach shook his head. He turned back to Cody, who hadn't flinched at her brother's words. "I don't have my sister's tender heart, but where she's involved, I am a soft touch, and I can see she's determined to hear your sob story, so have at it." He pointed a finger. "You're not out of here in five minutes, you'll meet the business end of my gun. I won't miss."

Willow grabbed his arm. "Zach, for heaven's sake. This isn't *High Noon* or *Shane* or *The Magnificent Seven*. Some gunfighter show-down on a dusty street in front of a saloon."

"All movies way older than I am." But he stomped off toward the tack room, evading the mess in the aisle. "This door will stay open. I'll be conveniently close by. Be careful what you say, Jones—and don't even think of touching my sister."

Willow's eyes threatened to tear up. Zach's reaction seemed over-the-top, which wasn't unusual these days, but it was probably what she deserved in this case. She'd made a hash of things with Cody once, risked the love and respect of her family, then been betrayed by him. That wouldn't happen again. For one thing, Cody had lied to her the last time they were together. And yet… She couldn't stop looking at him. His thick eyelashes swept down like fans to hide his dark eyes, and he stared at the empty space where Zach had been. He must have heard the same sounds she did from the tack room: Zach shoving trunks around, rattling bridles, kicking a bucket. Cody still wasn't coming toward her.

Instead, Willow went to him. In the glare of the sun, she said, "You're as bad as Zach. For your information, I'm no Rapunzel in some fairy tale either, letting down my hair so you can climb my tower."

His voice sounded husky. "I like your hair."

"Don't," Willow said. She would not let him charm her or shred her resolve. A loser, Zach had called him. She'd be better off to maintain a strict distance. A short silence followed before she pointed out, her voice sounding thick, "You've changed, lost some weight."

Cody pretended to examine his forearm, all corded muscle, his skin dusted with golden hairs. "Yeah, but take a look at my tan." And her heart turned over. His T-shirt read Navarro Correctional Facility. He'd seen her glance at it. "I did a lot of work outside there." His mouth set, he kept his voice low so Zach wouldn't hear. "How long, angel?" His once-familiar endearment for her went through Willow like a sword. "How long did it take you to forget? To start seeing Thad

Nesbitt, who, for one thing, has never worked outdoors a day in his life—"

So he'd heard about the engagement. "We broke up, Cody. You and I, I mean. What does it matter now what Thad does or doesn't do?"

"I cared plenty in court." He added, "I care even more now. Are you serious about this? I didn't think we broke up for good, not like this." He looked at her ring. "Didn't expect that to be all there would be between us. I don't see any diamond here. Just a plain silver band?"

"It's platinum." Her cheeks warm, she turned the ring around. It was a bit too large for her finger and needed to be resized. "A yellow diamond."

He murmured, "Go big or go home, huh?"

She gave a weary sigh. "Cody, stop. This is none of your business. We were through before you even went to trial."

He tilted his head as if trying to gauge whether she'd been lying. "Through? Then why did you come to see me at Navarro?" He paused. "For old times' sake? Or out of pity?"

"I've never pitied you."

His eyes softened. "Willow."

"You'd better go." Her voice shook. "I'm

glad your sentence was shortened. I hope that's behind you now. I wish you all the best—"

"Wow. That sounds like some Dear John letter."

"Yes," she said.

For a long moment Cody didn't speak again. Then, with his voice barely above a whisper, he asked, "Do you love him as much as you said you loved me?"

What she needed to say, what he needed to hear again, was yes, but the word stuck in her throat. Her lips pressed tight, she could only nod.

No sound could be heard in the barn, no stomping of hooves from the empty stalls on either side of the aisle, not a whinny or a whicker. All the horses were outdoors, and Zach was as quiet as one of the cats that kept the mice under control. Willow wished she could scurry into a hole in some wooden baseboard herself. She'd thought she would never see Cody up close again, hear his voice flow over her like water, smell the clean, fresh masculine scent of his skin near enough to touch. Hadn't imagined feeling like this. "Go," she begged him, then forced herself to say the rest around the boulder lodged in her throat. "For your own good, Cody. Don't come back."

The stunned look on his face shouldn't have been there. How could he not know what kind of reception he'd get at the WB? Even from her? And, especially, from Zach. He must have known. Yet he'd come anyway to see her again. He'd called her *angel*.

"Okay, then," he finally said. "If that's the way you really want it."

"I do," she managed to choke out.

With a shrug of his broad shoulders, Cody turned away. It seemed a dark cloud had descended over him. His head was down. She'd seen that posture before, in the prison. Willow watched him get into Derek Moran's yellow pickup—Cody must have borrowed it—and speed down the drive, raising a cloud of dust. Then she rushed away from the barn. She didn't want to face Zach again.

She ran through the gate into the nearest pasture and kept running until she came upon the small herd of mostly geldings in the far field under a stand of cottonwood trees, tails swishing the always-pesky summer flies. She called to her horse.

Ears pricked, the dapple-gray lifted her head, then broke from the others to trot toward Willow, who met her halfway. Silver's calm, deep brown eyes seemed to see into her. They always did. She whickered a greeting, as if in sympathy.

"Good girl," Willow murmured, throwing her arms around Silver's neck, clinging.

Then she buried her face in the mare's silvery mane.

And wept.

CODY'S OWN SHOUTS in the night jerked him awake, heart pounding, body thrashing on the bed in Calvin's guest room. *"Mom! Dad! Nooo!"* He could hear gunshots, echoing again down the years. The nightmare always rattled him. It never went away. He suspected it never would.

Now, trying to pull himself out of the dream, he feared his second night here— he'd stayed longer after all—could be his last. Becca might kick him out if he woke the baby, so Cody left the house before dawn, driving Derek's borrowed pickup, which he needed to return later that day. Yet he couldn't leave his memories behind. He couldn't forget seeing Willow yesterday, talking to her, not hearing what he'd hoped to hear. *I missed you. I'm glad to see you.* When he reached Clara McMann's ranch soon after sunrise, his take-out coffee from the town café sat untouched in the cupholder, and he was still shaking inside.

Determined to focus on reality, he spotted the foreman, Hadley Smith, in the barnyard, hosing down the dun-colored horse he called Trouble, which had been Cody's mount when he'd worked here before his arrest. Hadley glanced up at Derek's yellow pride and joy, at Cody behind the wheel, and his brows lifted. Then he went about his business again.

"Hadley," Cody called out, like he'd never been gone and had returned from town on some errand, but the powerfully built foreman who ran Clara's ranch didn't respond. "Got a minute?" Cody asked, climbing down from the truck.

Still no answer. Cody slammed the driver's door shut. As he'd told Calvin, Hadley had promised to help him once he left prison. Cody hadn't quite believed that, and yesterday after the WB, he'd stopped at several other ranches to ask for work.

That hadn't panned out, and after the latest mental showing of his nightmare, he still felt gutted. This was all he had right now.

"Heard you'd been released." Hadley turned off the water, then focused his attention on the scraper in his hand, sweeping it in broad strokes over the horse's wet hide.

"Yeah. I, uh…" Cody cleared his throat. "Thought I'd come see if you need—" He didn't get to say *help*. Hadley was already shaking his head as Cody had expected. He should have listened to himself instead of Calvin.

"Cody Jones. If that's even your real name…" Another swipe along the horse's side. Water flew everywhere. "Or should I stick with Cory Jennings? Close enough with the first name and both initials, but no cigar," he added.

"You have every right to be mad at me."

Hadley eyed him. "I don't need your permission."

"I lied, and I'm sorry." Which was Cody's first apology of many to come. Maybe he should have said that to Willow, too.

"Not the first time you lied, was it?"

"No," Cody admitted. The man didn't say

much, but when he did it usually counted. Hadley saw everything, even on the inside. "I don't expect you to trust me after what happened—"

"That's the point. I did trust you." Hadley turned his back, leading the gelding into the darker barn. Cody followed him, letting his eyes adjust to the dimness after being in the sun. He couldn't get his latest nightmare out of his head, and now it seemed he was in another daytime version.

He tried to explain. "My birth name is really Jones." Cody cleared his throat again. Seemed to be something stuck there. "After I came back to Barren, before the sheriff finally picked me up, I used that other name—Cory Jennings."

"Which you foisted off on me at this ranch. Why?" Hadley opened a stall door, and the horse ambled inside. Hadley closed the door, then latched it.

"I was on the run then," Cody admitted, "from that warrant on the arson charge." Hadley had known that existed, but he hadn't realized the Cory Jennings he'd later hired was actually Cody Jones. He'd been right here when, to Hadley's surprise, Cody got arrested.

"That was a dangerous game, *Cory*…Cody, whatever. I admit, maybe part of that was my fault. I took you on with no references, believed in you without question, and I even felt for you about that girl you were seeing. Willow Bodine, wasn't it?" His gaze homed in on Cody again.

"She's the reason I came back after running away."

Hadley shook his head again. "To a place where a lot of people might recognize you."

"While I was working here, I kept a low profile until Calvin saw me in town one day, and Willow learned from him I'd been working here and lying about who I was."

"Risky business." Hadley arched an eyebrow. "And now she's engaged to another man." He leaned against Trouble's stall door. The horse hadn't seemed to recognize Cody. No nicker of greeting, not a twitch of his jughead ears. Hadley said, "Be wise if you left that alone. The Bodines are clannish. They protect their own, especially Willow."

Cody knew that. Derek, Calvin, Hadley… They'd all advised him. Even Willow had.

That flashy ring on her finger should have been enough of a warning, without Zach.

Cody had been lucky not to meet the barrel of his rifle or shotgun yesterday. Maybe the only reason he was standing here now was because of Willow. Zach rarely denied her anything, even her talking to Cody for five minutes.

He started for the borrowed pickup, glad he hadn't begged for a job with the last ounce of his pride, when Hadley's voice made him turn back. "Don't run off. I'm curious."

Hadley crossed his brawny arms. He reminded Cody of his supervisor at Navarro, a burly guy who always looked as if he wanted to break Cody in half and had threatened more than once to knock some sense into him. Which he'd definitely needed. But, like Darryl Williams, Hadley only *looked* tough, and his gaze wasn't that hard now. "What did you do for work while you were in the pen?"

Cody told him about the Wild Horse Program, which was new and modeled after the one at Hutchinson, another correctional facility, his voice gaining confidence as he spoke about the mare, too. "A lifesaver," he finished, then flipped through his phone until he found his favorite picture, which he'd captured from the program's website. "I called her Diva, but she's not. She's a sweetie. I hope she goes to a good home."

"A nice-looking paint," Hadley said. He handed back the phone with the photos of the sleek brown-and-white horse with a snowy forelock, mane and tail. She'd been a beauty to train, maybe the best thing Cody had ever done. So far. "You got pretty attached to her, huh?"

"Yessir." He told Hadley about his dream to start a training business someday. "I'd like to focus on mustangs. If I could, I'd adopt her myself."

"Why don't you?"

"The application process might not be that easy for an ex-con."

"You're out now, and you told me once you were a big rodeo guy," Hadley murmured. "With your experience, assuming that's true—"

"I may have exaggerated a bit," Cody admitted. "Won some prize money on the circuit early on, but nowhere near as good as—"

"Dallas Maguire?" The name belonging to

one of the sport's major stars dropped through the air like a bomb.

Cody's pulse tripped. "How do you know Dal—"

"He's my brother, Cody." Ah, so that helped to explain Hadley's attitude. Dallas must have told him about the money Cody still owed Dallas, who, understandably, held a grudge against him, too. Cody hadn't heard from Dallas since then, but he knew Dallas had been injured at a rodeo in Lubbock, Texas, toward the end of last year. Had he fully recovered? Where was he now?

"Dallas is back on the circuit, winning again." Hadley waited a beat, his gaze boring into Cody. "He's working with me now in his off time. Let me check with him. We might be able to use another hand after all. If that would work for you."

Cody blinked but couldn't answer. Why would Dallas, or Hadley, do anything for him?

Hadley straightened from the stall. "You've made some bad choices, son. I were you, I wouldn't make any more. That's the voice of experience talking. I said I'd try to help you once you served your time, and—after all—I will."

Son. That one word to Cody was like a half-remembered song heard before his childhood had ended in violence. Hadley was about five years older than he was, and Cody was just shy of thirty, yet he'd called him *son*. After what he'd done. A few minutes ago, Cody had been a newly minted ex-con, without a job, still feeling the hurt Willow had caused him down to his bones. He thought about yesterday, that diamond she wore... And the way she'd avoided Cody's eyes when he asked, *Do you love him as much as you said you loved me?*

What if she still hurt, too? Over the way things had turned out between them?

He didn't have much time to find out.

"Well?" Hadley said. "What do you think?"

"I think—if Dallas doesn't mind—I'd like my old job back."

"It's a start," Hadley agreed.

A job, yeah, and he'd need a place to live if anybody would rent to him.

Hadley seemed to read Cody's mind. "Dallas lives in town, and so does Calvin Stern, who took your place. He works for someone else now. Guess you might as well take over the bunkhouse again."

Cody nodded. There, he'd be sleeping alone where no one could hear his cries. He hadn't been able to stop his mother's bloody death, or his father from killing himself, a scene that rarely left his nights be, and he'd certainly made the bad choices Hadley had mentioned, but he might get that fresh start now.

He breathed in a lungful of clean, if sultry, Kansas air. But this job and the place he would live—no longer behind bars—weren't all either. Cody was worried. He knew all about bad relationships. He also knew Thad Nesbitt. If Cody had read Willow right, she *wasn't* that happy, and as Hadley had pointed out, Cody was an expert on making mistakes.

He might just be able to stop Willow from making a fatal error herself.

LATER THAT DAY Willow met Thad at the jewelry store in Farrier. While they waited for someone to help them, Thad teased her.

"I thought maybe you were having second thoughts. Spinning this ring around as if you'd rather it wasn't on your finger."

He'd noticed her new habit, but his light tone seemed to mask a more serious concern.

She gave him a chiding look. "Thad, why are we here right now?"

"To get your ring resized."

"Exactly. I was afraid I'd lose it. How could I not like such a beautiful thing?" She straightened his tie, her touch lingering against his white shirt, feeling his warmth through the fabric, the heavy beat of his heart. "You should hear my mother. She's begged me to tell her the story of your proposal at least a dozen times. And every time she gets all misty-eyed. It's so cute," Willow finished, hoping she had reassured him.

Thad rarely showed a sensitive side—he usually seemed so sure of himself.

Leaning an elbow on the glass-topped counter, he caught her hand in his. "How did I get this lucky?"

Willow felt his pulse accelerate. "Well, it's not every guy who gets to call Jean Bodine his future mother-in-law."

"True, but I meant you." He paused, glancing around the shop to make sure no other customer was near enough to hear. At the end of the counter an older woman was trying to decide between a lavish diamond brooch encrusted with sapphires and an emerald necklace. Her husband paced back and forth from the display to the door. Across the way, another couple—younger than Willow and Thad—bent their heads over the case filled with engagement rings, none of them as splendid as the one Willow wore. No one was paying any attention to her and Thad. His brown gaze darkened before he leaned over to kiss Willow on the cheek, then lightly on the mouth. He drew away with obvious reluctance. "Let's get this over with," he said. "How do drinks and dinner at the Cowardly Lion sound?"

The extravagant restaurant sat in the center of Farrier's downtown, larger than nearby Barren was, and its menu was more elaborate than the Bon Appetit's. But Willow wasn't in the mood for an indoor meal. "Why don't we order burgers at the Cattlemen's Bar and take them to the park?" Its recently updated configuration also boasted a few paddleboats—when the creek was running high enough—that Willow thought would be fun to try. "It's going to be a beautiful evening."

Thad shook his head. "You'd rather have a picnic than a nice, thick steak?"

"I would. I always order the Lion's chicken, and yes I'd like a picnic. Tonight we let our hair down."

He ran his palm over his short, dark hair. "Not much to let down on my part." He trailed a finger down the length of Willow's hair, then slipped his arm around her waist.

"May I help you?"

The shop's owner had appeared from the rear of the store, which had been in business as long as the WB had been a working ranch. Willow's own mother's rings had come from this same place.

Willow stepped out of Thad's embrace. And held up her left hand.

"Ah," the man said. "I see we need a bit of adjustment." He looked at Thad. "How did she react when you flipped up the lid of that box?"

Thad laughed. "What would you say, Willow?"

"I was…stunned. Thad's proposal was a big surprise." She took the ring off her finger and handed it over. "He tells me this was a custom piece that you and he designed together. You did a beautiful job. I really love it."

The jeweler beamed at them. "My congratulations and best wishes to you both. Have you set a date?"

"Not yet," Thad answered, "but we will soon. I'm not going to let this girl get away."

His comment didn't strike Willow right, and neither had the two men referring to her in the third person as if she wasn't here, but they continued to discuss the diamond, and soon the shop owner took it into the back. "Was that necessary?" she asked. "My getting away? Now he'll think we've had a quarrel."

"That was only a figure of speech," Thad insisted, even though she felt certain he'd meant what he said, and her thoughts returned to Cody's unannounced visit yesterday to the WB.

"Are you sure?"

Thad straightened from the counter. Without answering, he went into the back room and Willow heard the low rumble of male voices, then Thad returned with a smile. "Let's go eat. We can pick up your ring afterward. He'll have it ready for us in another hour or so. Shall we?"

Thad held the shop's door open for her, and together they walked down the block to the burger place, where Willow ordered a double cheeseburger with fries and an iced tea to go. Thad did the same. "I hope I don't ruin my suit sitting on a park bench," he said, but with a smile. "On the other hand, it's different. We'll have plenty of formal events with the wedding coming up."

"And don't forget the first—my mom's party for us."

At the park they ate at a picnic table and talked about the "shindig," as Thad called it, and she could see him relax. He'd spent the day in court, but now he loosened his tie and rolled up his sleeves to bare his forearms. Willow kicked off her shoes. This was the kind of date she preferred—casual and low-key without any need to put on a show. She left that lifestyle to Thad's father and his new wife. "Was I right?" she said.

His eyes twinkled. "About what."

"Dinner in the outdoors. Doesn't your burger taste better in this fresh air?"

"Tastes like a burger to me." But he kept smiling. "Thanks."

"For what?"

"Getting me away from…" He waved a hand. "The job, the people I have to cater to every day, my own tendency to dress like a banker. It's always amazed me that Zach and I became such good friends. He's your basic, horse-loving cowboy in dusty boots, and I'm…wingtip shoes, as much city as can be had around here."

Willow laughed. "Zach's a cowboy, all right. He didn't expect to take over the WB, but he's doing a great job."

Thad hesitated. "Did he tell you Cody Jones is back in town?"

His question made Willow tense. "Yes."

Thad shook his head. "Did I just say that? I sound like some old Western movie."

Shane, Willow thought again. "You and Zach share the same opinion there."

"If only Jones was just passing through." He paused again. "Instead, he's on parole. He has to stay in the county."

That wasn't particularly good news for Willow either. She knew Thad and Cody didn't like each other. If she'd had any doubt, Cody had let her know yesterday.

"Have you seen him?"

She couldn't lie. "He came by the WB."

Thad didn't say any more, but she could tell he wasn't happy about that. Neither was she. "Thad."

"No, I don't need to know why or what he said." He rose from the bench, then held out a hand. By now, the light was fading, the setting sun casting a rose gold glow across the nearby water. "Come on, let's get your ring, then we can take that boat ride you told me about. I welcome the chance to show my more manly side."

Willow welcomed the chance to restore the romantic mood of their evening together. She wished he hadn't mentioned Cody.

She didn't plan to see him again.

CHAPTER FOUR

"CASS!" WITH A glad cry, Willow met her friend at the kitchen door. She hadn't seen Cass since she'd moved to Los Angeles about a year and a half ago, soon after Willow broke up with Cody, and Willow had been in a strange mood since seeing him a few days ago. Her picnic with Thad at the park last night hadn't helped enough to change that. Even the hour she'd spent this morning in the outdoor ring with Silver hadn't made her smile, but the news that Jean had hired Cass as the event planner for Willow's engagement party had finally lifted her spirits. "Come in, stranger."

After giving Willow a fierce hug, Cass glanced around the big ranch kitchen. She swept her auburn hair away from her shoulders. "Goodness, this place hasn't changed."

"Not yet," Willow told her, "but I'm sure you'll hear all about Mom's plans. She should be home any minute. She went into town to Fantastic Designs hoping to get more ideas. She apologized that she wouldn't be here when you arrived—I'm supposed to convey her regrets."

"I love your mother. She doesn't need to apologize." Cass dropped onto a chair at the table. "Gosh. How many times have I been in this kitchen? Remember when we used to come in after a horseback ride or when the school bus dropped us off? She always had some snack waiting."

"And while we ate, she wanted to hear all about whatever was going on at school." Willow's gaze softened. "She was as much your mother then as mine."

"Yeah," Cass said, her gaze turning inward, and Willow wished she hadn't brought that up. Willow's mom had been Cass's refuge, a safe haven, because Cass had always hated going home. "I hear my mother is a changed woman," she said. "I wouldn't know. I wasn't here when she got married again. She and Jack Hancock, I'm told, are lovebirds."

"They are. They have the cutest house in town not far from his restaurant. Different place, Cass, different man from your father…"

"Same old memories. I wouldn't really know about her new marriage either. I don't intend to see Wanda. I'm staying with my sister—until I can find a rental for myself." Cass brushed a stray hair from her cheek. "I'd rather talk about your mom. Jean must be over the moon about your engagement. When she asked me about the party, I did a double take—you and Thad Nesbitt?" Cass admired Willow's diamond. "I never would have guessed."

Willow worried the resized ring on her hand. Making it smaller hadn't ended her habit.

"Things change," she said. For a few minutes they talked about other things and caught up. Willow told Cass she didn't see their friend Becca, who kept busy now with her new baby and her job, as often as she liked. Then she said, "Tell me about yourself. The last time I saw you—remember our tearful goodbye?—you couldn't resist the lure of LA, the big city." When Cass had left town, she'd claimed she was never coming back. Life was obviously different now for both of them.

Cass pulled a paper napkin from the holder on the table, then began to shred it into pieces. Her amber-brown gaze, lighter than her mother's, avoided Willow's. "I had all these grandiose ideas. I was going to storm Hollywood, become every celebrity's first choice for an event planner, walk the red carpet wearing a gorgeous gown and watch my favorite clients accept their Oscars from a front-row seat. Which more or less worked for a while." She shrugged. "I was sure I'd meet the sexiest man alive, an actor who would fall madly in love with me and carry me off to his mansion in Beverly Hills. I did meet him, but—" She waved a hand. "He certainly was not *my* leading man, as it turned out. Fraternizing with an employer didn't help my career. Now I'm back where I started, where everyone must still see me as a loser."

"The loser was that guy in SoCal."

"Well, I learned my lesson."

"I'm sorry that didn't work out for you, Cass."

"Yeah, there I was, climbing the Hollywood ladder. Now my only option is to work at the WB—sorry, that didn't come out right."

But Willow could guess what she meant,

and why. "Maybe you should look around, not jump at this job. If you find something else, you can tell Mom you're quitting. I'm sure she'd understand how awkward this could be for you."

"How many big social events are there in Barren or Farrier?"

"Not that many," Willow agreed. "You might ask Jack at the Bon Appetit if he needs a server, a hostess, until you find something you really want, and the Sundown Café's a possibility. That's a more casual eatery so the tips wouldn't be as good—"

"I was a waitress, remember, all through high school. I'm not doing that again. I've already slid back to square one by coming... back." She didn't say *home*. "And let's not forget my so-called dad, who thank heaven isn't with us now. He never worked if he could avoid it, he stole things and didn't blink an eye. He treated his wife like dirt—and she took it. The day I left those five acres, I vowed never to step foot on that farm or in that house again."

"I know, Cass."

"And then what did I do?" Her gaze lifted. "I made the fatal mistake of letting myself think I was looking at a ring like the one on your hand. Bigger, even," she added with a twinkle in her eye. As good friends as they were, she and Willow had always been competitive with each other. "You do realize I'm pea green about this engagement. I never would have paired you with Thad, but it makes sense."

"Thad and I have a lot in common." Willow told Cass about his surprise proposal. Then she admitted, "Unfortunately, a couple of days after Thad proposed, and at exactly the worst time ever, Cody came to see me again. Can you believe he had the nerve to show up here at the ranch?"

Cass frowned. Just as Willow knew her background, Cass knew the whole story of Willow's past relationship with Cody. "I thought he was in Navarro."

"He's out now. I sent Cody away, but… I just hope that was that," Willow said. She was ready to change the topic. "Mom's probably breaking land speed records to get home. She's so excited about this engagement party, about your being here." She paused. "It won't be easy, Cass, working on the WB, knowing—" she waited a beat "—that 'he who shall not be mentioned' is always here."

Willow followed Cass's gaze to the back door. Zach would be outside at the barn. There'd been a time when Willow hoped she and Cass would become sisters-in-law as well as friends, but that hadn't happened. And now, in spite of Willow urging him to find someone for himself now that she was engaged to Thad, Zach was all about the WB.

"Face your demons," Cass finally said, then added, "I need this job, Willow. After what happened in LA, which seems to be the pattern of my life, maybe Jean shouldn't give me another chance—although knowing your mom, she probably will."

"Will what?" Willow's mother had opened the back door, a welcoming smile already spread across her face. She folded Cass into a warm hug and blinked at their reunion. "You dear girl, we're desperately in need of help. As soon as I heard you were home again, I couldn't think of a better person for the job." She said, "I've seen your Pinterest boards with those amazing ideas for parties. We're not Hollywood here, of course, but I'm hoping you can see your way clear to give us your valuable expertise."

"My time is all yours, Mrs. B." Her gaze fell. "I should tell you, though, I was fired from my last job."

Jean's hug only tightened at that. "Someone must not have had any foresight." She eased away, then took her seat at the table, where Willow and Cass joined her. "Let's talk. I'm eager to hear your ideas for *this* party."

SHORTLY AFTER NOON Cody cruised the aisles in Earl's Hardware. Hadley had sent him to town on a bunch of errands in one of the ranch pickups, his first assignment on the job, and afterward Cody had decided to browse for a bridle for the horse he'd been assigned to ride. The saddle he'd used for Trouble before was not in play. Dallas liked it instead, and it was a poor fit, anyway, on the ranch's third mount, the bay gelding Cody now rode named Thunder. He had decided to buy his own equipment. There was nothing like the comfortable feel of your own gear fitting like a glove.

He moseyed over to the side wall of the store, hat pulled low over his eyes. Earlier, he'd had to fight himself not to tell Hadley he didn't feel comfortable straying off the ranch just yet. He'd avoided such trips when he'd been on the run, hiding at the McMann ranch, and he'd spent too much time locked up in Navarro to welcome contact with free people yet. At times Cody still felt like a prisoner—of his own bad memories, too.

As he plucked a dark leather bridle from a hook on the wall, a voice spoke behind him. "Not a bad choice, but here." The man handed Cody a tan rig with brass fittings that cost twice as much as the one he'd been examining.

"Great," he agreed, the back of his neck prickling with awareness, "but my finances are pretty tight."

"Pair this with a good saddle, you'd be all set to ride. Out of town. That is, if you weren't stuck here because of your parole."

"Ah, what a surprise." Cody hung both bridles back on the hooks, then slowly turned around. Taller than he was, his dark hair cut in a fancy style and wearing a pin-striped suit, Thad Nesbitt flashed a broad smile.

"Cody Jones," he said, "or whatever you call yourself now."

"That'll do."

Cody guessed Zach had told Thad about his unwise visit to the WB. He was glad to see there were only two other customers in the store, one at the front register, where Earl, the owner, was ringing up purchases; another sifting through the men's shirt rack across the way. Cody didn't recognize either of them. "Nice to see you, too. Am I supposed to congratulate you on your recent engagement?" Might as well get that out in the open. That's probably why Willow's fiancé was here to needle Cody.

"Hey," Thad said, "you win some, lose some."

"I'm not looking for trouble," Cody told him.

Thad looked dubious. "I hear you kept your first appointment with your *parole* officer. Good friend of mine, by the way." His cool gaze swept the now-empty store. With the other customers gone, Earl had gone into the back room. "You know what they say about small towns."

"What do they say?" Cody knew, of course. Thad was keeping tabs on him.

"News travels with the speed of light. You

should have been here when the mayor's ex-wife took up with Dallas Maguire."

"Dallas is planning to marry her." At least according to Hadley. Cody hadn't yet seen Dallas, who'd taken the woman and her kids to Disneyworld. Cody dreaded Dallas's return. Their history wasn't much better than his with Thad. "What's your point?" he asked, unable to stop himself. "Are you trying to warn me away from Willow? Maybe because you're not that sure she wants to marry *you*?"

Thad pushed a finger into Cody's chest. He didn't need to raise his voice. "I'm just saying. You get out of line with *my fiancée*, I'll hear about it. And yes, I'm warning you."

Cody held his gaze. "Does Willow know about that temper of yours?"

Thad didn't answer. He'd delivered his message. He turned on his heel, then stalked down the aisle. With his suit he wore a pair of high-end boots from a brand that was one of Dallas Maguire's sponsors. Cody had coveted a pair for years. He heard Thad say on his way out of the store, "My temper is the least of your problems."

And Cody let out a long-held breath.

When someone laid a hand on his shoulder, he jerked around to find Earl wearing a hard expression. The older man was a fixture in Barren. He'd inherited this store from his father and had run it for years. For some reason, Earl had always seemed to like Cody.

"Don't pay him no mind," he said, his gaze sympathetic.

"You sure you want me shopping in your store, Earl? I did torch the Wilsons' barn," Cody admitted, owning up to his mistake. He had let his bad boy side get the better of him then, and he'd certainly wronged Grey Wilson, for one. "No telling what I might do next."

"I'm not worried." Earl glanced at the rack of bridles. "Hadley will keep you in check. If he can't, his brother will."

True enough, but Cody planned to keep himself out of trouble.

Earl held out a hand. "Glad you're back, Cody. Now, let's talk about a bridle." Earl went to the hooks on the wall, pulled down the dark one with nickel fittings that Cody had admired. "This to your liking?"

"Yessir. But I haven't made my first pay yet. Maybe I could put that on layaway? Come get it when it's paid off?"

Earl held out the bridle. "You'll take it now—for a deposit. I trust you."

Cody's throat tightened. "Thanks, Earl." He meant for more than the bridle. The man's easy acceptance of him was like finding gold.

"You need a saddle, too?"

Earl was already guiding him toward the display in the side room, which made Cody's heart beat faster. Beautiful models in every style and— Cody's eyes homed in on one that matched the bridle Earl had shoved in his hand. The leather, deep seat and sturdy cantle suited him fine. He tried the saddle for size. Perfect. So was the price tag, if he'd had any spare cash. "I, uh—"

"Sold." Earl's grin split his narrow face. "You should have seen your eyes light up. That's the one. Let's ring you up." He was already at the front register before Cody could process what had just happened.

"Earl, I don't know how to thank you," he said, digging in his hip pocket for his mostly empty wallet. "What's the damage on the deposit for both of those?"

"Twenty bucks'll do it."

"But we're talking hundreds for the saddle alone and I don't—"

"You don't need to thank me. Consider it done." Earl paused, not quite looking at Cody. "I always believe in giving a man a second chance."

Cody left the store with a brand-new saddle—he'd never owned one before, only used rigs—and a new determination to prove himself, not only to Earl but to the whole town, the county, the people he'd wronged and—if he was lucky—Willow, too.

CHAPTER FIVE

AFTER HER MEETING with Jean Bodine about the party, Cass left the house and immediately spied Zach coming from the barn in all his golden splendor. Yum. Summer tan, hair like clover honey, serious hazel eyes. Her footsteps faltered. Why hadn't he changed for the worse while she was gone? When he reached her, his gaze wasn't welcoming, not that she'd expected it would be.

"I thought LA was more your speed," he said, his voice a lazy drawl, and Cass's heart thumped, hard. His gaze tracked over her again from head to toe. Could he see the dark shadows beneath her eyes, her thinner frame, or did her everlasting crush on him show in every line of her body?

"Not anymore," she said, but she refused to explain except to say, "So here I am again."

"Cherry Moran," Zach said, his eyes shifting to the house behind her.

"It's Cass now." She'd altered her first name when she left for California. A new identity of sorts, or had she been hiding from the old one? Somewhere along the way she'd certainly tried to become someone else. Instead, now she would be like hired help again to the crown prince of the WB. Cass fell back on her old habit of using a sassy attitude as self-protection. A preemptive strike. "I can tell you don't want me here, but too bad. Your mother doesn't share your opinion, and Willow and I have been friends longer than you and I have been enemies."

"I'm not your enemy."

Which didn't convince Cass. As a kid, she'd gotten very good at reading people's faces, hearing the subtext beneath their words, and the message in Zach's eyes now seemed clear.

"But I'm getting a bad feeling," he said. "First Cody Jones turns up, then you. That combination never worked for me before. You're wasting your time, *Cass*. Willow's—"

"Getting married. Yes, I know."

Cass felt another twinge of envy. She hadn't lied when she'd told Willow she coveted that fancy ring and her engagement to Thad—though, to be honest, she wasn't that fond of him—and all their marriage would mean for Willow's future. A house bigger than the WB's, probably, a new luxury car or SUV every year, trips to Paris or Rome or San Francisco, a family of beautiful children who looked like their parents. Basically, the same lifestyle Willow had always known plus the babies she would likely have. Pretty much the life Cass had dreamed of once with Zach. A dream that had no chance of ever coming true.

The thought saddened her. She and Zach had started out better than this years ago, if not exactly friends, until Willow's relationship with Cody had changed that. And, of course, once even before...

"What makes you think I'd interfere with Willow and Thad?"

"I have a good memory," he said, making a certain day of her own life—a very personal memory of Zach—flash through her mind. She wasn't about to think or talk or dwell on that.

"So do I, but it appears we'll have to make the best of it, won't we?" Some things, like her beginnings, too, were better left alone. "I was never a bad influence on your sister," she said. "Yes, I supported her at first about Cody, but later I encouraged her to break that off, and after all, he's out of the picture now. I'm here to plan her engagement party. Nothing else."

Zach looked as if he didn't believe her. His gaze swept the area from the front lawn of the house to the barn and back to Cass's face. She watched a confusing mix of emotions cross his features. An attempt to trust, perhaps even that memory of what they'd once so briefly shared, then the same disbelief again.

Had she already overstepped the boundaries?

"I'll do my best at the WB." She had to. "And I'll try to keep out of your way."

She wasn't sure he believed that either, though his gaze had shifted. He tipped his tan Stetson, then turned his back and headed for the barn instead of the house. She hadn't realized how much it would tear her apart to see him again, looking a few years older but even better if that was possible, yet he was still tarring Cass with the same old brush he'd used since she was seventeen.

She ought to be used to it. She wasn't here for him but for Willow.

WILLOW KNEW ALL the signs. There wasn't a doubt in her mind that dinner tonight would turn into a well-mannered brawl of sorts. She was already at the table, which could seat a dozen people, when Zach finally appeared, fresh from a shower after working all day outdoors, and the determined set of his mouth told the same story.

He didn't say a word until their mother joined them. Before sitting down, she cast a look at Zach then Willow. "Are you two quarreling again?"

"Not yet," she said. When Cass had left earlier, Willow had seen her exchange a few words with Zach near the driveway. She'd been waiting for this.

As always, he came right to the point. "I can't believe you hired Cherry—Cass Moran."

Their mother unfolded her damask napkin, then laid it across her lap. "I hired Cass because she badly needs a job and I need someone with her experience to help put this party together for Willow and Thad. What exactly is your objection, Zachary?"

"You really think she's qualified to plan this thing?" He folded his arms. "This isn't a

backyard barbecue, Mom, or even Thanksgiving dinner for the whole family. The governor will be here, his staff, members of the
state legislature, every rancher in the area and
probably most of Thad's colleagues."

"I know that. I think she's more than qualified." Their mother passed the potatoes to
Zach. She watched him take a serving, hand the
bowl to Willow, then slid a platter of roast beef
his way. "Cass grew up with nothing. *Nothing*," she repeated, which reminded Willow of
Cody. "Honestly, I would have taken her in if
I could, but your father disagreed, I'm sorry to
say. I cheered when she finally left that run-
down farm to go to college," her mother said.

"On a full Jean Bodine scholarship," he
pointed out in a wry tone.

Neither their mom nor Zach looked at each
other. "She also had a grant that paid her
room and board," Jean said, "although none
of that concerns you. Cass has repaid every
penny I contributed. Not that I wanted her to."

When the food had been passed around
the table, forks were lifted and the three of
them began to eat. Willow's dinner seemed
to stick in her throat until, finally, she pushed
away her plate. Cass had poured her heart out

earlier. "Mom, I'm not that hungry tonight." And she needed to have her say. "Zach, Cass is my friend, and I'll expect you to treat her with the same kindness Mom will. She deserves this chance."

He had the grace to look shamefaced. "So, fine," he said, "let her try to pull off this party, but if she makes one mistake—"

Their mother slammed a delicate hand on the table. "You do not give orders to me, Zachary Bodine. *I* hired Cass. I'm the one who will pay her, which means you don't get a say. Like your father, you should stick to the business of this ranch—which, like him, is all you seem to care about. When you step through that back door, you're in my territory. And what I choose to do for that girl, whether that means giving her the opportunity to get a college degree or a job on the WB, is my choice alone."

Zach's mouth fell open. "Mom—"

"No, let me finish. I've watched you with her since the first day she came to this house with Willow when they were girls. I've seen you and Cass knock heads more than once. I think you should ask yourself one question— why do you make things difficult for her? Or is there something there that you refuse to let yourself acknowledge?"

"To paraphrase Shakespeare, maybe he protests too much," Willow muttered, her gaze on her abandoned dinner plate.

"You two think I could have some other interest in her?" Zach looked dumbfounded. He waited until they looked at him. "You're wrong. Or did you forget how she steered Willow to Cody Jones?"

"That's not true," Willow said. "She knew how I felt about him, and I appreciated her advice, but eventually Cass did urge me to break things off with him."

"That's what she said. Sure, after the damage was done. After Dad's health was broken—"

Their mother rose from her chair. "Stop right there." Her voice trembled, and Willow suspected she was on the verge of tears. "Your dad's death was no one's fault, if that's what you're saying, certainly not Willow's. Or, for that matter, Cody's. And as far as Cass is concerned, I don't care if you disagree." Their mom brushed past him. "She stays."

WHEN WILLOW LED a chestnut gelding into the outdoor arena at the Circle H the next morning, to her surprise she saw Cody standing at the rail. He couldn't have known she'd be here today, or any day for that matter, because Willow never knew herself. And why assume he was waiting for her? "Good-looking horse," he said.

Willow turned enough to see over her shoulder, silently asking him why he was here when he worked at the McMann spread miles away, closer to Farrier than to Barren and this ranch. After their previous encounter at the WB, she'd told him not to come there again, but the inference had been not to see her anywhere.

"Need to talk to Olivia this morning," he explained. Olivia McCord had acquired a reputation in the area as a fine trainer, but she must resent Cody. After all, he'd stolen her brother's cattle and burned down Grey's barn. It seemed odd he'd show up here, but at least Willow had been wrong. He hadn't been waiting for her. It was nothing more than a coincidence.

"It's a free country," he said, clearly in response to Willow's accusatory glare. "Hadley's newest horse has been giving us some grief. At first, Hadley thought he was settling in, getting acquainted, but now it feels more like Thunder was abused. When I'm not riding him, he stands in his stall or in the corner of a fence trying to look invisible." He paused. "Olivia around?"

"She's at her antiques shop in Barren. She should be back soon. She's the best trainer I know, but this morning you'll have to get in line."

"So, now you know why I'm here. I should ask you the same question."

Obviously, he hadn't forgotten Willow's parting words at the WB.

"I'm taking training lessons." She'd left the ranch right after breakfast, driving to the Circle H with her heart thumping in anticipation, feeling...carefree. "Olivia's been invaluable with my horse Silver, and she felt I was ready to try this one. I'll just warm him up until she gets back." Tugging on the lead rope, she positioned the horse in the ring so Cody could see him. He was something of a horse whisperer, always had been. She might not want him coming near her now, but she valued his opinion. "What do you think?"

"About you being a trainer?" Cody had a faint smile.

"No, about this horse. You knew what I meant."

Cody leaned against the fence, arms crossed on the top rail. "Might make a good cow pony," he said, squinting against the sun. "Let me take a closer look." He pushed off the fence, then stepped through the gate into the ring, slowly approaching and speaking to the chestnut, his voice low and soft. He ran his hands lightly over the horse's body, making its skin quiver, and the animal arched its neck around to nuzzle Cody's shoulder. "Kind eyes, and looks like he has some good bloodlines. Were you planning to show him instead?"

"He's not mine. He belongs to Finn Donovan. The sheriff wanted a reliable mount that his wife can ride or, in the future, their daughter." Willow's cell dinged with an incoming message, and she pulled the phone from her pocket to check the screen. "Oh no. Olivia's tied up until lunchtime. Then she has to run over to her other store in Farrier. I guess I wasted a trip today."

She started to turn the gelding toward the gate, but Cody said, "I've got a little time. I'll work him with you—if that's okay. Nothing personal."

Willow hesitated. She shouldn't encourage him, yet she hated to miss a lesson. With the party plans, her time was not her own these days. "All right, I guess so."

"What's his name?"

"Finn bought him at an auction under the name Buck."

Cody gave a full-out smile, his eyes with that mischievous look she remembered. "Does he?"

"Not that I've seen. But who knows how he was treated?" She almost smiled, too. "What would you call him?"

Cody assessed the horse again, looked into his liquid brown eyes. The gelding shifted his weight, took a couple steps, his hindquarters swaying, and Cody laughed. "Dancer," he said.

She couldn't help laughing, too. "Like one of Santa's reindeer?"

He trapped her gaze. "No, like at the road-house on Saturday nights." He and Willow had first met there, had gone together more than once, danced and held each other close, then kissed in the parking lot. Cody cleared his throat. "I always loved to hear you laugh." Then, watching the horse shift again, "He's got a nice two-step. So, why not Dancer?"

"You're crazy," she said. *Crazy about you*, his eyes seemed to tell her. Willow ignored that. "No," she said, "I think Prancer fits him better." With the lead rope pressing into her engagement ring, she led the horse toward the center of the arena. "Much better than Buck, although Finn may rename him."

"Then Prancer it is. For now," Cody agreed. "He does have a light, springy step as if he's in some parade—maybe to celebrate me getting out of Navarro."

Willow ignored that, too. She shouldn't talk to Cody at all, much less about *personal* matters like their shared memory of the roadhouse. She shouldn't stay here with him, their shoulders brushing now and then as they worked the gelding without Olivia. Together, as she'd never thought they would be again. And yet… She couldn't resist the chance to soak up his knowledge, to take the lesson that Olivia had canceled. Cody stayed with her around the ring as Willow lightly flicked the whip at the gelding's hindquarters to keep him moving forward on the lunge line. For long moments, they didn't talk at all until Cody broke the silence, as if he were continuing their conversation about his release from prison—without a parade.

"Matter of fact, I have some notion of opening a training center myself. Like you. Someday. First, I need to earn and save money, figure out how to make that happen."

"You'd be good, Cody," she said. Zach wasn't completely right about him. Cody had ambition. Like her. He had talents and certainly skills with horses, but was that enough? "Do you have real training experience? Other than wrangling horses at the McMann's? And I remember you did some rodeoing once."

His eyes lighting up, Cody told her about the Wild Horse Program. "One horse really caught me right here." He pointed at his solar plexus, the hard plane of muscle, then at his heart. "I don't mean kicked me. I fell head over tail for that mare. I called her Diva, but that's like an oxymoron or whatever. The opposite of how she really is. I thought the name would help build her confidence. She does— did—hold her head high, as if she's queen of the world, or something. Was," he added.

Willow's pulse skipped in alarm. "What happened to her?"

He shrugged. "She's still there, or she was last time I checked. I just hope they don't ruin her. She has a real soft mouth." He glanced at Willow's lips. "She needs a delicate touch. Some of the other guys could be pretty rough." He gestured at the horse. "I'd cool this big boy down a little now, then let him hang out in his stall. You don't want to overwork him, especially at first."

As they walked the horse to end the session, she said, "I've only worked with him twice so far, including today, but I think he has potential." Willow frowned a little. "I don't want to 'ruin' him, as you said about Diva."

Cody did a double take. "You've been riding all your life, Willow." She tried not to react to the gentle way he said her name. She seemed to be doing an awful lot of trying today. "You have a quiet manner with horses that they, as herd animals inclined to panic, appreciate. I'm sure you've noticed Prancer is a bit skittish. You don't believe in your own ability to train?"

"I competed in shows, but I got hurt pretty

bad last year, and as a trainer I'm a rank beginner. Maybe my brother was right."

Cody grinned. "I've never known that to be true."

"I meant about risking my health again, winding up worse than before."

"Just because you got hurt once doesn't mean it'll happen again." Then his smile faded. "He doesn't want you coming here." It wasn't a question.

"True, and he doesn't know about today," she admitted.

She paused, knowing their talk had delved into territory better avoided, along with this personal connection through horses. She decided a mention of her fiancé couldn't hurt. "Thad agrees with Zach. He's said I won't need a business once we're married. I disagree."

"Are they both stuck in some time warp?" His eyes sparkled. "Thinking women still belong in the kitchen or—?"

"Ha-ha," she said.

"If so, they sure have that wrong. When I was on the rodeo circuit years ago, I even knew a few female stock contractors and that's a rough job."

Willow grinned. "There's no limit to what we can do."

She and Cody walked on either side of the horse from the arena and into the barn. He snapped the newly named Prancer into one of the crossties, and Willow did the other side. Cody took a brush from the tack box against the wall, then began to sweep arena dust from the gelding's hide as if they worked together companionably like this every day. But the last thing Willow needed, even when she'd appreciated his support about women, was to feel that connection to Cody once more, to feel in sync as they had before their breakup and his incarceration and...Thad. She didn't want to lead Cody on.

She took the brush from his hand, taking care not to touch him. Willow swiped it along Prancer's near side, not quite looking at Cody over the gelding's back. Cody propped both hands on his hips and stared at her.

"Was I just told without words to leave?" he asked. "What did I say wrong?"

"Nothing. It's...nothing," she said, remembering. *Do you love him as much as you said you loved me?* That was a temptation she couldn't afford. She loved Thad. "Cody..."

He glanced at her engagement ring, "Yeah, I know." He patted Prancer's offside, straightened his forelock, then ambled toward the barn doors, shoulders back, head high. She wondered if Cody wasn't more than a little like a wild mustang himself. A mistreated animal that could break her heart. She wouldn't let that happen again. "Good luck with that horse," he called back, but then his footsteps halted.

Willow glanced up, and with the sun behind him, it looked like... Had Cody just blown her a kiss? Then he was gone, rounding the corner of the barn and out of view. A minute later, she heard a truck start, the wheels crunching along the gravel drive leading to the road. To whatever his future, so different from hers, might hold. She hoped his would be good, too.

Those clandestine nights at the local roadhouse she'd once spent in Cody's arms were part of her past.

She turned her attention back to Prancer, feeling guilty anyway. She shouldn't have let him tease her.

She needed to focus on Thad. The man she was going to marry.

CHAPTER SIX

THAD HAD BOOKED a table by the window—
once again—at the Bon Appetit, the fanciest
restaurant in Barren. He leaned closer to take
her hand, and she could guess what was coming. "I thought tonight we'd kick some dates
around for our wedding. What do you say?"

"Thad, we just got engaged. Do we need to
set a date so soon? Let's do the party first."

The smile lines showed around his brown
eyes. The candlelight gleamed off his dark
hair. "Here's a suggestion—we could announce our wedding day at the party. Everyone will be wondering anyway."

Willow glanced at the other diners, most
of whom seemed to be focused on their private conversations. Across the way, though,
Bernice Caldwell, a noted town gossip, was
eating dinner with her friend Claudia Mon-
roe, their always-curious gazes occasionally
homing in on Willow and Thad. She lowered

her voice. "I haven't fully absorbed what happened the last time we ate here. As I told the jeweler, I never expected you to propose then. You really swept me off my feet."

Thad didn't get to respond.

"Welcome," a voice had boomed out next to their table. "Willow, Thad, I am so *très* sorry I missed you the last time." Jack Hancock, tall and almost thin, wore his white chef's toque. The owner of the Bon Appetit, he fancied himself to be French, and had a tendency at times to lapse into the language or his version thereof. Willow didn't know if he had actually attended a culinary institute in France. He was now married to Cass's mother. "May I offer you a small amuse-bouche before your dinner? It will be my pleasure. Tonight, we have the freshest escargots."

Thad raised an eyebrow. "Willow?"

She wasn't a fan of snails, but the chef seemed proud of his menu. "Yes, Jack. Thank you."

He hurried off, greeting other diners as he went back to the kitchen, and Thad squeezed her hand as he resumed their conversation. He liked to touch. "Sweetheart, why do I have the feeling you're avoiding this issue?"

"Our wedding date? Of course not." She smiled. "I'm just a bit distracted."

He sounded amused. "Were you playing with your horses today?" Still holding her hand, he pulled back a little in his chair to let Jack set their complimentary appetizers in front of them.

Willow drew her hand from his. She was still trying not to feel guilty that she'd spent the morning with Cody working Prancer. One of their first bonds years ago had been that shared love of horses. Strange now that had almost happened today before Willow had squelched the feeling.

But alarm bells had started ringing in her head. "Training is what I've wanted to do since I was a girl. You know that, Thad."

His smile seemed indulgent. "Every girl is horse crazy at a certain age, but Zach's right. I don't want to have to worry about you. Besides," he went on, "after we're married, we'll be living in town. I need to be close to work and the courthouse. And often we'll be entertaining." He paused. "The engagement party will be your chance to slide into your new role. Soon there won't be time for animals."

Willow picked at her escargots. She was

rapidly losing what little appetite she'd had but tried to keep her voice light. "We haven't talked about where we'll live. Thad, it sounds as if you're trying to plan my life when what I want is to follow my dream. This can't be just about your needs. I have mine, too."

He glanced up at the elaborate tin ceiling. "Do you really think I don't have your best interests at heart? I love you. I want us to be happy."

"I do, too," she said.

"You're not upset, are you? I'm not trying to ruin our evening."

Willow forced a smile. "I'm not trying to be difficult, but I don't care to become just your supportive spouse. That's only part of any marriage. You're a successful lawyer, and I hope to become a successful trainer. Yes, it's that important to me. We need to get this right. Maybe we should consider living out-side of town, midway between your office and the ranch."

Thad pushed his crystal glass aside. He'd finished his snails, as if none of this conver-sation had distressed him. "We don't have to decide tonight." And yet he'd pressed her earlier about their wedding date. "There'll be plenty of time to work out all these details."

Which was true enough. She and Thad had known each other all their lives, yet that familiarity had centered around his friendship with Zach. Their own relationship as a couple was relatively new, and obviously they had much to learn about each other. "I agree," she said at last. Maybe she'd overreacted. Still, she couldn't help adding, "As long as my work is treated as equally important to yours."

Thad didn't blink. He sent her one of the loving looks he often used, then waggled his fingers. "Give me your cell phone, please."

Willow dug it out from her bag, then handed it to him. "Why?"

He opened the Notes app, then keyed in a few numbers. "These dates for our wedding will work for me." He'd obviously consulted his calendar before dinner. "Once you've had a chance to review, you can select the one that's right for both of us. Or we can revisit this. See how cooperative I can be?" He looked across the room. "I see our dinners coming. You ordered Dover sole, yes?"

"I did."

He beamed at Jack, who served their entrées himself instead of sending any of the black-jacketed waiters hovering near other tables. "Looks great, *monsieur*," Thad told him. "You never disappoint, and your *bifteck a là béarnaise* is my absolute favorite. I couldn't find better in Kansas City or New York." He dug into his steak as soon as Jack had disappeared again.

Her fish was flaky and tender, yet Willow couldn't dispel the notion that her fiancé had reminded her not only of his aspirations but had initially put her on the spot about the place he expected her to occupy in his life.

Willow hoped she had made herself clear. She would not give up her dream.

CODY SPENT THE next day rounding up strays with Hadley. The job done—if it ever really was—they were riding through the pasture nearest to the barn, keeping the cows and calves bunched together with the help of the ranch dogs when Hadley's SAT phone rang. For a moment he stared at it.

"I never get calls," he said. "The only one I remember was last summer about Dallas's adoptive mom being sick. I only carry this phone so my wife won't worry. This can't be good."

Cody didn't want to eavesdrop, so he rode on, chasing an independent-minded heifer that didn't want to stay with the herd; at the same time, he kept an eye on the rest of the Angus mooing and milling about. In the past couple of years Hadley had rebuilt Clara McMann's herd, turning her neglected spread from a barren wasteland into a functioning, prosperous ranch again. Cody had been there at the beginning, before prison, and he was here again now. As much as he wanted to help, he hoped he wasn't about to get caught up in some crisis that might trigger his old nightmares.

"Clara, slow down," Hadley said behind Cody in a taut voice. "I'm almost home. We'll be there shortly. Hang on," he added, then ended the call.

"What's up, boss?"

"Jenna's not feeling good." Hadley's wife was Cass Moran's sister. "I told Clara to phone the doc and see if Sawyer's there, but otherwise we'll have to go over to Farrier General's ER."

Cody could see anxiety in the man's

electric-blue gaze. Hadley could be a hard case, and he looked as tough as nails, but with Jenna he was a real softie. Right now, he looked scared.

At the gate, Cody leaned down to open it—then, calling on the dogs again, he let them push the cows into the adjoining pasture while he watched for escapees. By the time he shut the gate, Hadley was at the barn unsaddling his horse. He had already loosened Mr. Robert's cinch when Cody rode in and saw that Hadley's brother had appeared. Exactly what he'd dreaded. Just back from his brief vacation with his fiancée, Dallas didn't say a word as Hadley threw the reins at him. "Here, you're in charge. Take over, Dallas. Cody's going with us into town."

This was news to Cody, who lifted his shoulders in a shrug that said, *Who, me?* Hadley hadn't given him much responsibility yet, and Cody had assumed he was on probation here, too, not only with his parole officer. Now he was supposed to ride shotgun with a sick woman on board? This wasn't in his job description. "I can stay," he said. "Let Dallas go—" After all, he was family.

Hadley was already running toward the house. "I want you."

More likely, he didn't trust Cody to manage the ranch while he was gone. With a growing sense of doom, Cody followed him. He could hear Hadley call Jenna's name as he ran through the house, panic clear in his voice. In the front hall Cody met Hadley, with Jenna in his arms, clattering down the steps from the second floor. Normally pretty, with auburn hair and clear blue eyes, she looked ashen, her head against Hadley's shoulder.

"I don't know what's wrong with me," she kept saying in a weak voice. Hadley strode out the front door to the extended cab pickup. Clara, a slender older woman with graying brown hair and light brown eyes, hurried along behind, wringing her hands. "She seemed fine earlier," she told Hadley. "Then just before I called you, she fainted in the nursery."

"Take care of the twins," Hadley said. "Thanks, Clara." He turned to Cody, who kept thinking of his mother being murdered. Jenna wasn't hurt, she was sick but… Hadley tossed the keys at him. "Drive. I want to sit with Jenna in the back. Don't do anything tricky."

That stung, but Cody *had* lied to him, one of the few people who'd ever treated him kindly. They hadn't gone a mile along the road before he heard a siren. Blue lights flashing, a cruiser overtook them and pulled him over.

"Were you speeding?" Hadley asked Cody from the rear seat.

Finn Donovan, the sheriff, popped his head inside the truck. "Clara called. Said you need help."

"An escort," Hadley agreed. "Get us there as fast as you can."

Finn didn't ask questions. His sharp, gray-green gaze assessed Jenna's condition, then he hopped back in his car and led the way to the medical office in town, siren screaming. Cody thought that was a bit much, but what did he know? Sawyer McCord, the doctor and Olivia's husband, was waiting for them in the facility on Cottonwood Street.

Cody sat with Finn in the waiting room. "I hope she's all right," he said.

Finn, his dark hair tipped with gold, studied Cody's profile. "How'd you end up at the McManns' again?"

"I needed a job. Hadley gave me one."

Finn wasn't a fan of Cody. He had arrested him for arson. Before that he'd wanted all three of Cody's gang to serve time for cattle rustling. "Way I figure it, you have two strikes against you—three would mean a lot more time in Navarro or a max facility."

"Thanks for the vote of confidence, Sheriff."

Finn pointed a finger at him. "Listen, I don't like what I know about you. One false move again, and I'll be on you like a leech. Understand?"

"Yessir." Cody had just met the long arm of the law again. He hadn't felt comfortable around cops since his mother's murder.

"Decent people in this town deserve my protection. And they'll get it. Remember that." Finn went back to reading, or pretending to read, an ancient *People* magazine from the stack of periodicals on the corner table.

Cody sank deeper into his chair. First, Thad at the hardware store and now the sheriff. He wondered if he'd ever live down what he'd done, if he could atone for his crimes after all—or did he need to try harder? He considered mentioning Prancer, telling Finn he'd soon have a pretty good horse, but didn't speak. The plastic cushion dug into his backside, and briefly he wished he'd never had to return to Stewart County. Wished he'd never seen Willow and reinjured his broken heart. He couldn't seem to forget how she'd looked in the morning sun at the Circle H, her blond angel's hair and innocent blue eyes, her laughter when they'd named Prancer. How she'd smelled of lemon blossoms the way he remembered—until she'd sent him away with a flick of that grooming brush.

By the time Hadley emerged with Jenna from the exam room, Cody was ready to hit the road out of Barren—as if he could. What had he been thinking? He'd hoped to prevent her from making a mistake with Thad, but Willow was still engaged. She'd made that clear enough. *What part of that don't you understand, Jones?*

Jenna leaned again on Hadley's shoulder, but her color looked better. His arm was around her and hers was around his waist.

"I'm fine," she said. "Just a fainting spell." She glanced at Cody. "Thanks to you and Finn for bringing us here so promptly."

Sawyer, in his white coat, said, "Don't forget to eat lunch next time, Jenna. I'll let you know when the rest of the lab work comes back, but your blood sugar was a bit low."

Cody breathed a sigh of relief. Crisis averted. No nightmare tonight, he hoped.

On the way home, Jenna nestled into her husband's embrace, and Cody couldn't help but smile at the image of them in his rearview mirror. He envied them. And Hadley had trusted him enough to play chauffeur for the wife he cherished.

Cody was walking from the truck toward the barn, thinking about dinner at the bunkhouse, when Hadley stopped him. "While we were gone, Dallas fed the horses. The cattle have settled down out there for the night. You're good to go home now, but I'll owe you some overtime pay for the ride into Barren and back."

"No, you don't. I was glad to help. I'm even more glad Jenna's okay."

Hadley clapped him on the shoulder. "Listen. I've been meaning to mention this.

You told me about that horse you trained at Navarro, right? So how about this instead? Why don't you go ahead and apply to adopt that mare?" He paused while Cody tried to take in what he'd just said. Hadley already knew how difficult that might prove.

"That's a nice idea, but I don't have anywhere to keep her. I probably wouldn't get approved even if I did apply."

"You won't know unless you try," Hadley said, a smile playing on his lips. "You could stable her right here." Then he turned and went back up to the house, leaving Cody with his head turning around inside like that girl in *The Exorcist*. Had Hadley forgiven him for lying before? He'd let Cody stay on the job and live in the bunkhouse for as long as he liked? He'd even take in a wild mustang that could make Hadley's three horses look like Kentucky Derby winners? Not that she wasn't pretty.

An ex-con might not qualify to adopt, but then again, he might. Hope was not a familiar feeling for Cody, but just maybe… At least, if he couldn't have Willow, he'd have something.

With Finn Donovan's warning in his

mind, he decided to fill out the application. See where it led. Maybe somewhere good this time.

Him, too.

CHAPTER SEVEN

"WILLOW, WE'VE LOOKED at half a dozen caterers and you still haven't made a choice." Her mother slid the Bon Appetit's menu toward Willow, who couldn't help staring at the table by the window, remembering her most recent dinner with Thad. Close to lunchtime, the place was still empty. "If you're undecided, I think Jack's is an obvious pick," Jean said. "He's right here in Barren, his prices are reasonable and he's eager for our business." Jack had begun to cater events in the area, but would he be able to handle such a big party?

Willow's head was beginning to hurt. They'd spent the morning studying menus online from firms as far away as Kansas City or Wichita, then visiting a few places in Farrier before they'd ended up at Jack's, and his options of *boeuf en croûte*, steak Diane and chicken marsala blurred before her eyes. She didn't think Cass would welcome using the Bon Appetit; after all, Jack was married to Cass's estranged mother. "Mom, does it really matter who supplies the beef or chicken or shrimp? And this will all cost the earth. Dinner for two hundred people? I think we should do something simpler."

"You are your father's daughter," Jean murmured, and the light seemed to dim in her eyes. "He always pinched a penny twice before he spent it. Except on his cattle."

Willow felt an immediate wave of fresh guilt. She didn't think she was at all like her father, but she didn't want to disappoint her mother. "I just wish we weren't making such a thing of this. How many friends of mine have thrown elaborate parties to announce their engagements? None," she answered herself. "Becca and Calvin put a notice in the *Barren Journal* with a cute picture, had no party at all, and they've invited fewer than forty people to their wedding. Dallas and Lizzie—"

"That's not the same. We've already put an engagement announcement in the local paper with a mention of the party being planned."

"But you're threatening to redo the whole house, and what if it rains? The cost of the tents alone, which Cass is seeing about today, could probably pay for a much smaller gathering. All I can hear is the constant ringing of a cash register. Is this really necessary? None of those guests whose names you've mentioned are important to me."

"They will be." Jean pretended to study the Bon Appetit's new catering menu. "If I'm right, someday Thad will follow his father into politics."

Which didn't excite Willow—all that public pressure. "But in the meantime, there's no sense in bankrupting the WB. Let's wait to do anything more until we start on the wedding. I'm surprised Zach hasn't objected."

"Your brother would do anything for Thad, and not because Thad may have a great deal of power in the future."

"His dad already does." Willow didn't particularly like Grant Nesbitt, and she'd had the impression her future father-in-law found her lacking, too. She did love Thad, but how would his plans play out with hers once they were married? "Mom, this isn't me, that's all."

Jean arched a brow. "You're the bride, the center of attention, and my only daughter doesn't get married every day." She glanced around to make sure they were still alone. Something from the kitchen smelled amazing. The nearby tables were set for lunch, china sparkling, silverware gleaming on ivory tablecloths. Crystal glassware reflected the sun streaming in through the windows. Just like the other night, although then candlelight had shimmered in this same space. Her mom said, "That reminds me, we need to start shopping for your dress."

"My dress? We haven't even set our wedding date." Thad had mentioned that every time they spoke. She hadn't actually seen him since their dinner, and needing time to make her decision, she'd been avoiding him. Today she had four text messages, a voice mail and an email waiting.

"I meant a dress for this party, not the wedding." Her mother glanced at Willow's diamond, which she'd been turning on her finger. "You're sure about this engagement, honey?"

"Yes. Of course."

Still, an image of Cody in the Circle H arena shot through Willow's mind like an arrow aimed at a target. Hadn't she told him to keep away? He'd known what she meant the first time. Yet he'd shared that training session with her, they'd laughed together and, unless she'd imagined it, he'd blown her a kiss.

The ache in her temples began to pound, and she pushed the Bon Appetit's menu toward her mother. "Nothing has changed. I'm going to marry Thad."

She could see her mother visibly relax.

But Willow's stubborn thoughts ran on. She'd met Cody soon after she finished college. Then, after the barn fire he'd disappeared. He'd eventually come back, risking his freedom, to see her, and their relationship had deepened until he'd been arrested.

Jean said, "You've always had a shy streak, so I could understand how at one time Cody Jones's outgoing nature was a good balance for you. Now, the promise—or threat—of media attention because of Thad's father must seem a bit scary. Frankly, it's put me on edge, too. The WB has never produced such a show before, but I'm here for you. Cass is a big help. We'll manage. As long as you're sure about Thad—"

"I'm sure." No matter how much Cody still tugged at her heartstrings, how good he looked, or how closely they shared their love of horses, she couldn't throw away what she already had. He needed to prove himself before he built a life with anybody.

During Cody's time in prison, she'd come to love Thad, who treated her well and offered her the same kind of life she'd always known on the ranch—except of course for the public part. With Cody she'd rebelled, taken a brief walk on the wild side. She owed her family—herself, too—a better outcome this time. She wasn't about to cause anyone grief again. Including Thad.

Actually, she'd made her choice right here in this restaurant when he proposed. Because of the party and their upcoming wedding, they were both under pressure now, which probably explained his attitude the other night. It wasn't as if they'd actually quarreled.

"Let's go with the Bon Appetit," she said and, in spite of her killer headache, sent her mother a brilliant smile. Even Cody might thank her someday for being the sensible one who'd finally put that youthful indiscretion behind her.

In the end, that would be all they shared.

AFTER SHE LEFT the Bon Appetit, Willow wandered along Main Street looking into store windows, already having second thoughts about the steak they'd chosen for the engagement party dinner. Outside the restaurant, her mom had met up with a friend, and they'd decided to have coffee together. Willow had left them to catch up, pleased to have these few minutes to herself. Alone, as her headache began to ease, she gazed into the windows at Olivia McCord Antiques—and suddenly spied Cody's reflection in the glass. Before she could prepare herself, he'd crossed the street from Earl's Hardware. "Hey," he said.

She turned from her perusal of a mahogany side table on display, reminded of how small the town really was. She rarely shopped or even browsed here. Twice a year she and Jean spent a weekend in Kansas City, where they went on a spending spree, buying clothes for the season. Now, seeing Cody, Willow wished she'd sat in the car to wait.

Her mother's question about the engagement had shaken her. Cody's unexpected appearance made her remember him at the Circle H. And that when they'd finished with Prancer, she'd treated him rudely. Willow said, "At Olivia's, I didn't mean to snatch that brush from you. It was the right thing to do...but not that way."

"You mean give me the brush-off?" he asked, hat tilted back on his head. Had he made a pun to lighten the moment? But Cody sobered. "I didn't like leaving things like that."

"Me either, but *I* have to—because nothing good can come of us spending time together." Her ring flashed in the sun. "I'm going to marry Thad, and that's the best thing for you, too."

His gaze darkened. "Don't tell me what I need, Willow." He looked away. "Are you really that...happy with him?"

"Absolutely." After their dinner that night, Thad had taken her for ice cream at the café. They'd eaten their cones while they walked up and down Main—there weren't that many streets in Barren—and by the time they drove back to the WB, she'd nearly forgotten their earlier disagreement. At the ranch he'd kissed her sweetly good-night. She glanced now toward the Bon Appetit, wishing her mother would appear. "I don't want to hurt you, Cody. I've always...liked you. I think you're going to find yourself. I hope you'll train horses—"

"But will you?" He didn't seem to expect an answer. "After you and I finished with Prancer, Olivia showed up at the McMann ranch and gave me some pointers about Hadley's gelding—the depressed one? Thunder seems to be coming around."

"I'm glad that worked out."

"And I've already made a start trying to 'find myself.' I'm applying to adopt that mare at Navarro. Diva," he said. "Hadley told me I can stable her at the McMann ranch. Convenient, huh?" He tried a smile. "Maybe I could help you again sometime with Prancer."

"That's not going to happen."

"Why?" He half waved at a man walking on the other side of the street. Calvin Stern's gaze lingered on them before he moved on, and Cody returned his attention to Willow. "Because I went to prison?"

"This has nothing to do with Navarro." Which wasn't quite true. Willow's head pounded again. It was obviously time they had this out. Years ago, Cody had charmed her into believing *he* was the right choice for her, which had only led to disaster even after they'd broken up. Her father's death, Cody's trial and conviction... That had been enough turmoil for a lifetime. "What we had once is long past and that's where it should stay."

"Are you trying to convince me or yourself?" Cody's mouth tightened. "I probably ought to leave this alone, but I think you should know." He said the words as if he couldn't help himself, hadn't planned to. "I ran into Thad at Earl's not long ago. He didn't seem exactly pleased to have me back in Barren." *Near you*, he might have added.

"You don't like Thad because of your trial."

"I didn't much like him before, and certainly vice versa, but yeah. I couldn't help but notice you weren't in court then, so you probably don't know how the trial went."

Willow made an exasperated sound. "I wasn't there because I'd been hurt in that show ring. I was recovering then, and you were in enough trouble. People were still talking about us. And, yes, my family disapproved. What could I have done for you by sitting in that courtroom? Nothing I could do or say would have helped. You were guilty, Cody. And before that, you did steal Grey Wilson's cattle."

"He should have pressed charges for rustling his cows. I know that. And I can't blame anybody but myself about the arson charge. That fire was a bad move, a petty move, and I'm sorrier than I can say for that, too. What I did was a Severity Level 7 offense in Kansas, a nonperson felony, meaning no lives were lost. But getting sent up for arson was exactly the right call. Willow, I would never have forgiven myself if I'd hurt somebody, or any of Grey's animals…" He didn't go on, and Willow could see the pain in his eyes. "What did I think I was doing then? I love horses."

"And you want to make up now for what you did."

"Guess I had to learn the hard way. I'm not proud of that. But Derek and Calvin are doing all right now. And I'm trying." His gaze held hers. "If they can make it, so can I." He told her he'd even had a beer with them one night, talked about things, which had helped. "The judge gave me a real tongue-lashing in court—again, richly deserved—and the maximum sentence with no previous record." He paused. "Eleven months. Could have been life if someone had died—which I don't even want to think about. And yet I do, all the time. I have to. Willow, I've been messed up since the day my dad murdered my mom."

A sobering thought, indeed. Willow looked toward the Bon Appetit again, but her mother still didn't appear. "I take your early release for good behavior as a sign you've started down a better road, so do yourself a favor and concentrate on your future. That's what I'm going to do. Even if you'd like to just be friends, I don't think that would work for me."

Her pulse was now a drumbeat in her ears. She couldn't afford to feel sympathy toward him, even when she recalled the earlier tragedy of his parents' deaths, especially his mother's. Cody's behavior after that was understandable. Or it had been for a time. "And about Thad, he may have contributed to your being sent to Navarro, but he was just doing his job."

"I don't care about him. I care about you."

"Cody, I don't want to hear any more."

She edged away from him, walked to the corner across from the Bon Appetit and, to her relief, saw her mother coming out of the restaurant. Jean hailed Willow, then noticed Cody and her brows rose.

Without looking both ways, Willow stepped off the curb. A horn blared, and Cody's hands shot out to pull her back, Willow already beginning to shake from the close call. She'd nearly been hit by a car while trying to get away from him. Just as quickly, he released her arm. "Don't do this, Willow. Thad's not who you think he is. He's not."

"You're wrong." *You have to be*.

She was across the street before Cody could say another word.

CHAPTER EIGHT

ON HORSEBACK, WILLOW rode with Cass across the WB toward a far-off stand of trees. They were supposed to be working with Jean on the final guest list for the party, but neither of them had felt like staying indoors or even sitting on the swing at one end of the house's wraparound porch. The next day had dawned even warmer than usual, and by noon, with the sun high overhead, the temperature had become scorching hot. Now, in midafternoon, a slight breeze had finally begun to cool the air.

Cass hadn't been on a horse in years, and never anywhere but the WB, but the gentle gelding Willow had chosen for her from the ranch string of cow ponies was more than forgiving, and soon Cass had settled into the saddle. Also, the short getaway gave them a brief respite from the flurry of party activity that seemed to increase by the minute.

Yesterday, Cass had negotiated the best price for the rented tents and chosen where all the fairy lights and lanterns should be strung around the property, while Willow had studied catering menus and agreed with her mother on the Bon Appetit. As expected, Cass hadn't been pleased about the choice.

"My mother is ahead of me on every phase of this party," Willow admitted, "and she's ready to start on the wedding itself."

Cass's horse had stopped to rip up a few tufts of grass, and she pulled his head up. "Have you and Thad chosen the date?"

"I'd love a Christmas wedding—I've always dreamed of that—except December's not on the list he gave me. A few of his choices wouldn't work for me, but I've promised to discuss those that will tomorrow night. Thad has a black-tie event at the bar association in Farrier."

"Oh, what are you wearing? Men have it easy. A sexy tuxedo—and done."

"Mom wanted me to buy a new gown, but I'm going with the royal blue I wore to the Cattlemen's Association ball last winter. Thad shared our table that night with Zach, Mom and four other people. I assumed that was a one-off event, but then he asked me out, making clear our second evening together wasn't because I was his best friend's sister."

Cass's hands tightened on the reins. "I rarely go to fancy events like that, except, of course, to work."

"I don't think you'd want to go to this one—a dinner/dance with Thad's colleagues." Willow wasn't looking forward to it either.

"Sorry, that did sound like jealousy. You mean your dress with the crystals on the bodice? That's gorgeous, Willow."

She rolled her eyes. "I've worn it on at least two other social occasions, but why not? Enough money's being invested in this engagement party. Mom's lending me her diamond studs for a bit of bling." Her father's gift to Jean on their last anniversary. "So, no cost to me. The earrings, and Thad's ring, should be all the jewelry I'll need. Unless you think—"

"You know what I think." Cass probably didn't mean gems. "A night out is always fun, but in this case, the company...not as much."

Willow ignored that. She'd heard enough about Thad yesterday from Cody, and she told Cass about seeing him again in town.

"He wasn't right about Thad, and I know you agree with him, but I hated to give Cody what amounted to an ultimatum," she said. "We seem to keep bumping into each other, and maybe he'd like to pick up where we left off—but I can't."

"You wouldn't." Had she heard a slight question in Cass's voice?

Willow concentrated on the view ahead of her horse between Silver's ears. "If it were a simple matter of training Prancer—the new horse at the Circle H—that might be okay, but it's not simple. Thad would mind. Zach would, too."

"Maybe we shouldn't talk about men." Cass clearly wanted to avoid any mention of Zach. She edged her horse away from Willow. The gelding and Silver had been nipping at each other's ears. "Oh, I forgot to tell you. I've started looking for a place. Grey and Shadow don't need me taking up space in their house much longer. My sister would probably like her privacy back."

Willow said, "There aren't many rental properties in Barren, only one apartment complex miles from the WB, and you have to start work early. Mom has a list for this, a list for that every morning…"

Cass pushed hair from her eyes. The wind had picked up, blowing loose dirt in rising swirls like dust devils that made Willow's eyes burn. "I've seen that apartment building. You're right, it's pretty far from the WB."

Willow hesitated. "Maybe I shouldn't suggest this, but Finn Donovan and Annabelle have space above their new garage. They've been renovating everything, and I know they'd like to rent that space to make extra money. It's going to be a cute apartment."

"At my parents' old farm? You can't be serious." Cass's trembling fingers combed through the gelding's thick mane. "I'm sure it hardly looks like the same place now, but it is," she pointed out. "I'd be opening a Pandora's box of memories."

Cass had been scarred by her past, but Willow wasn't going to nag her about resolving her issues with her mother or her feelings about her father.

"I wish I could help, Cass. And that situation in LA didn't help your confidence either, but my engagement party will be your chance to shine again."

Cass's horse stopped to nibble a large clump of overgrown grass, and she pulled its head up again. After so many years of not riding, her arms must be starting to ache. Willow could only imagine how her backside would feel by tonight.

Cass sighed. "I guess I'll just have to hope I haven't worn out my welcome with Shadow and Grey completely yet."

"I'm sure you haven't." Willow reached over to take Cass's hand.

"Too bad I'm not a cowboy. I could probably find lodging then on somebody else's ranch."

Willow gently pulled on Silver's reins. "Whoa," she said, not merely to stop her horse. "I do have another idea. You're spending most of your time here anyway, and the closer the party gets, the more you'll be needed. There will come a time, believe me, when Mom's hyper-enthusiasm becomes full-blown panic. She so wants this event to be successful."

Cass's expression shuttered. "What are you getting at?"

"Mom said last night she hated to ask you to show up every day at the crack of dawn.

If you were already here, you'd only have to come downstairs."

"You mean stay here? And each morning run into your brother on my way to the bathroom?"

Willow grinned. "Dreams do come true."

But Cass wasn't amused. She murmured, "I know where I stand with Zach."

Willow didn't understand. "But why, Cass? Years ago, you two got on well enough. You practically lived here then, and he told me more than once that he liked you."

"He did?"

Willow toyed with her reins. "So, what changed that?"

Cass shook her head, and Willow knew she shouldn't push at the same time she said the words. "We have six bedrooms, only three of which are being used. The spares won't be needed until the actual wedding when family from out of town arrive, but that will likely be months from now."

"Are you really saying move from Shadow's into *your* house?"

"Rent free," Willow added. "I'd love to have you here and so would Mom."

"You're still forgetting Zach." As they

neared the stand of trees where they planned to sit before going back to the barn, Cass twisted in her saddle to look behind them as if she were seeing him there.

"My dear brother may object at first—" just as he had about her being hired "—but really, doesn't this make sense?" Willow asked. "You can't keep trying not to run into him. It would also do Zach good not to call the shots for once, and this time I'm making the decision."

Cass spurred the gelding into a faster lope, just shy of a canter, and Willow hurried to catch up. She couldn't miss Cass's response, though. "I'm not that desperate."

CODY SAT AT the desk in the McMann ranch office and wished he hadn't started this. After seeing Willow yesterday, and his own determination to make those amends they'd talked about, he'd pulled up the application form on the Wild Horse Program's website. He'd filled out only half the information requested, his heart rate increasing with every keystroke, before he'd quit for the night. Busy with work all day, he hadn't had the chance to try again until now.

Hadley had urged him to use this new laptop, yet Cody wondered if his encouragement, like his trust, had been misplaced. Maybe he shouldn't fill out the form after all. Did he really think he'd get the nod to bring Diva here?

If so, could the mare truly become the rudimentary basis for his training business, as he'd hoped? At Navarro he'd come to believe in his developing skills. He'd even realized that he'd wanted to train professionally for a long time. But then he'd been released, and now he was a hired hand again, not a trainer, even though he'd worked with Willow and Prancer that one day.

The chestnut gelding at the Circle H wasn't his responsibility. After their conversation in town, Willow shouldn't be either, and he—

The office door opened, and Hadley's brother, Dallas, dark haired and blue-eyed like Hadley, stood there with his hand on the knob. His gaze flickered over Cody. "Sorry, didn't know anyone was in here."

"Hey, Dallas." Cody had seen him briefly the day Jenna had her fainting spell, but they hadn't talked then, and Cody had been waiting for, fearing, this showdown.

Dallas frowned. "How was prison?"

"An experience I don't plan to repeat." Another reminder, like Thad's at the hardware store, and Willow's, that Cody now had a criminal record. Plus, he and Dallas had history from their days on the rodeo circuit, which he didn't care to revisit. He attempted a casual tone. "In case you were wondering."

"Cattle rustling, then fireworks...and last time I saw you was at a rodeo—where was that?"

As if Dallas didn't know exactly where. "Laredo," Cody said. "I haven't forgotten."

"Me neither."

Willow's words ran through his head again. She hadn't let him off the hook about his crimes, not that he'd wanted her to. He'd taken responsibility. If Cody was really a changed man, this was also his chance to start atoning for what he'd done. "Listen, Dallas, I...uh, need to apologize. I shouldn't have run out on you then." Cody began to sweat. "I know I still owe you that money I borrowed."

"Doesn't seem to me 'borrowed' is the right word. You swindled me out of five hundred bucks. You knew when I handed it to you that you'd be gone by morning."

"That was a mistake. One of many. I intend to pay you back, if not all at once. I can't." He reached for his wallet. "Fifty now, the rest later?"

Dallas shook his head. "Let me get this straight. So, you work for Hadley, then hand me money that's actually his. Huh," he said, "that's quite a deal."

"Money I earned honestly," Cody assured him. "I'll work my tail off to pay that debt."

"Yeah? Why should I trust you? Hadley's free to do so, but when I got back from Florida, I couldn't believe he'd hired you a second time." Dallas drilled him with a look. "See here, Cody. I'm a reasonable man. In fact, these days I've become downright domesticated. Lizzie and our kids have given me the roots I never knew I needed until them."

Dallas would soon marry Lizzie Barnes, a woman with four kids, the youngest being Dallas's biological baby daughter. His recent trip with her and the children had included a series of rodeos in surrounding states. A combination of work and vacation.

Dallas said, "Rodeo—the prize money I win—doesn't matter as much now as it used to, and I'm on the downswing with that career, anyway." Cody wondered about that;

from what he knew, Dallas's star was higher than ever in the rodeo sky. He was on track to win the world championship he'd always aimed for. "Another year or two, I'll probably be ranching full-time with Hadley. So I don't have a problem with you paying me back on some installment plan. But if you ever cross my brother the way you double-crossed me in Texas, I will make you hurt. Big-time."

"Fair enough." Cody swallowed. "I'm not the guy you knew back then. I swear, prison gave me plenty of time to learn I'd been taking the wrong path over and over, to realize I didn't want to be that guy anymore, and I promised myself I'd never make another mistake like that." And maybe he'd hoped that, as a better man, he could win Willow's approval again. "I really am sorry," he said, then ran out of words except to tell Dallas, "I'm a changed man."

Cody started to close the computer window, but before he could Dallas's gaze homed in on the screen. "What's that? Wild horses?" The banner showed some of the herd in the prison's outdoor arena. "At Navarro, right?"

"I was lucky enough to try my hand at training there. They're not easy animals to work with, but many of them make it worth the effort. I'm thinking—I've thought—about adopting a mare I gentled." He wouldn't say broke. That wasn't Cody's way of gaining a horse's trust. He preferred a softer approach. Maybe he needed that with people, too.

"Why not?" Dallas bent closer to scan the form. "Not many places you can buy a horse for a little over a hundred bucks. That's twenty percent of what you owe me."

"Plus, Hadley says I could keep her here. I'd pay board, of course, even though he didn't ask me to." He talked more about his dream to start his own business until Dallas straightened.

"Sounds good, Cody. You need to begin somewhere." He paused. "You'd have Hadley's expertise. And mine. As long as you keep your nose clean. Back in the day, I would have kicked you in the pants for what you did in Laredo," Dallas said, a smile appearing. "But I'm going to take my brother's advice and cut you some slack. Let bygones be bygones. You can thank him for that, too. He seems to see the good in you."

Cody stared at the computer screen. First Earl had offered to let Cody take the saddle and bridle for a small deposit—he'd told Cody he could pay as he found it convenient to do so. Hadley had urged him to send in the application to adopt. Cody wasn't doing so well with Willow, but there were people who seemed to believe in him.

That was sure something. He couldn't quite take it in.

His amazement grew when Dallas pulled another chair up to the computer now and sat down beside him. He read what Cody had filled in on the application. "I don't know what all this hesitation is about. Let's get this done."

WILLOW SET OFF the next morning for the Circle H. Olivia had promised she'd be there this time for their lesson. What if Cody came again today? Willow couldn't say whether she felt disappointed or relieved to find that he hadn't.

Olivia, her blond ponytail swinging, met Willow at the gate to the outdoor arena. Prancer was already in the ring, and Olivia carried the lunge line and whip. "Ready to roll?"

Willow hugged her. "More than ready."

As they entered the ring, Prancer's ears pricked up. With one eye he studied the training whip as if to say, *Really, you think I'm going to work? I'd much rather stay in my stall eating hay or in the field munching grass.* He sauntered to the center of the round area, then flopped down and proceeded to give himself a dust bath, all four legs thrashing the air.

Olivia murmured, "Let him have fun for a bit, loosen up." She turned to Willow. "Talk to me," she said. "You look troubled today. In this pen you can't afford to lose focus. Thinking about something else can lead to serious injury."

"My brother would certainly agree," Willow said.

"I'm sure he would—after the dreadful spill you took at that show."

Willow wasn't sure she should confide in Olivia. Although they were different ages—Olivia well into her thirties and Willow still in her late twenties—and they were not close friends, she and Olivia did have much in common. And Willow could use a listening ear about her concerns. "I hope you don't mind, but Cody Jones helped me with Prancer the last time I was here."

"Yes. He told me."

"He knew exactly what to do with this horse. But it wasn't the first time I've seen him since his release from prison. Cody, I mean."

Olivia gauged Willow's expression. "Ah, I see. I remember you and he were an item for a while. What about Thad?"

"I would never jeopardize our engagement."

"You feel *nothing* for Cody now?" Olivia paused. "He's a good-looking guy, a bit of a bad boy—don't forget he was part of the gang that stole my brother's cattle—and he's rough around the edges, but I'm willing to give him another chance. Are you? Sometimes, Willow, love doesn't die, even when you think it has. I was in love with Sawyer for years—he was worth the wait—before he and I finally got married."

"I do feel something for Cody," Willow admitted, more miserable by the moment. "Maybe, though, that's just residual compassion because I know some of what he went through as a kid. He watched both of his parents *die*, Olivia, and I can empathize. I nearly lost my family when Daddy passed away. It *was* my fault his heart gave out after the stress and strain he felt about me seeing Cody—" She broke off. "So I know that kind of loss has to change a person—in his case not for the better, and yet Cody has a heart of gold. Not many people see that."

"But you're afraid now of causing more distress, alienating your family again."

Willow nodded. "There's that, sure. I keep seeing my dad that day, collapsing in front of me. He died a few hours later."

With a small sound, Olivia drew her close. Across the ring Prancer had gotten to his feet and was pacing along the opposite rail, blowing through his nostrils. "Shh, it's all right, sweetie. But you aren't marrying Thad to somehow make up for your father, are you? For the anguish that created for your mom and brother?"

"No." Embarrassed that she'd revealed so much, Willow pulled back from their embrace. "Sorry, I didn't mean to get sloppy. I shouldn't have laid this on you." Cody was her problem when he shouldn't be—she couldn't stop seeing his face in town, hearing what he'd said about Thad. Her mom had questioned her, too, about Cody, and now Olivia had done the same. She also knew Cass's opinion of Thad, even when she liked the idea of the lifestyle he offered Willow.

"Are you still okay with coming here for lessons?" Olivia asked. "Knowing Cody might be here?"

"Of course. You're a wonderful teacher. It'll be fine." She hoped.

Olivia touched her shoulder. "You're doing great, Willow. Come on, then." She marched to the center of the ring. "Let's get Prancer moving in the right direction."

Willow needed to do the same. She wouldn't ruin things with Thad.

She needed to get Cody out of her mind.

CHAPTER NINE

"You look especially beautiful tonight." Thad's deep voice and his easy compliment made Willow smile for the first time that day. In the entryway she turned in a circle, her long skirt sweeping the floor. The royal blue gown was a definite hit, and Thad's approval showed in his eyes as he took Willow's hand, then drew her to the long mirror on the wall, where their gazes met in the glass. He paused. "Have I seen this dress before?"

"The Cattlemen's Association ball last year," she reminded him.

"Our first date." He'd liked her dress then, too—one reason she'd chosen to wear the same one tonight. Pleasing Thad made her happy, reassured her that, after her talk with Olivia, she was indeed doing the right thing.

"Many of those people will be at the bar association tonight," he said. "I love what you're wearing, but maybe a different choice this time."

It wasn't a question, but Willow had no other options. The half dozen or so brides- maids' dresses she'd bought for various friends' weddings had been sold or donated to charity. Other than this one, she owned not a single long gown at the moment. "I would have bought a new one, but I've been busy with our engagement party. There hasn't been time, Thad."

"Ah," he said as if he completely under- stood. His immaculately tailored tuxedo and pleated, snow-white shirt were most likely custom-made. Black patent loafers—the height of fashion this season, she'd read in one of her mother's magazines—and an inky dark cummerbund to match the tux completed his evening attire. "I may have the solution," he said with a look she couldn't interpret.

Willow had thought she looked fine, her hair a straight shimmer down her back, her mother's diamond studs at her ears, silver heeled sandals on her feet, but her confidence ebbed. It wasn't as if she and Thad could stop at a local store in Farrier to buy anything else, and Barren wasn't known for high style either. The emporium carried mostly rancher's garb.

Raising one finger for her to wait, Thad called up the stairs. "Jean, would you come down now?" His tone hinted at some secret, and he sounded very proud of himself. What had he done?

Willow met her own perplexed gaze in the mirror before she turned to see her mother bustling down the steps carrying a large white box. At the bottom Thad took it from her. Willow recognized the store's logo, an expensive boutique in Kansas City. "Thad, Mom, what is this?"

Jean avoided her eyes. "I was sworn to silence," she murmured.

Willow faced Thad. "If you don't like what I have on—"

"I like it very much. But wait." His smile was tender, yet Willow had a bad feeling. Then, with a flourish like a magician, he opened the box.

Her breath caught as he peeled back a mound of tissue to reveal a gorgeous red satin gown. Thad drew it out, gently shaking it to reveal thick folds of lustrous fabric. Strapless with a band of the same satin around the top of the bodice, the dress nipped in at the waist before its skirt took a plunge to the floor. Light from overhead pooled in the pure, rich color. "Oh, Thad. This must have cost a fortune."

"Money is not the object." He held the dress up to her as if to measure its size. "I should have let you in on my little secret, but I wanted to surprise you. I only wish I'd come earlier so you didn't dress before, but I got held up at the office," he said. "Go try it on and let's see how you look."

Holding the red satin, Willow drifted up the stairs to her bedroom. Quickly, she removed the blue gown, and as she set it aside on her bed, a few crystals pinged onto the floor. Obviously, she hadn't set as much store by tonight's bar association event as Thad did. Now, as she put on the red dress, she couldn't help but feel inadequate.

His generous gift humbled her. How could she be ungrateful?

Willow picked up her evening bag, then hurried downstairs.

When she reached the last step, her mother gasped. "Oh, honey. You look…"

"Fantastic." Thad took her hand. He led her

to the long mirror in the entry hall again and stood behind her, his hands warm on her bare shoulders. In a husky tone, his eyes holding her gaze, he said, "I knew I was right. In all my choices."

After a long moment Willow broke their stare. An uncomfortable thought had crossed her mind—Cody saying, *Thad's not who you think he is*—and she remembered Thad at dinner trying to plan her life. "The dress is lovely, thank you, but I don't think this silver bag goes with it. Mom, do you have something I can borrow?"

"Never mind, Jean. I have just the thing." Thad thrust a hand into the white box again and out came a gold evening purse. He rummaged through the tissue and held up a pair of strappy gold sandals in her size. The last item was a silk wrap lined in the same red satin for Willow to wear, even on such a hot summer evening.

"Look at the two of you," her mom said. "Glamour right here on the WB. You'll be the belle of the ball tonight, Willow."

"And in tomorrow's newspaper," Thad said.

"Quite the transformation," Willow murmured, "for this ranch girl who's most comfortable wearing jeans and on a horse, not teetering in high heels."

Thad's brow creased just enough for her to notice. "You're amazing." Then he hesitated. "Oh, one more little adjustment. I love your hair loose the way it is, but maybe a bit more…" He circled his hand in the air. Willow didn't know what he meant, but her mom seemed to understand.

"You mean an updo," she said, looking to Thad for his approval.

A few minutes later, with Willow's hair brushed into a casually elegant style that showed off her neck and shoulders, she was ready at last.

She couldn't fault Thad. She should be grateful he cared so much. How could she resent his generosity? His choices, as he'd said. And yet… She did.

It promised to be a long night.

WILLOW AND THAD made the drive into Farrier in silence. Had he picked up on her mood? It wasn't until they'd reached the hotel and Thad had given his keys to the parking valet that he spoke. "Sweetheart, are you okay?"

"I'm fine." She let him help her from the car, then stepped away from him.

And then, before she felt prepared, she was being guided through the lobby to the grand ballroom, which glittered with light from dozens of chandeliers. At the threshold, Willow stopped. She heard the tinkle of glassware, the buzz of conversation and laughter. There were more people here than she'd even envisioned, the women in glittering gowns, the men in tuxedos so alike they could all have been Thad.

Her stomach clenched. "This is a far cry from the WB," she murmured, her hand through Thad's arm. At the entrance to the vast room, thickly carpeted in an elaborate pattern, he'd stopped with her. As he surveyed the dozens of large round tables set for dinner, she was grateful he'd hung back, too. Then she realized why. Thad was searching the area, as if to make sure that every eye was upon them.

Finally, he took a step—and dozens of cameras went off, blinding Willow who saw stars.

She wanted to turn and leave. This wasn't her environment. She could smell enticing aromas from the kitchen, but instead she yearned for that picnic with Thad at the park or the clean air of the ranch, the blue sky, Silver's whinny of greeting, the feel of her own saddle with the reins in her hands. For the arena at the Circle H. Without Cody.

Thad patted her hand. "What you see in there is the crème de la crème of society in this state. People have come tonight from KC, Wichita, Topeka…lawyers, donors, political stars, the sort who will help make our future." He glanced around the ballroom again. "Ah, there's Dad."

Thad hesitated for another moment until he caught Grant Nesbitt's eye and his father started toward them, winding his way through the curious throng, greeting people as he came. "Showtime," Thad said with a bracing smile for Willow. "Come."

She didn't have much choice but to let Thad lead her into the fray, her hand tight in the crook of his elbow. She'd never liked crowds. Her mother's annual barbecue at the WB was normally the height of Willow's social season. As a girl, she'd gone to the yearly fair in Barren, competing there with her pony and, later, on her first horse. At heart, she was a country girl, not a city-bred socialite. *Help*, she wanted to shout. *Thad, this isn't my world.* But now, having taken her first steps through the entry, with the state's attorney general headed their way, she couldn't back out.

Thad's father clapped a hand on Thad's shoulder. "Glad you could make it, son. Let me introduce you to some people." He didn't appear to notice Willow.

For that matter, her future father-in-law didn't acknowledge his second wife either, as if she were part of the wallpaper, or an ornament. She had trailed after Grant to meet them, looking every inch the successful politician's mate, her dark hair in a perfect French twist, her flowing white gown, diamonds and silver heels making her the very picture of an ice queen. Willow wondered if, like Elsa in the movie *Frozen*, she might wave her hand and turn the ballroom into winter. Grant's bride wore a vague, interested expression but said nothing.

Thad turned to Willow. "Dad, you know Willow. Tamara, meet my fiancée."

Grant dutifully air-kissed Willow's cheek, then turned away. Still handsome, he looked to her like an older version of Thad. "Our table is at the front. I'm supposed to make a few remarks after dinner." On their winding path through the ballroom, he stopped half a dozen times to talk with men and women Willow assumed to be his constituents. Each time he introduced Thad as "our future attorney general, perhaps governor," with a beaming smile and a great deal of eye contact to show sincerity. Always ignoring his wife and Willow. He still hadn't said a word to her.

When they were seated, she laid her napkin across her lap. Their two families knew each other, of course, but weren't that close. Leaning down to put her evening purse under the table, she said, "Does your father think I'm a country bumpkin, or what? I can never tell."

"Excuse me?"

"He rarely speaks to me directly. I think you wasted your money on this dress," she added, as if Thad had dragged a mannequin to this event rather than a flesh and blood person. "If this is what I should expect when we're married—"

"Dad gets distracted," Thad said, keeping his voice low. "Give him a break. He likes you. I know he does."

But Willow thought her fiancé must have

a blind spot. Perhaps he wanted to please his father—she'd noticed before that he often did—as much as she wanted to atone with her family. And Thad seemed to walk in Grant's shadow.

Thad turned to the man seated next to him. "Harold, I haven't seen you since we won that case last May."

Not included in their shared remembrance, Willow tried to talk with Tamara Nesbitt, who had ended up sitting beside her, but beyond a few pleasantries—"I like your gown, Willow"—the conversation quickly died. Feeling very much on display yet not a part of things, Willow fidgeted with the stem of her wineglass. Thad had known when they started dating that she was WB–born and bred. And not the type of woman his father would have chosen for him.

It wasn't until dinner was over, and Grant had spoken before the gathering of lawyers, political types and other *stars* that Willow relaxed a bit. Thad asked her to dance, and they twirled around the ballroom in each other's arms. He stole a light kiss or two, then asked, "Having a good time?"

"Trying," she said with a smile.

"This event is annual. Next time we'll be married, and you'll feel more comfortable."

Willow wasn't sure about that, but she did her best to go along with Thad. Tonight was obviously important to him. He appeared to thrive in this atmosphere, which was something of a surprise. Her brother would never put on a tux and endure such an evening. Even more than Willow was a rancher's daughter, he was a country boy.

She didn't have to respond to Thad, though. Someone had tapped him on the shoulder.

His father again. "My turn," Grant said, and Thad handed her over to the attorney general. Grant was no dancer, so they simply shuffled around the floor in one spot, his gaze on other couples who danced by them. "That's the state treasurer," he pointed out, then, "Oh, and— Good evening, Governor." Grant's wife was dancing with him. Earlier, Tamara had covered every inch of the floor to greet and talk with the other guests. Not so quiet after all, then.

As the song finally ended, Grant said, for her ears only, "That's quite a dress."

"A gift from your son," she said, flushing. "Do you like it?"

He hesitated. "I always like Thad's choices."

Willow wasn't convinced that he meant her, too. She was certain that, from the start, her impression of Grant, and his dislike of her, had been correct.

"About *your* choice…" he went on. "Thad will go a long way in this state, not only because I have the power to help him. When he told me he was seeing you, and he thought it was serious, I didn't interfere. He's a grown man. But then he asked you to marry him— and I wondered."

"If I'm good enough for him?" Willow wished she'd stayed home.

"No, I wonder if you're ready to make the sacrifices that will be required. Are you prepared to fully support my son? I've been watching you tonight. I saw you freeze before you entered this ballroom. I see the uncertainty in your eyes now. I heard it in your question. Tamara, too, has sized you up, and she'd be the first to tell you the political game isn't for everyone."

"I'm a fast learner," Willow murmured, but her heart rate had jumped.

"Are you? Or are you more like Thad's mother? She never did like playing in this arena." By now, they had reached Thad, and his father gave Willow a small bow. "Thank you for the dance. Enjoy the rest of your evening."

THE NEXT MORNING Cody went from the barn up to the house for a second mug of coffee. He'd spent most of the night before on the application to adopt Diva, which he'd finally submitted, and he didn't like feeling this groggy working around horses or riding fence. The cattle seemed to have a favorite hobby: pushing down wire, then plunging through as if they might escape confinement. They most always got caught, but only a few days ago a neighbor had phoned the barn to tell Cody a McMann steer had wandered across her property.

Cody understood the animal's wish. He'd dreamed often enough in prison—when he wasn't plagued by his recurrent nightmares about his murdered mother—of finding a way out of Navarro. Which would have only earned him a longer sentence.

"There's fresh coffee," Clara McMann told him now, coming into the kitchen from the other room where she'd been overseeing

Hadley's twins from his first marriage. Cody could hear them giggling as they played some game.

He filled his cup, then dropped onto a chair for his morning break. He wouldn't be worth a nickel until he achieved the right volume of caffeine in his blood. He pushed aside a copy of the *Barren Journal*, reached for the coffee cake in the center of the table—Clara always had some treat waiting—then did a double take. Cody forgot the application, forgot his morning stupor. He wasn't seeing things, but he wished he was.

Next to the cup Clara must have left earlier, the paper lay open to the society page, never a big item in Barren—except today, it seemed. Clara sat across from him. "I seldom read about who's who and what's what here, but that was quite the do last night at the hotel in Farrier. Everyone who's anybody was there, at least in the legal and political realms."

Which sure left Cody out.

Next to the write-up about the bar association dinner/dance, he studied an array of pictures, one of them in color of Thad, Willow standing so close to him their bodies appeared to merge at the hip.

No wonder she hadn't wanted to believe Cody's warning about Thad. He should have known. And wasn't he dense not to have gotten her message the last time? Yet he couldn't stop looking at the photograph. The caption underneath read:

Farrier's favorite engaged couple out on the town. Assistant DA Thaddeus Nesbitt and Willow Bodine of the WB Ranch.

"Such a pretty girl," Clara said, cutting a slice of cake. "And look at that ring. My goodness, that young man didn't spare any expense."

Cody looked away from the big yellow diamond—Thad had placed Willow's hand in a prominent position for the flashy stone to be photographed. "You know Willow?"

"Not well, but I've known her family for years."

Another photo showed Thad's father with his second wife. Grant Nesbitt wore the same broad smile his son did. The new missus and Willow both looked like golden trophies. Hc looked at her picture again. Why had Willow worn her hair up like that instead of flowing like a sleek waterfall down her back? Which must be bare in that dynamite strapless dress. This wasn't the Willow he knew.

Cody took a first sip of his coffee and burned his tongue. He couldn't help but see the tight look on Willow's face, her frozen smile. He knew every one of her expressions. And was that irritation he glimpsed in her cornflower blue eyes? Whatever it was, it sure didn't look like the kind of love she and Cody had known together, once.

"Oh," Clara said, obviously distressed. "I forgot you were close to Willow."

"Before I ended up in prison." He should push the paper away but couldn't move. For a moment he savored the sharp pain of the burn he'd caused himself with the coffee. Like everything else. If only he'd never gone bad and they…

"You're not in prison now, dear."

"Well, that part of my résumé didn't impress her."

Clara shook her head. "I've always liked her mother. I have no use for Thad's father, though." She pointed at the picture of him and his wife. "He left Thad's mother for that woman. A nasty divorce. Grant Nesbitt tried to leave her with practically nothing until public opinion made him see that he wouldn't do his political career much good by turning her into a pauper. Just so he could remarry and pretend he's twenty years younger than he is." Clara touched Cody's hand. "I didn't mean to open an old wound. Willow is, however, engaged now. I assume that's because she loves Thad."

A hard truth Cody couldn't seem to accept. He didn't need the reminder that he was no match for her, the girl her brother called the Bodine princess to Cody's… What? The son of a crazed father and his tragic victim, Cody's own mother? He hadn't been able to stop her murder.

"I know," he said. "I should let it go." *Willow*, he meant.

Clara's expression filled with sympathy. "Advice isn't always easy to take."

"My own included."

"Cody, maybe this would help take your mind off things," Clara said as if she'd had a sudden inspiration. "Last summer Dallas put on a rodeo here, which the townspeople loved. He's too busy this season on the circuit to do that again, but I'm helping set up a small festival in town instead. We hope it'll please people. Maybe you'd like to be part of that, too?"

"I'll think about it," he said, then shoved back from the table just as Hadley walked in.

He sent Cody a look. "Dallas is waiting for you."

"On my way," Cody said, his burned tongue still tingling. He topped up his mug even though the *Barren Journal*'s society page had woken him right up. "How could I miss riding fence on such a nice day? It must be nearly a hundred in the shade."

"Close," Hadley agreed.

Cody grabbed his coffee, then headed for the barn. It wasn't as if he didn't know that Willow had chosen Thad instead of him. Still, he'd never actually seen them together, and seeing the proof on paper, like evidence presented in court, had shaken him. Cody's life seemed to have slipped out of his control again. Willow being the best example.

CHAPTER TEN

WILLOW'S MOM ADDRESSED another envelope, then tucked an invitation inside. At the dining room table, she pressed a seal to the closing flap and set it on the ever-growing stack. She, Willow and Cass sat among what Willow hoped was the last of this chore.

"Thad's father called," Jean said. "From his head count last night, the governor will be a definite yes, four members of his cabinet, Grant's staff, of course…and so for them these invitations are a mere formality." Jean fanned her face. "I'm exhausted."

Willow had spent a mostly sleepless night herself, due only in part to the after-dinner coffee she should have refused at Thad's event. Obviously, it hadn't been decaf. And unlike her mother, she wasn't just tired—as if she needed another reminder of last night, her feet still hurt from wearing the gold sandals. Willow yearned for her favorite cowboy boots. This morning she couldn't keep quiet any longer.

"Mom, I can't believe you let Thad buy that gown, then made sure I wouldn't see it until he had you bring the box downstairs. At Jack's that day, when you mentioned my getting a dress, you must have already known what Thad did, and last night I felt…embarrassed."

"Why? Your blue dress was lovely, but how could I tip you off? And spoil his surprise? Besides, Thad wanted you to really make an entrance."

"Well, he got what he wanted. He did everything but hire a trumpeter to announce our arrival. Have you seen the paper, Cass?" She looked to her friend for support, but Cass only glanced down at the next invitation, consulted the guest list, then began to write the address on the envelope.

She seemed to have taken on the role of a distanced observer. "I saw it. Great picture of you both," she murmured.

"I don't care if we looked like the Duke and Duchess of Cambridge." Willow sat back in her seat. Did she know Cass or her mother at all? Cass wasn't wild about Thad. So what was going on here? "Mom. How could you be his willing accomplice? Because that's how it seems to me. I was not only humiliated to have Thad practically dressing me—I was also betrayed by my own mother."

Jean's pen trembled in her hand. "Buying a lavish gift for the woman you love is not a crime. Naturally, I wish Thad hadn't blind-sided you, especially when you'd already dressed for the evening. He might have given the gown to you sooner. I wish he hadn't asked me not to say anything, and I can understand how that might make you feel."

"Might?" Willow echoed, vaguely hearing the back door open. A glance at her watch told her Zach had probably come from the barn for breakfast after doing chores. "You should have been there at the hotel in Farrier. When we stepped through the door, I must have been blushing from the roots of my hair to my toes peeking out beneath that red satin." And by then Willow had been in no mood to smile. "Everyone in that ballroom stared. Thad's father, of course, took it all in and was beaming."

"He's proud of Thad. He's happy about your engagement."

"I'm not sure about that," Willow said, recalling his veiled comments when they'd danced, "but he's always playing to the media. So was Thad." She'd managed to do her social duty as his date but choked her dinner down, unwisely drank a second glass of wine to cool her temper and still seethed inside all night. This wasn't the first time Thad had taken matters out of her hands, or tried to, and Willow was beginning to wonder if she was little more to him than arm candy. They would see about that.

Jean fidgeted in her chair. Her hand shaking, she added another envelope to the pile.

But Willow wouldn't back down. "Whose side are you on, Mom?"

Cass laid a hand on Willow's arm. "I don't blame you for being irritated. Thad should never have surprised you like that, but it's over and done."

Willow gaped at her. Why would Cass also defend him? "No, it is not over," she said. "I intend to speak to him about this, too. Maybe you should wait, Mom, to send out all these invitations."

Her brother chose that moment to wander from the kitchen with his steaming mug of coffee. He propped one shoulder against the dining room doorframe, his gaze lingering a second too long on Cass. "Ladies. How's it coming?"

"It was coming fine," their mother said in a hurt tone, "but Willow—"

"Did us all a favor last night." Zach's gaze actually looked mellow. "Because of that mention of the WB with your picture in the *Journal*, I've had a dozen calls this morning offering us everything from prize Angus bulls for breeding to satin runners for the aisle at the wedding. The ranch is in the news, thanks to you and Thad."

"I'm glad to be of service," Willow muttered, but no one at the table seemed to hear the sarcasm. And she could see from the look on Cass's face, the faint color in her cheeks and the way she avoided looking directly at Zach just what else was going on here. Friendship or not, and aside from her opinion of Thad, Cass wouldn't do anything to annoy Willow's family and risk losing her job as she had in LA. Or her chance, if one existed, to at last win Zach's affections.

Willow pushed her stack of invitations across the table toward her mother, then stood and walked from the dining room out into the front hall.

Cass's reaction she could understand, even though it didn't please her. Willow's mother was another matter, but she had stated her position. Next, Willow needed to talk to Thad without a hundred other people around.

GOADED BY THAT picture in the paper, Cody sat on the top step of the McMann's back porch after lunch, searching the Wild Horse Program's website on his phone for a video of Diva. He had never cared much what other people thought. After his folks died, he'd used his teens to act out, and his bad boy image had followed him right into a prison cell. He liked to think his work at Navarro with Diva and his supervisor had helped straighten him out, but the rest of his reform was up to him.

As he clicked on the video he'd found, Hadley looked out the kitchen door and saw him sitting there in the sun. "I'm headed for the ag store to get some feed. Their truck's broke so there's no way for them to deliver. You and Dallas can finish riding fence this afternoon."

"Sure, boss." Cody rose to his feet. Since the day he'd driven Hadley and Jenna to the doc's office in town, he'd been determined to maintain Hadley's renewed trust in him. Cody's days of showing up for a job only when he felt like it, and disappearing when he didn't, were over. He had aspirations now to become a solid citizen. To repay society.

"Didn't mean to stretch my break. I was watching some tape of the mare I want to adopt, but I'll do that later."

"Come back inside. The light's better, and I need to tell you something."

Cody's gut tightened. What had he done? Dallas had seemed to forgive him the other night, and Cody had already paid him the first of the money he owed him, but what if Dallas still didn't trust him, had changed his mind and griped to Hadley about the rest of the five hundred bucks?

The kitchen where he'd talked with Clara was empty. Cody avoided looking at the newspaper still lying open on the table. "Let's watch that video," Hadley said, leaning over Cody's shoulder. "See what you're getting yourself into."

This was more camaraderie than Cody had known in his entire life. The kind of thing he'd once hoped for with his dad—teaching him to play ball or ride a pony or fish—none of which had happened.

The video wasn't long, only thirty seconds or so, but it was enough to make Hadley whistle. "Good mover," he said. "Has a lot going for her. You might reconsider her future."

"If my application gets through." Almost as fascinated as he had been by the still photo of Willow in that red satin, Cody hit Replay, his eyes glued to the short film of Diva gliding around the pen at Navarro in the glaring sun, light glinting off her sleek hide. The brown-and-white mare was indeed the entire package, from her conformation to that springy trot. He'd half forgotten how beautiful she was, even more than Prancer.

"I hope you get her, Cody," Hadley said after they'd watched the clip a third time. "I don't know much about mustangs, but I'd sure like to see you put her through her paces on this ranch."

So Cody hadn't done anything wrong after all. "The mustangs aren't really wild horses. They're descended from domestic stock brought here by the Spanish long ago, and it's kind of amazing they've managed to survive, even thrive. The Bureau of Land Management culls them every now and then. There are thousands available for adoption or held to keep them off the range. Without that, they can multiply fourfold every four years." He tucked his phone back in his pocket. If things worked out, he'd buy other mustangs at such a reasonable price, build his business around them, too, and make a tidy profit. "I'd sure like the chance to train Diva to a higher level. Guess all I can do is cross my fingers." And pray that the powers-that-be deemed him worthy.

Hadley cleared his throat. "Tell you what. Let Dallas finish the fence. You can come with me to town, help with the feed bags."

It wasn't until they were turning onto Main Street that Hadley seemed to remember he'd had something to tell Cody. "Remember when Jenna fainted, and we had to bring her to Sawyer's office?"

"Yeah, the doc said she had low blood sugar."

"Or something," Hadley said with a sudden grin. "We thought—Jenna always thought—she couldn't have kids. She tried everything when she was married to her first husband,

and finally she did conceive but lost that baby. I don't think she ever got over it, but now—" his smile got even broader "—she's pregnant again. I thought, since you were with us that day, you should be one of the first to know."

"Congratulations, Hadley. That's great news."

"Yeah, we think so."

"I didn't want to ask how Jenna's other blood work turned out. It wasn't my place since I'm not family, but I've been wondering if she was okay. More than okay, huh?"

Hadley couldn't stop smiling. "If you want to tell Jenna you think so, too, that'd be fine with me." As Cody pulled into a parking space in front of the ag store, still amazed that his boss had shared such news with him, Hadley hopped out. "Let's get this done. I promised Jenna I'd take her to dinner tonight. Before we head back, I'll stop at Jack's to make the reservation."

"You should buy her flowers, too," Cody suggested. "Women like that."

He'd once picked some wildflowers for Willow, and they made her so happy she'd cried.

"Good idea," Hadley said as if they were

more than boss and employee, almost as if they were, well, friends. Confidants. Cody remembered Hadley calling him son. They were at the door to the store when he spied Thad Nesbitt walking toward them. He was all decked out in his three-piece suit even in this heat, his striped tie snug against his throat. And Cody's buoyant mood evaporated.

"Jones, wait up." Thad's voice stopped him before Cody could duck inside with Hadley.

"Go ahead, I'll start loading the feed," Hadley said with a polite nod at Willow's fiancé.

After he walked off, Cody said, "What do you want, Thad?"

Had he come to gloat about last night? He wore the faint smile that in court had made Cody want to deck him. *Willow and I had a great evening*, he might say. *Dinner, dancing, then afterward...* His tone would imply they'd spent hours in each other's arms. Like Cody with her at the roadhouse not that long ago. As he waited for Thad to speak, his insides knotted. He felt as he had during his trial, seated at the table next to Thad's team for the prosecution, and he itched with the need to say, *You want to know the truth—I don't think she looked that happy.*

"I hear you've applied to adopt some horse from Navarro," Thad finally said. "You should have saved yourself the trouble. You don't have a chance in blazes for that adoption to go through."

He hadn't actually made a threat or said the words *I'll personally see to it*, and he hadn't mentioned Willow, but he left Cody rooted to the sidewalk, certain Thad had meant just that. In both cases.

WILLOW LED PRANCER through the gate into the outdoor arena, inhaling the familiar scents of horsehide and hay, rich grass and the clean late-afternoon air. This, not a hotel ballroom in Farrier, was the sort of environment she preferred. Last night's red satin gown now hung in her closet, and the invitations to the party were in the mail. As for setting a wedding date, she'd put Thad off again last night. Mildly regretting her strong words this morning to her mother, Willow had decided she needed this hour of respite at the Circle H.

Olivia came from the barn, looking ready— she always did—for business. Whether in town at one of her two antiques shops or on this ranch, she exuded a sense of purpose.

For a few moments, they watched the chestnut gelding circle the ring, then Willow flicked the whip behind the horse's hocks to urge him faster into a breezy lope. Their gazes meeting, Olivia grinned at her.

"Lord, I love the way he glides, almost like he has some Arab in him."

"He might," Willow agreed. "He has that same dish-y nose." The slight scoop in his profile rather than a bolder, more convex Roman style was typical of the breed.

Olivia said, "But he has some habits we'll need to break. For one thing, he keeps heading for the rail, and I'm sure he'd stand there all day watching that cute little filly in the next paddock. He's not listening to us, that's for sure."

A voice behind them said, "He doesn't like being between you and that fence. He'd prefer to ride the rail, telling himself he's near enough to freedom." Cody walked into the arena. "Naturally, that filly plays a part, too." He added, "You have to read his cues just like he should read yours, Willow. Olivia knows that already, so I'm just sayin'. That was my experience, anyway, with mustangs."

Olivia went to greet Cody, but Willow stayed in the center of the ring, her attention focused on the gelding. She was here to train, not to chat with Cody. Whatever he'd come for this time wasn't her concern and, after the earlier awkwardness with her mom at the dining room table, she had enough on her mind, counting the hours before she would confront Thad about last night.

Cass's betrayal had also hurt. She seemed more concerned with pleasing Jean and Zach to keep her job than in being Willow's friend. Willow could have used some support. Maybe she should call Becca instead, though, as always now, she was probably tied up with her baby.

"Can I have a minute with Willow?" she heard Cody ask Olivia.

"Sure." Willow glanced over her shoulder to see Olivia raise one eyebrow as if to ask, *What have we here?* And Willow thought of their previous conversation about Cody. "I'll just go take another look at Blue's leg," Olivia said. "He's had some lameness that worries me." Her big horse was the crowning achievement of Olivia's training skills, but his personality could be difficult, and he still had a tendency to nip anyone near him. Surprising that she hadn't been able to cure him of that bad habit, but some things defied being fixed. Like Willow's former relationship with Cody. She wasn't going there again.

He waited until they were alone. Prancer had stopped moving and was standing at the fence again, gazing at the filly.

Cody rubbed his neck. "I didn't dare set foot on the WB again, so I decided to come here, see if you'd managed to get away today." His tone was overly casual. "Did you have a good time last night, angel?"

His pet name for her went through Willow like a favorite tune. "I assume you saw the morning paper, but don't start, Cody. I don't need another of your warnings about Thad."

"You looked miserable to me."

Willow's heartbeat tripped. "How could you possibly see that from a photo?"

"True?" he pressed.

"No," she insisted, rejecting the notion that her mood had shown so clearly, wondering if anyone else had seen her resentment.

Cody said, "Maybe I'm wrong—again—

and you wanted to be exactly where you were, getting shown off to all of Thad's friends. Like some blue ribbon he'd won."

That came too close to what Willow had indeed felt. But letting Cody know he'd seen the truth wouldn't help either of them. "I don't have to care what you think." She held up the hand holding the whip, Thad's diamond catching the sun.

"Willow, I know you. Less than two years ago, and even before that in the beginning, I probably knew you better than anyone else. I recognized that look in your eyes last night, the set of your shoulders. I could see you all but flinch away from Thad's touch."

"I did not. If I winced, which I doubt, it was because of all the cameras."

"He had his hand clamped over yours, displaying that diamond to best advantage. Why won't you see that?"

"Why don't you stop interpreting my every move and expression for me? I'm not one of your mustangs to train. I'm perfectly happy where I am. With Thad."

Cody's gaze dropped. "Willow, I want you to be happy, but I don't feel that you are." He let out a breath. "I saw him in town again an hour ago. I dropped Hadley off at the Mc-Mann's then headed over here. I'd bet even he knows he doesn't have you where he wants you. Under his control."

"That's your opinion, which I've also heard before." But to Willow's dismay, her voice had quavered.

"You haven't heard this." His tone hardened. "I applied to adopt the mare, as I told you I would." He didn't wait for her reaction. "I'd guess you don't want to hear this either, but I'm pretty sure your *fiancé* intends to prevent the adoption from going through."

Willow blinked. "He said that?"

"Not in those words, but yeah."

She could tell Cody wasn't lying, but Willow hadn't counted on this. Would Thad really interfere? Just as he had last night about her dress? She'd never thought of him as someone who needed control… There was no reason to let Cody know how she was feeling, though. She had to settle the matter with Thad, not let Cody sway her.

She turned toward Prancer, then flicked the whip at his hindquarters. The horse's head jerked up, his hide quivered, and he took off running, wrenching Willow's shoulder as he tore the lunge line from her grasp.

At least she hadn't tried to hold on to the line or she'd have been dragged.

Cody whistled through his teeth, but the gelding didn't stop. Prancer tore around the ring at a vicious gallop, hugging the rail. The filly next door startled then bolted for the barn. The panicked horse's eyes were wild, showing the whites, and Willow realized she'd made a rookie move.

Olivia, probably drawn now by Cody's shrill whistle, chose that moment to step around the corner from the barn. Worse luck for Willow, she knew accidents seldom happened because of a single factor.

Prancer spun on his hocks and veered off the rail. He changed course, charging at a dead run straight toward her and Cody in the center of the ring. Willow took a step by instinct but the wrong way—right into the horse's new path.

Cody reached out to grab her arm, but the horse thundered past, grazing Willow with enough force to knock her off her feet before Cody touched her.

She was unconscious when she hit the ground.

CHAPTER ELEVEN

CODY'S HEART HAD lodged in his throat. He ran to Willow while Olivia did her best to corral the chestnut gelding. As soon as the horse no longer perceived a threat, Prancer began to quiet down, but Willow was out cold in the dirt. As Cody dropped to his knees beside her, he knew he shouldn't move her but couldn't stop from gathering her gently into his arms, saying her name over and over. Her body sagged against him. His heart pounded, his pulse echoing through his body. "Wake up, angel. Come on, baby."

Olivia said, "I'm calling 911." Her cell in one hand, she led the sweating horse past them to the barn. "I'm so sorry. I shouldn't have moved that quickly."

By the time she'd disappeared, Cody was in a full-blown panic. He gazed down at Willow, thinking, *Let her live and I'll never come near her again. I'll leave her to Thad*, even when that was the last thing he wanted for her. *I'll pray she isn't making a mistake. I'll give her up after all. I will.*

And like an answer to his prayers, Willow finally started coming to. She blinked up at Cody, her eyes dazed. "What…happened?"

He couldn't seem to speak.

She struggled to get up, but he only held her closer. In those few seconds, seeing her lying here, he'd lost ten years off his life, scared enough that he'd made a bargain with God.

Finally, fully conscious again, she wheezed, "Cody, you're crushing me." She'd had the wind knocked out of her, but so had he, figuratively speaking. What if she'd died? Cody had seen enough accidents around horses to know how easily that might have happened. He'd suffered a few himself, and for that one terrified instant he'd imagined Prancer hitting her full force, slamming Willow to the ground, dead on impact from a thousand pounds of danger on the hoof. She could have been badly hurt, maybe was. He'd learn soon enough if he needed to worry even more, but all that mattered to him now was her being alive.

Cody laid his cheek against her hair. "God, when I saw him swerve, then head for you…"

Willow shifted enough to see his face. She was breathing easier again but laid a limp hand against his cheek. "I'm sorry I scared you. That was stupid on my part. I knew better…or I should have."

"You couldn't have predicted that. Prancer's a rank beginner," he said.

"So am I. All it took was that split-second lack of focus. My knee-jerk instinct to get out of the way."

"No blame necessary. When Olivia suddenly appeared, all Prancer could think of was running from whatever threat he imagined. I'm just glad you're with me right now." He meant her being conscious again, coherent, but also in his arms. Cody probed her skull for damage, and she winced.

"Don't fuss," she said.

"Keep still. You could have a concussion or a back injury." Remembering her accident last year, he cupped her face in both hands. "We'll see what the paramedics have to say. Or what if Sawyer's home? Maybe Olivia called for him, too." His hands were shaking. "We'll wait."

"Cody." Willow's eyes had filled with tears. "I know you care about me, but…"

"I'll always care." She was in his heart, in his blood, and all he could think of was that he'd nearly lost her, even when he didn't really have her. "I couldn't move fast enough to get in front of that green horse…"

Just like years ago, when he hadn't been in time to save his mother.

Instead of inviting the nightmare into his head again, or replaying today's mishap, he thought of Willow in her red satin dress standing beside Thad. Did Cody wish she would end her engagement? Sure, and he'd tried his best to tell her Thad wasn't what he seemed, wasn't the right man for her—in Cody's biased opinion—but he'd failed. He couldn't give her what she seemed to want, the things she'd had all her life. The very things Thad could give her while Cody was punching cows again on someone else's ranch, paying off his saddle, repaying Dallas the money he owed him.

At the moment none of that mattered. She was in his arms again, as she'd been so many times before, his hands cradling her face, her mouth mere inches from his. He studied her tear-filled eyes, her cheekbones, her nose as if to memorize them. Then, for a few more hard beats of his heart, Cody gazed at her lips before he closed that small distance between them—the tiny gap that might soon become an emotional chasm—and bent his head to the angle they'd both preferred once, then covered her mouth with his.

He hadn't kissed her in a long time, and he shouldn't now. He wasn't good enough for her. But what had started out in his mind as relief for her safety, an attempt to comfort and reassure himself that she'd be okay, ended up being something else he couldn't resist.

Willow moaned a little, then wrapped her arms around his neck and held on tight, as if she knew this couldn't last and was also giving up. The kiss went on until Cody heard someone running from the house toward them, and still he couldn't end it. Not yet, at least.

Giving her up would be his penance, the bargain he'd made and would keep.

He didn't even care that Olivia had seen the last, dreamlike kiss he might ever share with Willow.

"Don't make this harder for me," Willow's mother practically begged her as she tucked Willow into bed before nightfall. "You need to rest."

Willow thought of making another protest, but her mom was always a mother first. After Willow's accident, the paramedics had soon arrived, then Sawyer's truck had roared up the drive from town, and Willow had been surrounded by well-meaning people. But it was Cody's shaken expression she remembered best. His kiss. What had she done?

She should have stopped him, pulled away, gotten to her feet and run toward the ranch house to…well, safety. Instead, she'd let Cody hold her, touch her, lower his mouth to hers, and Willow had welcomed his kiss, remembering every other one they'd ever shared. She'd gotten lost in him again.

Willow tried to shut out this new memory of him. "I don't want to sleep at seven o'clock," she told Jean, even though her body ached in places she'd forgotten she had. Her muscles were stiffening up as they had before whenever she'd suffered other accidents, the worst in that show ring last fall. By tomorrow she'd probably need this bed, but tonight… And what about Thad?

Would he somehow sense her guilt?

She couldn't tell him about the kiss, not after his implied threat to Cody about the horse adoption. Maybe he hadn't meant it that way, but she wouldn't give him reason to retaliate. She wouldn't make things worse for Cody. Besides, it had been one kiss that wouldn't happen again. Still, how could she make up to Thad for what she'd allowed to happen?

Willow cleared her throat. "Thad and I were supposed to see a movie, Mom."

"Tonight?" Zach, who was standing on the other side of her bed, his hazel eyes reflecting his lingering concern for her, said, "You can't be serious. A movie?"

"I've talked to Thad," their mother said. "He's coming over to see you instead, Willow." The doorbell downstairs was already ringing. "That must be him now." And she left the room, leaving Willow with Zach, who moved even closer to her bed.

His tone was exasperated. "Mom's worried. So am I. What kind of a stunt was that? I had no idea you were still working with Olivia at the Circle H."

"As I have every right to do."

"And look what happened. Willow—"

"I apologize for making you worry, but did I jump down your throat when you cut your hand on a rusty saw at the barn? When you got thrown off that stud horse Daddy bought that no one—not even you—could ride? Or when you were six years old and fell out of the hayloft? No, I did not, Zach."

He held up both hands, the hint of a smile on his lips. "All right, I see your point."

"And don't remind me that being your kid sister makes things different."

"It does. But that's not all," he said. "I hate to bring *this* up, but Olivia wasn't the only other person there today."

"Cody," she said for him. "Yes, he was, and I can assure you we didn't plan that, but he was a big help after I got hurt." Willow wasn't about to say that Cody had sought her out. She'd had no way of knowing he'd come to the Circle H again.

"When I walked into the hospital in Farrier," Zach said, "and saw him with Olivia in the waiting room, I couldn't believe my eyes. Neither could Mom."

"What am I supposed to say? Except that I'm not sneaking around, Zach." Even when it felt as if she had. "Or have you forgotten— I'm marrying Thad?"

Willow still had plenty to say to him, too, about the bar association dinner/dance, but she hadn't expected to be hurting all over when she got the opportunity to tell Thad how he'd made her feel then.

"I haven't forgotten," Zach said, holding her gaze as if to say *see that you don't forget it either*, but he refrained from voicing the thought. Maybe she'd truly gotten her point across.

Just to be sure, Willow added, "Your best friend is safe with me."

Zach relented. "I'm glad you're going to be okay, Willow." As Thad's footsteps pounded up the stairs, her brother leaned close to kiss her cheek, then straightened as Thad rushed into the room.

"Hey," Zach said, stepping away from the bed. "Good to see you, Thad."

"You, too—not under the best circumstances. We still on for Rowdy's at the end of the week? I owe you a beer. It's not every day my best friend agrees to be my best man."

"Who else would you pick?" Zach asked with a grin. They exchanged fist bumps, accompanied by a quick male hug, then Zach said good-night.

He lingered in the doorway. "Call if you need anything. Or if there's any change in Willow's condition. You'll take good care of her, Thad?"

"Always," he said, which had been Cody's word, too. *I'll always care.* As soon as Zach left, Thad bent over Willow's bed, one hand tenderly pushing her tangled hair back from her face. "You scared all of us today. Zach's a good big brother. And he's like a brother to me."

For a moment, her heart melting, Willow considered not ever mentioning the red dress. "True," she said. She'd been lucky Zach hadn't taken her to task worse than he had. "But he's still a thorn in my side sometimes."

"That goes both ways. Part of being siblings, I guess." Thad couldn't know. He was an only child. "Zach once showed me a picture of the day your folks brought you home from the hospital. He was holding you for the first time, studying your face with this look I've never forgotten. It said a lot about his feelings for you. Love at first sight." Thad held her hand. "We can see that film another night, but I had to see you, make sure you were all right. Now, what can I do to help you feel better?"

"I'm fine, Thad." If she kept repeating that, his name, too, she might believe it herself. Gingerly, she shifted position, and another bolt of agony shot along her spine.

"I've spoken with Sawyer," Thad said. "He found nothing in your tests to alarm us but—"

"My scans were normal, well, except for a *slight* concussion." In the past, after getting thrown while riding Silver, Willow had banged her head once or twice, but she wouldn't share that. Thad didn't need those details, though he already knew about her show ring mishap. Beyond her other injuries, Willow hadn't been able to focus her mind for months. Did anyone think she'd want to relive that time? She hadn't imagined getting hurt today when she'd been working Prancer from the ground, not in a saddle.

Thad frowned. "Slight? What were you doing on that horse in the first place?"

Willow avoided his gaze. "I wasn't *on* him—he's not ready to ride. I was standing in the arena when Olivia accidentally spooked him."

"Another example of an animal with no sense. You'd work with him, or any other horse, taking that kind of risk each time you come near them?"

"Again, Thad? Do we really need to have this conversation? I've lived around horses all my life." She gestured at her bedroom wall, where an array of red, blue and white ribbons attested to Willow's skill. Not for training, but such minor incidents were part of learning the trade she hoped to practice. She shouldn't have mentioned the concussion.

"I really wish you'd stop this training business." Thad's gaze had clouded. "I can't bear to see you hurt again like you were today or, God forbid, worse."

"I'm sorry. I don't want you to worry."

He eased away to give her an assessing look. "Then we're agreed? This is going to be a busy year, and we don't need anything to interfere with the party or our wedding. Do we?" He didn't wait for her answer. "Did you see the piece in the *Journal*? That picture of us last night?"

"I saw it." This would have been her opening to confront him, yet she didn't take the opportunity. Willow was hardly innocent herself. Thad's gift of the dress didn't seem as serious now when, because of Cody and that kiss, she was guilty, too.

"Everyone said how great we looked together." Thad smiled. "I couldn't have been prouder of you, and I'm glad you decided to wear that satin dress."

His comment changed her mind. If not now, when? Aches and pains aside, she had to speak her mind after all. She needed to let him know she didn't intend to hand him the reins to her life. "Frankly, I didn't feel I had much choice."

He drew back farther. "You think I forced you to change clothes?"

"I think you're forcing me to change right now. Trying to. I apologized. I did not agree to stop training. I'll just have to be more careful." She took a breath, and the motion sent a sharp reminder along her back that she was, indeed, hurting. "And since you mentioned last night first, you didn't *force* me to wear the red dress, but you made your wishes clear, and with Mom taking part… Thad, I was mortified. Please don't do something like that again."

"What?" His eyes narrowed. "Buy you something expensive?"

"This isn't about the price or the dress, which is beautiful." She remembered her discomfort on the threshold of the ballroom, Thad's obvious attempt to make sure they were the center of attention, to wait for the cameras to go off. "It's about wanting to show me off, as Mom said—"

"Of course I did. I do," he said. "That was my way of *showing* you how much I care. And today when Jean called to tell me you'd been hurt, I was so scared for you that I barely got through the summation in my court case."

Willow straightened, then winced. "You weren't so afraid that you left the courtroom." He hadn't come to the ER.

Thad looked astonished. "I couldn't. That's my job."

"Which should work both ways. I've promised to support your career. Why shouldn't you support mine, too? If this is to be a real partnership, that's only fair."

"Sweetheart." He shook his head. "They're two different things." He motioned at the ribbons on her wall. "I'm not likely to end up in bed from practicing law."

He had a point, but Willow toyed with a loose thread on her comforter. "I still want to work with Prancer."

"Yes, you've established that," he said. Then, as if he'd just thought of something, he added, "Oh—by the way, Zach mentioned Jones was with you at the hospital and before at the Circle H."

Her heart sank. Of course, Zach would tell him. She wondered if Thad had been saving this part for the right moment, just as she'd planned to talk to him about last night. His voice stayed soft, too soft. "Should I be concerned?"

Her pulse leapt. "He was helping Olivia—and me today by chance—with Prancer."

"Do you think that's wise?"

"Do you mean Cody or the horse again?"

Thad waited to answer. Then, instead of pursuing things further, he said, "Let's not quarrel. While you're convalescing, why don't we talk about our wedding date? Have you had a chance to narrow down my choices to a date that will work for you?" When she didn't respond, he said, "Really, Willow… You haven't looked at them? If I sound over-eager, I apologize, but that's because I can't wait to have you as my wife."

Willow was glad he couldn't see her thoughts—her guilt about the unexpected kiss she'd shared with Cody, her fear that, like Zach, Thad would keep trying to discourage her from doing work that fed her soul. "I still have several conflicts to resolve."

His expression gradually cleared. "Fair enough. By the way, I've been looking at real estate online. I've found some houses between Farrier and the WB." He paused. "Naturally, I won't tour them or make a de-cision until you've seen them. How does that sound?" Thad glanced at the window, which in the dark showed nothing but his reflection. "I know you're not happy with me about the dress. But I'm not happy about Cody Jones, so let me tell you this." He leaned closer, spac-ing out his words. "I don't share."

He hadn't given up on that after all. "Don't give me orders, Thad—about training horses or anything else. And *by the way*," she said, repeating his earlier words, "did you threaten

Cody? Would you really try to block his application to adopt a mustang?"

His gaze flickered. "I wouldn't waste my time."

Her head was still foggy after her fall, but Willow didn't believe him, a first for them. If she hadn't wanted to please her brother—Thad's best friend—and ease her mother's grief, too, over the wrenching loss of Willow's father, she might have asked Thad to leave.

Fresh guilt kept her in place. She needed to make sense of Cody's kiss and hope Thad never learned about that. In one foolish move, Willow had jeopardized their happiness.

Still. Cody had warned her. And tonight, Thad had shown her that dark side.

CHAPTER TWELVE

CODY AVOIDED THE Circle H for the next week. Hadley kept him busy at Clara's, not that Cody's mind didn't make a quick trip now and then to the other ranch, the outdoor arena with Willow in his arms, the softness of her mouth under his once more. For those few heart-stopping moments before she'd regained consciousness, when he'd bargained for her life, he'd feared losing her in a very different way. But in hindsight—which was always perfect—Cody regretted giving in to the urge to kiss her. It hadn't changed things—she still wore Thad's ring. And Cody had promised to let her go.

This morning, on his way to meet his former supervisor in the Wild Horse Program, he told himself to keep his mind on his job. And he'd just bought a used pickup that he and the bank now owned.

Darryl Williams was waiting for him outside the feed store. They exchanged a few pleasantries before Darryl said, "I took a new video of Diva." Cody's spirits lifted at the same instant they sank, as if he were on some perpetual roller coaster. "She's making real progress."

Darryl handed him his cell, and Cody couldn't resist taking a look at the mustang. Just as he hadn't been able to keep from kissing Willow. "Wish I could see her in front of me rather than on this screen," he said, "but thanks, Darryl."

"No problem." Williams had been one of the few people he'd trusted at the prison; he was a talented trainer who'd taught Cody a lot. He watched Darryl's calm manner on-screen in the ring. It was almost like being there. Starting Diva's training was the best thing Cody had ever done.

Darryl scratched the thin spot on the crown of his head, the dark hairs not quite covering his scalp. Cody could see compassion in his brown gaze. "How you doing on the outside, Cody?"

"Doing okay." He hit the Watch Again button to restart the video, then told Darryl about working with Hadley, who'd become a different sort of coach, expecting Cody to toe the line and meet his responsibilities. All part of his reform.

When he stopped torturing himself with the video, Cody glanced at Darryl. "I need to give you a heads-up," he said. "I filled out an application to adopt Diva."

"I heard." The tone of Darryl's voice had changed. "In fact, that's why I called you this morning. I didn't want to send an email or text. People in high places have been nosing around, asking about you."

"You mean the warden?"

"Not yet." Darryl's gaze didn't waver.

Cody groaned inwardly. "Thad Nesbitt."

"His father, too," Darryl said. "Doesn't get much higher than Grant Nesbitt. Maybe I shouldn't have shown you this video. No sense getting your hopes up." He paused. "You didn't hear this from me—but if I were you, I'd withdraw that application. Take seeing Diva today as a nice goodbye, then find another horse." Darryl added, "Oh, and, Cody, watch your back."

"I appreciate the warning. Think I'll let the process play out, though," he said. "It's not in my nature anymore to cut and run." He wouldn't add he was too stubborn to back down, to let Thad win this time.

"Your choice," Darryl said. "If anyone asks, I'll put in a good word for you, but that's all I can do. Got a wife and kids to feed, if you know what I mean." He clapped Cody on the shoulder, then headed for his state-issued truck. In the back were sacks of feed—his excuse, Cody assumed, for making the trip to town.

"Thanks, Darryl," Cody called after him. At least now he felt better prepared for whatever came next.

Or was he? When he finally reached the Circle H and pulled up at the barn, he spied Willow in the ring and hesitated. Should he turn around and hightail it back to Clara's? He'd stopped by to talk to Olivia but hadn't expected Willow to be here this soon after her accident. Prancer was jogging around the pen, one ear pricked in Willow's direction, the other laid flat against his skull, his irritation a bad omen.

Keeping one eye on the pair, trying to decide what to do, he sat in his truck and pulled out his phone. Through the windshield he watched Willow for a moment, then opened his browser. The clip he'd shown Hadley from the website wasn't as new as the video Darryl had taken, but they made Cody say, "Aw, darling, look at you."

He remembered Diva's hide glistening even on a gray, overcast day, her surprisingly delicate hooves pounding the ground as she cantered around the ring. The mare's movements were nervous but flashy. He didn't want to think about the day he might learn Diva would never be his.

When he looked up again, his vision had blurred, and Cody blinked to clear it. Olivia had entered the nearby ring, but Willow was no longer there. Remembering last week's mishap, his heart lurched then settled as he spied her crossing the dirt between the arena and his truck.

"I thought you might've gotten knocked down again," he said. She'd been limping slightly as she walked over to the pickup. "You feeling better?"

"I still have a little soreness, nothing major." She sent him a tentative smile that turned Cody inside out. He'd already decided she was lost to him.

"You here to work?"

"We're just getting started. Who were you talking to?"

"Myself, mostly," he admitted.

Willow peered through his open window to look over his shoulder. The mare was still on the screen. "Is that Diva?" He handed her the phone, making sure their fingers didn't touch. "Oh, she's beautiful. I can see why you like her."

"She's done well since I left there. I just saw my old supervisor. He had a new video but didn't send it to me."

"Have you heard about your application?"

Cody wondered if he should go on. She hadn't believed him before about Thad, but this was something she should know. "Your fiancé made contact with the prison."

Her eyes widened. "He claimed he didn't threaten you but…"

Torn between staying here or turning his truck toward the road, he said, "I'll find out soon enough just how far that will go, but in the meantime, you'll be happy to hear, I've warned myself. About you. I shouldn't have kissed you, Willow."

Almost as if he'd been given a cue, Prancer chose that second to act up again in the arena, and Cody envisioned another bad accident in the making, with Olivia this time. He jumped out of his pickup, then took off with Willow right behind him. "Olivia! Watch him!"

By the time they reached the ring, Olivia had control of the gelding again, but the horse still eyed her as if he might run her down as he almost had Willow. Neither would be on purpose, considering the gelding's edgy nature, but Cody said, "Prancer must think he's a wild mustang. They're sensitive, on high alert all the time. They live in this constant state of potential fight or flight, intent upon survival. Never take your eye off him. Like them, he'll obviously need a lot of patience, so don't expect his training to be quick."

He'd really been talking to Willow, but.

Olivia blew a damp strand of hair off her forehead. "I've never trained mustangs, and Prancer clearly has problems I haven't encountered before."

Cody made a spur-of-the-moment decision. "Then I have a suggestion—you've helped me with Thunder. I can help you during my lunchtime some days. I'll drive over from Clara's, eat a sandwich on the way, then work with Prancer. I can even stay for a while now. If you want."

"Do I want?" Olivia grinned. "I think you'll be a big help, Cody." To his surprise, she turned then to Willow. "We might both learn something, but I wouldn't blame you if you want to quit." Did she mean because of her accident or Cody?

"I'm all in," Willow said, her gaze on him a challenge. She knew as well as he did that this wasn't a good idea, yet Willow had an air about her today that he couldn't quite decipher. Cody didn't know whether to feel glad or to take off running himself. He'd have to keep his distance from her. Which would be a challenge all its own.

Cody walked toward Prancer, slow and steady, taking the lunge line from Olivia, who looked a bit shaken. He started reeling the horse in, alert to every twitch of his ears, each lash of his tail in annoyance. Cody would accept that dare, too. Prancer would be worth the effort to train him, but because of Willow it wouldn't be easy for Cody either.

"None of us have been watching this guy close enough," he finally said, keeping his voice low. "Let's get to work—and try not to get our brains kicked in."

WILLOW SHOULD HAVE her head examined—oh, wait, she already had at the ER. Today she'd made it through her lesson at the Circle H—after her talk with Thad, she'd gone in the first place to demonstrate her determination to do as she pleased. The training had gone well enough. At its end, though, after being unable to keep her eyes off Cody, she'd gotten in even deeper there. Olivia had asked him to help with the upcoming town summer festival. He'd agreed and Olivia had suggested they do pony rides for the kids. Somehow, Willow had ended up sharing that responsibility. Not knowing how that had happened, she'd hurried off, leaving him and Olivia to cool Prancer, using an appointment with Cass and Jean as her excuse to leave.

In fact, they were in Farrier now seated around a small table in the florist's shop, the air heavy with the scents of various blooms.

Willow's mind wandered—which was becoming as bad a habit as playing with her engagement diamond. Ever since Cody had kissed her, she'd been more aware than ever of the attraction she'd once felt for him. Over several weeks, his summer tan had deepened, and his shoulders looked broader than she remembered, his muscles even more well defined. Hoping her disappointment in herself didn't sound in her voice, she told Cass, "We seem to be on a roll with this party," trying to concentrate on the here and now, but she'd barely heard a word her friend had said before.

Maybe her renewed awareness of Cody wasn't because of that kiss, but because she felt irritated with Thad. After falsely claiming he wouldn't waste his time, he'd stepped in about Diva. It was beneath him to try to interfere with the adoption.

Cass, however, seemed delighted about the coming party. "We've had RSVPs now from almost everyone on the guest list, and I imagine the rest will come in by the time we need to let Jack know the final count for the dinner. These flowers are next. Then I'll need to reserve chairs and create some wonderful party favors."

Willow's mom said, "Right now, I'm thinking white roses, greenery, in crystal vases for our centerpieces..." She looked more closely at Willow. "You should have stayed home today, honey. I think you're doing too much after that nasty accident."

More like after my talk with Thad. And seeing Cody again... Willow couldn't seem to summon any interest in flowers. "I'm okay, Mom. Let's get this over with."

"I think we should hire a few people as valets to park cars that night," Cass added just as the florist stepped into the room.

"Afternoon, girls." She sat at the small round table with them. "Now, let's discuss. These choices are of course dependent upon the budget you have in mind, but the selections are all flexible. If you decide, say, on carnations rather than roses or alstroemeria instead of hydrangeas..."

Willow stopped listening even marginally. She didn't want to be here, and she sensed her mother wished she'd stopped at home to shower and change after being around horses all morning. Suddenly, she couldn't sit still another moment. Willow scraped her chair back from the glass-topped table, hoping she didn't leave a whiff of the barn behind on the silk upholstery of her chair. This beautifully appointed shop virtually screamed *wedding*, and she and Thad still hadn't even chosen their date.

She turned toward the shop's entrance. "Sorry," she murmured. "I need a breather."

"Willow." Her mom stood, too. The florist was staring at them.

"I'll be right back," Willow said, then practically galloped to the door. Out on the street she gulped in quick lungfuls of oxygen, surrounded by the less appealing scents of car exhaust and dust. She leaned against the side of the building, one hand over her eyes, wondering why her life suddenly seemed so complex, but she wasn't alone for long. Fortunately, instead of her mother, it was Cass who'd stepped out.

"Hey." She leaned beside Willow. "Are you okay? Your mom's about to have a cow and the florist is falling all over herself trying to smooth things out. I bet she's never seen a bride-to-be act like that."

"I bet she has. Cass, everything feels so messed up." She told her about Thad's reaction to her fall and about training horses that morning at the Circle H. "I know I shouldn't have stayed there when Cody came, but I want so badly to help with Prancer. And frankly, I didn't want to let Thad run all over me. Working with horses is my choice."

Cass let out an exasperated-sounding breath. "But seeing Cody must be awkward."

"Not just that." Her words rushed out. "Cass, he kissed me."

She blinked. "What?"

"After I fell last week. I feel so guilty I let that happen. Now it feels strange to be anywhere near him, and he told me he's trying to stay away from me." Willow gazed across the street at the row of shops, biting her lip. "I never expected this, but he…still attracts me."

"Cody's hot, and from the beginning I could see the sparks between you. They may be there even now, but, Willow, you're with Thad…and Cody went to prison."

"He's done some bad things, I know that, but he's trying to be better, he already is, and he has this…sweetness that rips my heart to pieces. Cody had an awful time as a kid, while I was growing up on the WB in the lap of luxury. I always wanted to make that up to him somehow." Just as she did with her family over her father's loss. Just as she did with Cass, who'd never had the same advantages Willow had. She told her about his video of

Diva, and Thad's notion to derail the adoption. "Thad lied to me about that. I'm not sure I can trust him."

Cass hesitated. "You know I'm not crazy about Thad. But I also know he'll give you the kind of life I've only dreamed of, so I'm not the best person to give advice here."

"I could use some. I also feel disloyal. Thad loves me, and there's no reason not to marry him."

"Except one." Cass hesitated. "Do you love him, too?"

"I do, of course. Thad and I practically grew up together. He was always at the ranch with Zach…" Willow gestured toward the florist's shop. "And look how I freaked out my mother whose dream, like Zach's, is to see me marry Thad. To them, it's the natural thing for me to do."

"If you don't feel right about that, Willow, you'll be making a serious mistake. Like me with Zach." The words were out before Cass clamped her lips shut.

"What does that mean?"

"Forget I said that."

"No, it's not the first time I've picked up on this, but you always clam up," Willow pointed out. "What really happened between you and Zach, Cass? Please tell me."

"Nothing good. Nothing important now," she murmured.

Cass and Willow had few secrets from each other, but apparently this was one. Whatever she wouldn't talk about must have changed Cass's possible future and Zach's view of her. Knowing she shouldn't meddle, Willow was about to push her anyway when Jean opened the door and peeked outside. "Girls, we need to make our choices. The florist has another appointment."

Willow knew her mother well. With a slight arch of an eyebrow, she could say a thousand words, yet she only needed a few. *Come inside. Now.* Willow would have to find another time to probe Cass about her past with Zach, but for now she needed to reassure her mom that everything was fine. Willow's renewed attraction to Cody must be nothing more than a reaction to her disappointment in Thad. Conflicts happened in any relationship. Through their years together, there would be quarrels, but they'd make up again then, and soon she'd be the bride she'd always wanted to be, although she doubted there would be a Christmas wedding. But would even that ease her mind?

Thad had lied to her about Cody's application, though he seemed remorseful.

Willow wondered how she'd feel if, instead, things had worked out for her with Cody. Which they hadn't, she reminded herself. And one shared kiss meant nothing.

Unless Willow had never gotten over him.

CHAPTER THIRTEEN

IN TOWN, CASS had tried to walk that fine line between supporting Willow and making another wrong move. She'd avoided talking about Zach or her family, but maybe she should have stepped more lightly about Thad, as well. Now, finished with work for the day, Cass wheeled into the driveway at Wilson Cattle. Unprepared for more drama, she walked into the house—and, to her shock, found her mother sitting on the living room sofa.

Wanda Moran—no, Hancock since she'd married Jack—jumped up. "There's my baby," she cried, but where she would have hugged Cass, Wanda met empty air.

Cass had stepped back. "I'm not your baby. I certainly didn't know you'd be here."

Wanda hurried to explain, as she always did. "After I had lunch at the Bon Appetit—" her husband's restaurant "—I dropped in to see

Shadow. She invited me to eat here tonight. Jack's working the dinner service, so I thought, why sit home alone?" She gave Cass a smile as shaky as her reason for being here. Clearly, Cass had been set up by her own sister.

This was the "mother" she remembered— always covering for her first husband. Long ago, that pleading smile would have silenced Cass. "I guess I should say congratulations on your second marriage, but I have no intention of talking to you beyond that." Cass hadn't attended the wedding, and she'd met Jack only once, when they'd set the price for catering Willow's party.

Wanda's brown gaze fell. She fingered a few strands of her dark hair, worn now in an attractive, layered style the opposite of the dull, unfashionable look she had in Cass's memories. Instead of the plain tarnished silver band she'd worn when Cass was a girl, there was a simple gold ring on her finger. "Sugar," Wanda tried again. "We're family. We always will be, yet you've turned your back on me. Why, Cherry? You're living in your sister's home, but I haven't seen you once."

The use of her birth name was another

symbol to Cass. "I'm not *Cherry*. I left that farm a long time ago."

"The farm belongs to Finn and Annabelle Donovan now," Wanda said. "They even have a herd of cattle on the property rather than my chickens scratching the dirt, and Finn has bought extra land. Remember when those people next to us—"

"I don't care who lived on that adjoining acreage. I don't care who lives there now. Every minute I spent in that old house is still right here—" Cass jabbed a finger at her chest "—and that's never going away."

"I know your daddy wasn't the best f—"

Her voice trembled. "See? You're doing it again. Don't even mention him to me. Or didn't you get my message when he finally died? I didn't come for his funeral, I've never visited his grave site and he's more than dead to me."

"He wasn't the way you still see him."

"Oh yes, he was." Cass's body felt as tight as the hold she'd tried to keep on her temper. She didn't like herself at the moment, but Wanda needed to know where she stood. "You *knew*, and yet you always protected him."

Wanda held out a hand. "Then, all right, maybe I did. But he's gone. Please, I want us to find our way back to each other. I'd like you to see our new home. Jack and I have lots of room, and Shadow tells me you're looking for a place. There's no need for you to pay rent. I'd be happy to have you stay with us as long as you want."

"You don't get it, do you? It's not just about him. It's *you*, Mama…" She bit her lip. The last word had slipped out as unbridled as her anger. "I can't be anywhere near you. I don't need to know Jack better." It was bad enough that he'd be supplying the food for Willow's engagement party. Cass would have to deal with him for one night. "I always wonder why I seem to pick the wrong guys—but I guess I learned from you. That's what you did years ago."

Wanda bristled. "Jack's a good man."

"Maybe he is, but I'm sure not living in the same house with him—or you."

"Then what brought you back to Barren?" Wanda held her gaze. "To the WB, no less. The memories aren't all good for you there either."

She meant Zach, and the copious tears Cass

had shed over him in her mother's arms, the tears no one else knew she'd cried here again in the upstairs bedroom she'd borrowed from her sister.

"You'd make excuses for Zach Bodine, too—if I let you."

"What really happened, then, Cass?" Her question was the same Willow had asked earlier. "What did your daddy do?"

With a sharp, indrawn breath, Cass turned away, striding into the front hall toward the door. Wanda came after her. She touched her arm, but Cass flung off her hand. "I came back because I had nowhere else to go. Are you satisfied? Stay away from me, *Wanda*."

"Cass..." But the warning tone she heard hadn't come from her mother. Shadow stood in the doorway from the dining room holding a stack of plates, and Cass's temper erupted again like a volcano spewing ash. Or was it her fear of revisiting the past?

"This is your doing," she said, pointing a finger. "Don't bother to set a place for me." Cass whirled to face Wanda, then pushed past her to the door. "You wasted a trip from town on my behalf. I don't ever want to see you again."

WILLOW WALKED WITH Thad out of the theater—they'd seen the film that they'd missed because of her accident the week before.

Now that the flowers for the party had been chosen—roses and camellias—the engagement party plans were nearly complete. The only thing Willow still had to do was buy a new dress. So the next step was finally choosing a wedding date. Despite Cass's hard questions earlier, and Willow's tangled feelings for Cody, she needed to move on. Losing her head again over him, letting her stubborn attraction overwhelm her, wouldn't be the best blueprint for her life—and definitely wasn't a way to atone with her family for her father's loss.

As she and Thad walked along Main Street, he put his arm around her. "I'm glad you called me about the movie. I had that bar association meeting tonight, but I canceled."

"But weren't you supposed to give a speech?"

"One of the junior prosecutors gave it for me. I told him I wanted to be with my best girl tonight. My only girl," he hastened to reassure Willow. Thad guided her into the café, where they ordered coffee and dessert. "Now what did you want to talk to me about?"

She took a breath, knowing this would please him, but waited until their server had delivered their order. "Our wedding date." Willow cut into her German chocolate cake with a fork. "Late October?" She named a day not far from one of Thad's choices, when the autumn leaves would be at their peak with red and gold still on the trees.

Thad took a sip of his espresso. "That week wasn't on my list, was it?"

"No, you did have one at the beginning of the month, but that's a bit early in the fall, and wouldn't it be lovely to use all that leafy splendor as a backdrop?" Willow was already thinking of the colors she might pick for her bridesmaids' dresses, and as soon as she told her mother what date she and Thad had picked, it would be game on for that, too, in Jean's view. She'd been raring to go from the start. There wouldn't be a whole lot of time to segue from the party to the wedding, but she knew Thad was eager to marry soon, and this was one way to confirm her commitment to him.

He frowned. "I have a conference in Vegas then. What else have you got?"

They discussed several other dates, which Thad rejected for one reason or another. Willow took a bite of her cake but set the rest aside. She and Thad had gotten along well enough since clearing the air about the red dress and even his lie, and he'd been more solicitous than usual, but this wasn't proving to be as easy as she'd hoped.

Willow ran through the last dates on her list, but Thad rejected them, too. Except possibly the final one. "Valentine's Day?" she said. But that wouldn't be until next year. "We'd never forget our anniversary that way."

"You'd make me wait that long?" His smile teased her. "Let's keep our wedding anniversary to itself, okay?"

Willow thought for another moment. "If October's out, then we'd soon run into the holidays, Thanksgiving—" She took a breath, thinking she might as well go for it. "Why not Christmastime?"

"The end of December? That would be a compromise," he agreed. "It should give you and Jean plenty of time to put a wedding together."

"We'd have to start right after the party."

He tilted his head to study her. "If your heart is set on Christmas, let's do it."

"Are you sure?" She could scarcely believe she'd gotten her dream choice. "I want you to be happy about it, too." Willow envisioned their holiday wedding, white and red and green with lots of fairy lights, or maybe she'd choose white, silver and gold.

"If you're happy, I'm happy," Thad assured her and began to embellish her idea. "I'm thinking a horse-drawn sleigh after the ceremony, bells and harness jingling..." He paused. "Let's have our reception at the bar association, what do you say?"

That wouldn't be Willow's first choice, and her mother might prefer using the ranch as they were for the party, but Willow agreed. She'd imagined a problem where there was none.

"The weather could be freezing," he said.

"I'd love to have snow that day."

"Then we'll wrap you in an ermine throw."

She twined her fingers in his. "Brrr, and maybe I'll wear glass slippers."

Not that she actually would—this wasn't a fairy tale but real life.

Thad looked into her eyes, and the warmth in his gaze nearly took her breath away. "Are we okay, then?" he asked.

"We're fine," she said. "We're absolutely fine."

AFTER SHE AND Thad had said good-night at the WB with lingering kisses, and he'd driven off toward town, Willow went upstairs to get ready for bed. Soon after, she heard the front door open, and voices came from the hall below. Her brother's deep baritone, and was that... Cass's husky tone?

"I thought your workday ended at five," Zach said.

"Is Willow home?"

"She's gone to bed," he told her, but by then Willow was on her way down the stairs wearing pajamas, a robe and slippers, her hair caught up in a ponytail. She carried a book she'd been reading, *Training Horses*. Maybe Cass had come to apologize for that afternoon. "I'm right here. Cass, are you all right?"

"Not really." She swallowed. "I know it's late. I don't mean to intrude—"

Willow slipped around Zach. "What's happened?"

Cass looked as if she'd dragged her hands through her hair. She'd obviously been crying, which even Zach should see, her mascara streaked underneath her eyes. His gaze surprisingly thoughtful, even sympathetic, he looked Cass over from her messy hair to her boots, but at least he didn't say anything to make her feel worse. He just stood there, looking as if Cass's distress had changed his view of her. There was something else, too, in his eyes.

Willow said, "Come on, we can talk in my room."

She felt her brother's gaze on them all the way to the landing, where the stairs turned toward the second floor. Neither she nor Cass said another word until the door to Willow's room closed behind them. Willow tossed the book on her side table, then sat down on the bed. "Take a seat."

The bed was king-size, with plenty of room. Cass took the other side, piling pillows behind her head and still looking shattered. "I saw Wanda tonight."

Willow's tone softened. "Aw, how did that go? Not well, I can see." She reached for a tissue and handed it to Cass.

Cass told her how shocked she'd been to find her mother at Wilson Cattle. "I said things I shouldn't have, but it all just came out. I'm so angry with Shadow I could chew nails."

Willow said, "You're also hurt."

Cass wadded the tissue. "I know why Shadow did that, and I know you urged me to talk to Wanda, but seeing her in person was like being back at the farmhouse with my whole childhood running through my head again, me hoping that, somehow, I could get out when I knew I couldn't. And he…" She hesitated, but of course she must be remembering her father, too. In her teens, Cass had turned up here at times just like tonight.

"Your talk with Wanda must have happened hours ago," Willow said. "Where have you been all this time?"

"Driving around," she admitted. "I almost stopped at the café to eat something—my stomach was growling by then—but when I got to the restaurant, I saw you with Thad inside and went back to my car. You were holding hands, smiling at each other, and I wasn't in the mood for conversation. Maybe those hunger pangs weren't because I needed a meal—I've been so stressed I must be getting an ulcer."

"Cass, I'm sorry, but I'm also glad you talked to Wanda. Maybe that's a first step."

"I doubt that," she said. "Can I stay here tonight? I can't go back to the ranch. I can't face Shadow yet. And since Jack's working late, what if Wanda decided to spend the night? I can imagine the heart-to-heart she and Shadow must have had after I left."

"Of course you can stay." Willow had offered her a room before, but obviously Cass felt desperate enough now to sleep in this house for one night. "I told you. Move in if you want."

Cass laughed a little. "Yeah, imagine that. Zach's head would explode."

Willow didn't agree. "Remember when I said you might not be seeing him clearly? Didn't you notice how he looked at you downstairs?"

"Actually, I did—that pity look. And then there was that same look I used to get from other guys here."

That was true—but at the same time false. Cass was a pretty girl. Willow knew from their late-night talks when they were in school that she'd had a boyfriend now and then. Things had never gotten out of hand, but they hadn't treated her all that well. She was wrong about Zach, though, and Willow had always wondered why. "I think my brother looked at you tonight with a very different kind of interest, much more complex."

She scoffed. "I doubt that. Willow, you can't have forgotten my reputation in Barren."

"Cass, why do you put yourself down like this? That's coming from you, no one else. So your family wasn't the best, and maybe *their* reputation rubbed off on your self-image, but you're not them. Besides, you've all managed to turn your lives around, to gain respect. Look at Shadow and Jenna. Your sisters are very much part of the community." Willow drew Cass closer, an arm around her, her other hand easing Cass's head onto her shoulder. "You're such a good person," she said.

"You still think so?" After a moment Cass straightened. "Listen, I'm sorry about this afternoon. I didn't mean to question your engagement to Thad. That's your decision—I shouldn't interfere." She waited a beat to say, "About Cody either…except to tell you please be careful."

"Friends are allowed to speak their minds." Willow decided it was time to lighten things up. "Guess what? Tonight, Thad and I *finally* picked our wedding date. That's what we were doing at the café." She added, "I'll ask Becca to be a bridesmaid. Will you be maid of honor?"

"If that's what you want." Cass was blushing. "You realize that would mean me enduring all the events—the rehearsal, the dinner, the wedding and reception—with Zach there. He is Thad's best man, isn't he?"

Willow grinned. "Who else could it be?"

"Well. As long as you're okay with my being in the wedding party, too, I'll try not to embarrass you."

"Don't be silly." Willow smiled. "We'll all have to be on our best behavior."

Which reminded her that Cass's caution about Cody was well-timed. Tomorrow was the town festival they'd both volunteered for. They would be together all day.

CHAPTER FOURTEEN

WILLOW MET CODY at the park the next morning, wishing she hadn't agreed to help with the pony rides. Today promised to be beautiful with no clouds in the blue sky, and the temperature wasn't unbearably hot for once. Yet the idea of spending this time with Cody kept sounding an alarm deep in Willow's conscience—she hadn't forgotten Cass's words. Thad hadn't come—he was working on a brief for an important case next week. What if he turned up later? He knew where she would be, if not with whom.

Cody was in the makeshift ring saddling Hero, the horse Olivia's son, Nick, had lent them for the event. All of the horses were borrowed. Stormy had been named after a pony in Shadow's daughter's favorite book. Then there were Ginger and Trig from the Circle H and Cinders from Wilson Cattle. Of varying sizes, the five should suit kids of different ages. Willow picked up a saddle for Stormy.

"These are the gentlest horses around," Cody said as he adjusted another cinch. "They define the term *bombproof.* Imagine bringing Thunder today—even the improved version I'm riding now."

They'd had a lot of choices, but most ranchers' mounts weren't this easy to handle. She couldn't imagine Prancer here either; he wasn't ready for an afternoon carrying anyone around a ring.

"Silver's not used to children either," she agreed. "I think we'll be fine with these."

Cody looked Willow over from her hair to her everyday boots. "Did you bring a hat?"

She gave him a cheeky grin but didn't want to encourage him. "No, sir. Did you?"

Cody clamped his dark Stetson on his head. "Let me know when the sun gets to be too much. We can share."

Willow wished she'd remembered her hat. In fact, she should have stayed home, sent Zach instead. Lessons with Olivia, in close proximity now and then to Cody, were going well—he'd been nothing but a gentleman, and she'd kept space between them whenever he was there—but this was different.

And, to be honest, she enjoyed it. After the first few rides, hearing the laughter of children, especially those from town who didn't have opportunities to ride, seeing their eyes light up to be on a horse or pony, Willow began to relax. She followed Cody around the ring, their horses nose to tail, chatting with Finn Donovan's little girl and Lizzie Barnes's younger son. Willow loved hearing the clip-clop of hooves on the packed dirt of the ring, the occasional snort when dust got up a horse's nose.

They were making the last loop on one of their regular runs when she nearly ran into Cody. He'd abruptly stopped Ginger, his gaze trained on someone walking across the park from his truck. Cody looked suddenly pale under his tan. "Grey Wilson," he said half to himself. "Can you take over? I need to talk to him."

Willow took Ginger's reins, walking between the two horses. The kids chattered away, as if in seventh heaven, while Willow's attention remained on the two men nearby. As they met up, she wondered how this would turn out.

"GREY." CODY STRODE across the trampled grass toward the parking area. People had been arriving since ten o'clock, and the park was now filled with fairgoers. Food stalls lined either side of an improvised aisle. "Got a second?" The air smelled of hot dogs, hamburgers, popcorn and funnel cakes. It was getting hotter by the minute, yet that wasn't why Cody was sweating in his pearl-buttoned Western shirt and new blue jeans.

Grey did a double take. "Heard you were in town." He started to turn away.

Cody stepped in front of him. This was his chance, after explaining to Willow, apologizing to Hadley and Dallas, to make amends with Grey, too. If he meant to stay in the area, Cody needed to clear the deck. The last time he'd seen Grey was at Clara's ranch when he'd been working there under an assumed name. Grey and Derek had found him out. And Cody had been arrested on the spot.

"Grey, I did my time in Navarro. I wanted to say—"

"I don't want to hear it, and I got nothing to say to you, Jones." He added, "I cut you, Derek and Calvin a break about those cattle, but I'm not inclined to forgive you burning down my barn."

"I don't blame you."

Grey's blue-green eyes snapped. "You don't blame *me*? I refused to press those rustling charges for my wife's sake, for her mother, because Derek is their family, and they'd suffered enough. I didn't do it for you. And that barn? My grandfather built that. My dad kept it for me, and I would have passed it to my kids. Instead, after the fire, and by the goodness of their hearts, this town had an old-fashioned barn raising—and I've got a brand-new barn, no thanks to you for running off like you did."

"I was wrong. I'm sorry."

"What if my horses had been in that barn? The ranch dogs and cats?"

Cody swallowed. "I think about that a lot. That fire was a reckless thing I did and I'm thankful every day that no one got hurt—or killed."

"Yeah? What if I'd lost my daughter or my baby boy? You're damn lucky they weren't there or I'd have found a way to put you behind bars for good. Got me?"

Cody flinched. "Yessir."

"Finn Donovan and I see eye to eye on that. I can't keep Hadley from taking you on, and I understand his brother thinks you're worth saving, too, but I don't. Are we clear?"

"Yessir," Cody said again, his stomach in knots. Grey wasn't about to listen to Cody. He'd known he couldn't count on Grey's absolution, but he wouldn't try to make excuses. He looked toward the ring where Willow was managing the five horses and about two dozen kids who were lined up waiting their turn to ride. She sent him a look. Sympathy, or did she need his help? He needed to get back. His apology, this time, hadn't worked, and he figured Grey Wilson would be watching him from now on like the sheriff, hoping he'd step out of line.

"I— All I want you to know is, I'm trying to turn myself around. I promise I'll never do harm to you or yours again." He turned. "That's it. That's all I've got."

Cody took a few steps before Grey's hand landed on his shoulder. For a moment he expected to get a fist plowed in his face, and maybe he deserved that—he'd done the worst to Grey, worse than he had with Hadley, Dallas or Willow, who had trusted him—but it never happened. Cody stared at him, the sun glinting on Grey's light brown hair.

"You mean that?"

"What?" Cody asked.

"About turning yourself around." He paused. "I've seen Derek do that. Calvin appears to have gone straight, too. You think that's possible? For you?" He shook his head. "What a bunch you guys were. But I'd like to see that happen, Jones."

"I'm trying real hard, Grey." And he'd made progress, including with Derek and Calvin. They were all friends again, a good influence on Cody after all.

"Okay, then. Here's the deal. You keep trying, but if I get wind of the least little transgression on your part, you'll answer to me. If you behave yourself, we'll have no problem."

"Yessir," Cody said for the third time. "I understand. I won't let you down."

"Don't worry about me," Grey said, starting to walk away. "Don't let yourself down."

THE SUN WAS sinking in the west, a red ball headed for the horizon, when the last of the would-be riders and their parents drove out of the parking lot. After Willow saw Cody talking with Grey, he'd come back to the ring, plopped his hat on her head, said, "Your turn," then lifted the next little girl onto Cinders's saddle. Since then, he'd only said a few words to Willow, and her curiosity had finally gotten the best of her.

She hauled the last rig off Trig's back, then slung it into the bed of Cody's pickup. He led the horse up the ramp into the attached trailer, then shut the gate. And Willow couldn't stay quiet any longer.

"Cody. What's the matter?"

He looked at the ground. "Nothing."

"I saw you with Grey."

"Yeah, well. That turned out all right, sort of, but I've been thinking. I'm not sure it's possible to change every person's mind about me." Did he mean her, too? "I'm thinking, maybe once my parole ends, I should…ride off into that sunset." Cody strode over to the ring again, taking the remaining blankets from the rail. He added them to the pile in back of the truck. "Thanks for helping out today. I'll finish here. Should be a crew coming soon to take down the ring. Before nightfall. Olivia said we're to leave the park as we found it. The food people have already cleaned up."

Her truck was parked next to his. "I was glad to help."

"Were you, Willow? Or did you spend the whole day hoping Thad didn't show up? See you with me? Make you feel guilty for…nothing?"

Willow leaned against the side of the WB's truck. He saw too much. "This wasn't nothing. It was…fun." Until he'd gone to talk to Grey. Willow had the familiar urge to make things better for Cody. She hated to see him in such a downcast state. They seemed to have switched moods since that morning.

"I was surprised," he said, "when you agreed to work the pony rides…and when you decided to keep training at Olivia's."

"Why? That's what I want to do."

"With me there? After you told me we couldn't even be…friends?"

Willow sighed. "That might have been a bit harsh. And Thad doesn't own me, Cody. Neither does my brother—or the WB."

He studied her in the fading light. The sky had turned into a ball of fire; Cody's skin had a ruby-gold glow over his tan. His eyes looked dark as night. "Willow."

"What are we doing?" she asked, because he wasn't in this alone. She couldn't deny her attraction to him was still there, her concern for him. Without thinking, she moved to the McMann's pickup, laid a hand on his forearm. "Cody…"

Then neither of them said another word. Before the sun slipped an inch lower on the horizon, she was in his arms, and in the next blink of an eye she was raising her mouth to his, savoring the warmth of his lips again. Cody gently pushed her back against the side of the truck. Still kissing her, he braced his arms at either side of her head. He broke the kiss, nuzzled her earlobe, her throat, then went back for more. "I never forgot this," he whispered. "Never forgot you."

She could hardly lie. She'd touched him first. "I didn't either, Cody." Then Willow slipped out from under his embrace. "Forgive me," she said, and ran for the WB's truck, guilt at her heels.

TWO DAYS LATER, still thinking about Willow's sunset kiss, Cody pushed through the main doors of the prosecutor's office, startling the receptionist at the front desk. He braced his arms on its glossy wooden surface. "Morning. I need to speak to Thad Nesbitt."

"Do you have an appointment?"

"No," he said.

She looked at her computer screen and likely an online schedule. "Sorry, Mr. Nesbitt's on a conference call," she informed Cody.

"Tell him to end it."

Darryl Williams's text this morning from Navarro had been etched on Cody's brain, as deep as the memory of last weekend with Willow at the town festival.

Taking a chance here. FYI—somebody else has applied to adopt Diva.

That wouldn't be Thad, who was no horseman, but this had his name written all over it.

Cody had barely taken time to tell Hadley he'd be back in an hour before he'd hopped in his truck.

The receptionist glanced at him again. "I'm sorry, but Mr. Nesbitt is not to be disturbed. I can have him call you later."

Cody didn't wait for her next excuse. "I'm here now." Bypassing the desk, he yanked open one of a pair of doors to the corridor that must lead to the offices. Too bad he was in his everyday jeans and boots, and everyone else would be wearing a suit, but Thad was going to answer to him now.

"Sir, *sir*—" The woman ran down the hall after him past the cubicles where presumably junior lawyers were at their desks. People stared, but Cody kept going until he reached a hall of private offices.

Most of the doors were closed, blurred images visible through the wavy glass beside each name plaque. Cody jerked open Thad's door, surprising him at his desk. He wasn't on the phone.

The receptionist was right behind Cody.

"I'm sorry," she said. "I tried to stop—"

"It's all right." Thad arched an eyebrow at Cody. He must have been expecting him, which meant he knew about that other application. Maybe about Saturday with Willow, too.

Thad straightened his tie. "Thanks, Susie." She looked close to tears. "We'll be fine." He waited until she'd left the office then said,

"Start talking." Thad shot his shirt cuff to check his watch. "You have exactly two minutes before I'm due to leave for court, and you crash in here without an appointment? Why am I not surprised?" Thad drawled. "What's on your mind, Jones?"

"I understand you've made good on that promise."

"To you? I don't know what you mean. I never promised you anything."

"There's another application pending now for my horse's adoption."

Thad didn't blink. "I still don't know what you're talking about." He leaned back in his chair. "That horse from Navarro? The Wild Horse Program? I haven't been near the place in weeks."

"You have a phone. You have your father's ear, and he has influence, all the way up to the governor if need be. It wasn't hard to connect the dots."

Thad folded his arms. "That's ridiculous. My dad hasn't the slightest interest in you."

"But you do, and I know why." Cody stepped closer, fighting an urge to jab a finger in Thad's shirtfront, but he wasn't about to mention Willow first. "I understand mustangs, Thad. I can support Diva, train her, finish her off real nice and give her a good home."

Thad looked him up and down. "A home where? If you didn't have such a thick head, you'd already be on your way out of Barren with that new saddle. No reason to stay, or is there—other than seeing your *parole officer*?" He studied Cody for another moment. "I hear you're training at the Circle H. I know you were there the day Willow got hurt. You went with her to the ER when you should have let Olivia handle that." He added, "If I were you, I'd stop helping out. Seems to me you should have enough work at the McMann ranch. I'm surprised Hadley hasn't fired you."

"I'm working with Olivia in my free time," Cody said.

Thad straightened in his chair. "With my fiancée there. Not to mention running the pony rides with her at that festival." Okay, so he knew. Did he also know about the end-of-the-day kiss Cody had shared with Willow? Was it his being near Willow, then, that had triggered Thad's interference? But Cody meant to finish what he'd started.

He leaned over Thad's desk. "I knew guys

like you in school," he said, "picking the wings off flies, making girls cry. I don't care what you think of me, but don't ever hurt Willow. If you do, even if I'm on the other side of this world, I'll come back. I'll—"

"Careful, don't threaten me." Thad didn't seem intimidated by Cody standing over him. "You should have given up on that mustang when you had the chance. Which you don't anymore. Back off, or losing that ugly nag will be just the start. And *that's* a promise."

Thad must mean he'd find some way to get Cody's parole revoked. He'd find some minor violation Cody didn't even know existed, or a loophole… How could Willow not see the kind of man she intended to marry? Or did Thad only show this darker side to Cody?

Both hands raised in surrender, Cody stepped back. Maybe he'd lost his mind in coming here, and quite possibly, if Thad guessed how Cody had heard about that other person who wanted to adopt, he'd risked Darryl's job, too. *Taking a chance here*, he'd texted. Cody hoped that wouldn't get him fired.

Thad stood, then rounded his desk and strode to the door, waiting for Cody to step out into the hall. He lowered his voice so no one else in the prosecutors' office could hear. "No charge for the consultation," he said in a dry tone.

Thad closed the door behind him, and Cody started toward the reception area. "She's not ugly," he said to the walls.

CHAPTER FIFTEEN

AFTER THE TOWN FESTIVAL, Willow knew she could be playing with fire, yet she couldn't stay away from the Circle H. She and Thad had chosen their wedding date, and her mother's planning had already shot to the next level, Jean's excitement doubled now by two events. After a hectic morning, Willow had fled. When she arrived close to noon, Prancer was already in the ring with Olivia. Trying not to make any quick motions that might scare the horse again, Willow entered the arena, closing the gate softly behind her.

Olivia said, "I didn't expect you today, and you usually come earlier."

"I'm escaping," Willow told her. "My mother is out of control with that party. How's Prancer?"

"Mondays must not be his best either. Cody said he'd require a lot of patience. Maybe we should let Prancer take it easy. And speaking of Cody..." She glanced toward the barn as he rounded the corner, surprising Willow, who'd hoped this wouldn't be one of his days for a lunchtime training session. He wore his usual jeans and boots with his Stetson pulled low over his eyes. Olivia said, "We were just about to start."

"Then let's do it." Willow crossed the ring to lay a hand on Prancer's warm neck. Olivia gave her the lunge line, and Willow heard the gate creak open. A few heartbeats later she sensed Cody behind her, close enough to feel the warmth of his body. Willow stepped away, handing him the line without touching. "I'll let the master take over," she said, not meeting his gaze. A remembrance of him, caging her in against the side of the truck, holding her in his arms, kissing her, had derailed Willow's attention. She wouldn't cause another accident because her mind was on Cody, not the horse.

He said, "These horses teach me more than I could ever teach them."

"I'll be learning, too." Willow stood beside Olivia against the rail by the gate, but before he started Cody had an idea.

"Let's try something different. We don't

need this lunge line," he said and gave it back to Willow. "I never used one at Navarro."

That wasn't the way Olivia worked, but after a brief discussion she did as he'd asked. For a few minutes, they watched Prancer freely lope around the ring, loosening up, until Cody said, "All right. Now, we'll get his attention."

His training method was simple. He never touched the horse. Instead, he pointed in the direction he wanted Prancer to go. If the gelding obeyed, moving into an easy trot, Cody was satisfied. If he didn't, he combined that with a quick cluck of his tongue. When both cues failed, he added a snap of the whip at the horse's rear yet never making contact with its hindquarters.

"He learns pretty fast," Cody finally said, flicking a glance at Willow and Olivia. "Now let's see if he'll turn in. Focus on me." Prancer objected at first, but as the session went on, he gradually got the idea that Cody was in charge and he had to do what the man in the ring expected of him. "When he does what I want, I let him stop, reduce the pressure on him, allow him to rest." And as he said the words, Prancer obeyed.

"He's just standing there facing Cody," Olivia remarked. "Quiet as a little lamb. I haven't seen him this calm since he got here."

"He must be thinking things over," Willow said, impressed.

Once the brief rest period ended, Cody pointed in the opposite direction, and to their surprise, Prancer trotted briskly around the ring as he'd been told. "Pretty smart," Cody murmured. "He knows now that when I tell him to move, and keep moving, that's what he needs to do." Whenever Prancer didn't pick up on Cody's cues, which happened less and less often, the horse had to go back to work.

"Cody's good," Olivia murmured. "I've never seen anyone with such natural talent." That didn't seem to threaten Olivia as a trainer at all.

"Me either. Those first few sessions," Willow said, "I knew I was out of my element."

The time was almost up for today when Olivia's cell signaled an incoming text. She looked at it, then groaned. "Becca—my acting manager—has a problem with a customer at the shop. The woman's impossible. I'd better handle this. Lizzie could have, but she's still on maternity leave with her new baby. I need to call."

Olivia had just disappeared into the barn when Cody took the line from Willow then caught Prancer and, leading the horse, walked over to her. She would have stepped back to let him pass through the gate, but Cody stopped. He slackened the lead enough to let Prancer poke his head through the fence to sample some grass outside the arena. Willow heard the familiar munching sound she loved and looked up to find Cody smiling at her. "This makes you happy, doesn't it?"

"Yes," she said, "more than almost anything."

More than Thad? he might have asked. But Cody didn't say that, even when she could see the question in his eyes. Clearly, though, he was troubled.

"Is something wrong?"

He ran a hand over the nape of his neck, then spoke, and Willow's heart sank. Cody told her about the text from Darryl Williams. He'd confronted Thad in his office. "I don't know who the other person is who applied— guess I don't need to know. Maybe one of his coworkers' daughters who's horse crazy, or someone from his dad's circle with a stable better than where I live… All I know is, I have practically no chance to get Diva now."

"You can't be sure that's Thad's fault."

Willow suspected Cody was right, though, especially after Thad had lied to her once, which only made her angry with Cody in self-defense. She didn't want to reexamine her choice. Yes, she'd worked with him on Saturday, kissed him again, and she shouldn't have, but she also couldn't back out of her engagement now—even if she'd wanted to, which, she told herself, she didn't. Things weren't perfect with Thad, but what relationship ever was? Look at her with Cody, years ago—there'd been a time when they fought more than they loved. "What on earth made you breeze into his office in the middle of his workday when you should have been with Hadley? You don't know that you've actually lost your chance to get Diva. All you have is a text from your supervisor. Am I right?"

"Right." Cody's mouth firmed. "I'm not asking you to feel sorry for me. You wondered what was wrong, so I told you. Don't blame me for what he said. I didn't make that up, Willow."

"I never thought you did." Yet it seemed easier at the moment to hold Cody responsible rather than herself after the pony rides. "All I'm saying is—why antagonize Thad, and without proof? I don't blame him for throwing you out of that office."

"He didn't throw me. He ushered me out. Like the gentleman he is."

"I know you don't mean that." Willow turned aside. Was Thad really to blame for this new application? Had he convinced that other person, presumably more qualified on paper than Cody, to apply? Or was Cody trying to turn her against Thad after the kisses they'd shared at the park? She was guilty there, too, but she didn't know what to believe. "Please stop telling me that my fiancé is a jerk!"

Cody rubbed Prancer's side. "I told you my view of him way back. That hasn't changed. I guess neither has yours."

She couldn't look at him, couldn't bear her own growing frustration, her confusion, or to see the loss in his eyes, the way he moved closer to Prancer and away from her.

"I know better than to keep banging my head against a brick wall," he finally said.

"Or am I missing something else here?" He ran his free hand over his neck. "Do I need to apologize for last Saturday?"

The tone of his voice compelled her to lift her gaze, and the memory of that other kiss, the one they'd shared in this very ring, threatened to overwhelm her. She and Thad were a couple now, not Willow and Cody. She'd lost her senses last weekend, that was all. A trip down memory lane.

"No apology," she said. "I kissed you then, too, but… Cody, that didn't change my plans. I need you to know." She took a deep breath, hoping that once she said the words, he would heed them. And Willow would, as well. "Thad and I have set our wedding date."

Cody flinched but didn't respond.

"Did you hear me?"

"Yeah. I heard. You really happy with that, too?"

"Yes," she managed around the ache in her throat.

"That's that, then." Cody sent her a look that virtually said she'd be sorry. "Just don't invite me to the wedding, okay?" He knew she wouldn't. Maybe he'd meant to remind himself that anything between them was out of reach forever.

Together, she and Thad had taken their next step toward holy matrimony—he'd agreed to fulfill her longtime dream of a Christmas wedding. One day maybe Cody would finish straightening out his life; he'd find someone new, as she had with Thad. He'd be as happy as she intended to be. And yet… "Cody, I don't like to think Thad would deliberately try to sabotage your chances with Diva." As if he'd heard the mention of the other horse, Prancer's head came up, grass still hanging from his mouth, and under other circumstances Willow would have laughed. Cody probably would, too, but he wasn't smiling now. "What if I talk to him?" she asked.

"Don't" was all he said, and then he walked Prancer from the ring.

IN THE BUNKHOUSE that night, Cody worked saddle soap into his new gear. He had as much chance with the horse as he did now with Willow—not to put them in the same category.

"Hey, Cody," a male voice called from outside his door. "You there?"

Putting down the soap, he answered, "Yeah," then found Dallas on his doorstep. "Come on in," he said, thinking *did I forget to do some chore today?* His run-in with Thad had unbalanced him again, and his talk with Willow hadn't helped him to refocus. *Thad and I have set our wedding date.* "What's up?"

"I wanted to ask if you're planning to attend the christening."

Cody gazed at him blankly. "Christening?"

"Our baby girl. Next Saturday. A small gathering." Dallas stepped inside. "Lizzie didn't send you an invitation? Shoot. Everyone from Clara's, of course, will be there, which includes you, I hope. Hadley and Jenna are going to be godparents, but he just told me she hasn't been feeling well the last couple days. The doctor wants her to take it easy for a while, and Hadley's concerned enough that he backed out, too, to look after her. So, before I go home, thought I'd ask… Would you be willing to stand in for him?"

"I'm not a churchgoing guy," Cody said, surprised Dallas would even think of him. They'd made a sort of truce before when Dallas helped him fill out the application, and he'd repaid most of the money he'd taken from him on the rodeo circuit, but it wasn't as if they were best buddies.

"Hadley thinks a lot of you. I'm coming around," Dallas said with a half smile to show he'd been kidding. "On the female side, Lizzie thought of Becca—they worked together before her maternity leave—but Calvin's off at a rodeo next weekend and Becca will be home with their baby. She suggested Willow Bodine, but we're still short one godfather for the day. How about it?"

"Willow's going to be there?" The mention of her had sliced through him like a knife blade. "I don't think so, then."

"Why not? I'll help you with morning chores that day, then drive back into town. Lizzie's excited and the kids are beside themselves, not that they haven't been every day since our baby was born." Dallas raised one eyebrow. "So…?" he said again.

Willow would be there, standing next to Cody. There'd be no buffer between them like Prancer or Olivia— "Why not Sawyer and his wife?" he asked. "Lizzie works with Olivia."

"Yeah, they were invited, but they already had plans. They'll be on their way to Tulsa to look at a gelding she'll maybe train here. Some fancy owner with a bunch of million-dollar horses. She didn't want to miss the chance. Lizzie didn't invite them in time for Olivia to change their plans."

"I don't know, Dallas. It's not as if I'm family or anything. There must be someone else you could ask for that one day, and with Willow there..." He trailed off, not wanting to make her his excuse.

But Dallas had already heard his hesitation. "What's with you and Willow?"

"Nothing," he tried, which was the absolute truth after today. "I just wouldn't fit in on such a special occasion."

"That's another feeble excuse. Hadley thought you'd jump at the chance once you heard Willow will be part of this, too."

Cody almost groaned. He regretted having ever confided in Hadley about her. "She's engaged to Thad Nesbitt."

"I know, but he won't be there. Thad's speaking to a group of incoming first-year law students at KU that day. What do you think, then?"

"I think in small towns like Barren or Farrier there must be some other friend who could fill in." That didn't sound friendly to Cody, but he'd already said it.

"Man, you're a tough case. How am I supposed to go home tonight and tell Lizzie I came up empty?" He paused. "Sorry, I don't mean you were our last choice—"

"Which it seems I am," Cody muttered.

Dallas wouldn't quit. "I mean, I know all about the WB's magnificence and that big house, those thousands of acres, and how Willow grew up. Thad must seem to all of them, and her, like the perfect choice. I'm guessing you have another idea about that."

"Based on what?"

"The way you looked when I mentioned her name. And from Hadley."

He had Cody backed into a corner now, even though he was standing in the middle of the bunkhouse's main room, arms folded, his heart beating like thunder in his chest. What else could he do to redirect Dallas's interest in Cody's hopeless yearning for Willow? But, although his apology to Grey Wilson— number three on his list—had gone okay in the end, Cody still had amends to make with Dallas. *I'm coming around* didn't mean they were square yet. Why not do him this favor?

"All right," he said, "I'll stand in for Hadley. Wouldn't want to tick off the boss and risk getting myself fired."

Dallas's expression brightened. "Man, that's a relief. I'll work for you some weekend so you can get time off, how's that?"

"Fine by me."

Dallas pushed off from the doorframe, crossed the room and shook Cody's hand. "Thanks. A few years back, for obvious reasons, I had a low opinion of you, but you're a pretty good guy after all."

Surprised by the acceptance from someone he'd once cheated, Cody only said, "Give Lizzie my regards."

He watched Dallas walk out to his truck, then drive off, red taillights glowing.

What had he gotten into? He didn't know how he'd get through the ceremony—which he hoped would be brief—standing next to Willow, realizing how out of reach she was for him now. Making him think of a different scenario: her and Cody christening their own baby. He still wished she'd break her engagement, but in spite of his vow weeks ago to save her from making a mistake, to eventually win her love again, and the bargain he'd made after she got hurt in the ring to let her go, he had little to offer Willow. Maybe not even the horse that could be the foundation of his business as a trainer.

"You've been awfully quiet all evening," Thad said in his warmest voice. He'd picked Willow up at the WB hours after she'd worked with Prancer, and she'd spent the drive into Farrier for dinner with one of Thad's colleagues and his wife mostly in silence— as she had the night of the bar association dinner/dance. At the restaurant she'd picked at her meal, contributing little to the conversation. She kept seeing Cody's face when she'd told him about her wedding date, hearing him say, *That's that, then*. She couldn't stop thinking about how he'd asked if she was truly happy.

She and Thad were still parked outside the restaurant in his car, its engine idling as he'd made his comment. Willow had decided not to listen to Cody when he'd said *don't*. Had he just been trying to make things easier for her? But she needed to clear the air with Thad— not to always fear that he might lie to her again. She needed to know the truth. "Quiet, yes," Willow said at last. "I've been trying to think how to approach this, but there's no easy way."

Thad reached for her hand, his thumb tracing her engagement ring. A strange look crossed his face. "You're not going to break my heart, are you? Give this back when we already set the date?"

"What makes you think I'd do that?"

He looked relieved, his tone wry. "My own insecurity, I guess."

Willow's pulse jumped. She'd seen him with his father at the dinner/dance, and how Thad seemed to walk in his shadow. His upbringing hadn't been ideal, she knew that. *I never imagined Thad was this vulnerable.* Getting this glimpse of him not feeling so confident for once surprised her.

Had he sensed her wayward feelings for Cody? After the festival, she'd really gone haywire with those kisses. This would be her chance not only to reassure Thad but to come clean herself, to confess that, without meaning to, she'd gotten too close to Cody. But she also remembered Thad saying *I don't share.*

Could admitting her betrayal only make things worse? For them—and Cody, too? Obviously, Thad felt insecure, but at the park with Cody she'd given him reason to be. It was up to her to fix things, to insist that would never happen again. If she didn't tell him, *she'd* be lying by omission. What would that do to their relationship?

And yet…first, she also had to know.

"Thad, I'm not going anywhere, but something has been bothering me." She took a breath, then told him she knew about Cody's visit to Thad's office. "Did you try to block his application to adopt a mustang mare from Navarro?"

She'd been shocked to think he might really try to influence the state's decision about the horse, even to the point of using his father's power.

Thad drew his hand from hers. He didn't admit anything. "Sweetheart, where did this come from?"

"Soon after he left your office today, we ran into each other."

Instead of addressing her charge, he tried to divert her. "At the Circle H? Again?"

"I know my spending time there doesn't please you." She reached for Thad's hand, but he edged farther away, and she felt almost sorry for him. "You have no cause to feel jealous, though."

"I'm glad to hear that." Thad ran a finger around the steering wheel of his new Tesla sedan, which he certainly hadn't bought on his salary as a prosecutor. Yes, his family was rich and one day he might be, too, considering his bright future, but he wasn't there yet. Even with the engine running, the car barely made a sound. "Now that we've settled on our wedding date, do you really want to keep getting your hands dirty with some ornery hor—"

"Prancer isn't ornery, he's a bundle of nerves. If we can get him to trust, then I will keep doing my part. You needn't worry about our wedding plans. I can walk and chew gum at the same time, you know." Her weak smile slowly faded. She'd seen the vulnerability in his eyes, as she had in Cody's, and heard it again in Thad's voice.

He stared out the windshield. "I remember when you were seeing him, Willow, long before you and I began to date. I remember how you looked—all starry-eyed—every time you managed to slip past your dad, went to some movie… trailered your horse to meet Jones somewhere for a ride. He's not good for you now either."

"You don't really know him," she said. "He's changed." But that made her wonder… Did she really know Thad?

He stared at her. "I'm still an officer of the court. If Jones violates one law, any one at all, it will be my duty to hold him accountable. Which I did before."

"Yes, he was guilty then, but—"

"He's still a *felon*, Willow. For the rest of his life. He might as well be wearing a brand."

"Cody's not breaking any law now. He applied to adopt through proper channels—and you didn't answer my question."

"Willow, if someone else wanted to apply for that horse, or half a dozen people, nothing was stopping them. Still isn't. Frankly, in my view, Mill—whoever—is probably more suitable than Jones anyway."

Willow stiffened. He'd just made the admission after all. How else would he know that there was another applicant? And Thad knew the identity of the other person, but the partial name—first or last—didn't ring a bell.

He'd been jealous all along. He more than disliked Cody. That would explain his interference about Diva. With Cody at the ranch, she'd tried not to believe Thad's possible meddling was true even when she feared her own instincts could be right.

Having been caught, Thad didn't attempt to explain. "Never mind the horse. I'll do whatever's necessary about Jones."

For a second she hesitated. "But to deny him his best chance to make something of himself—"

"I have to wonder," he murmured, looking troubled again. "Is this about some wild mustang, another horse at the Circle H, or your seeing Cody Jones?"

This was worse than she'd imagined. Clearly, Thad had intervened about Diva. If she told him any more about Cody, as she'd thought she should, he might retaliate again. Possibly, worse the next time.

She stared out the side window of the car. When Thad murmured, "I will not let that... *cowboy* ruin our relationship," she still didn't respond.

Would Thad even destroy Cody in order to keep Willow?

THE NEXT SATURDAY in church, wishing he'd said no to Dallas, Cody stood beside Willow among the small circle of people at the altar while the pastor droned on about the joys and responsibilities of parenthood. Cody fought an urge to fidget—his shirt collar felt too tight and his suit didn't fit as well as Dallas's did. The new father shot him a sympathetic glance before his gaze returned to Lizzie, who held their five-month-old baby girl.

Willow whispered in Cody's ear, "Be prepared for tears when the water hits her."

Cody hoped the baby wouldn't cry. He had little experience with kids except for Hadley's twins now and then, and all he seemed able to envision, bathed in a stream of light through the stained glass windows, was another fantasy of himself with Willow in some church like this, saying their wedding vows, starting their life together.

He would have been better off spending his Saturday at the Circle H with Prancer. Why had Olivia chosen this particular weekend to go to Tulsa? Cody couldn't wait for this ritual to end. Standing close to Willow was pure torture, especially since their last training session together.

He supposed from now on she'd avoid him, having given her heart, and her full commitment, to Thad. Cody had issues of his own.

He hadn't heard another word from Darryl Williams, but any day now he would get the state's decision on Diva.

Dallas's baby didn't cry. When the baptismal water trickled over her head, she stared up at the reverend with blue eyes that were turning green like her mother's. Lizzie had dressed the kid in a white lace gown, the same one her three other children had worn, its skirt cascading nearly to the floor at the baptismal font.

"Hannah Elizabeth Maguire, I baptize thee in the name of the Father, the Son and the Holy Spirit," the pastor intoned, and Cody bowed his head in prayer, too. He wished the sweet infant every good thing in this life, few mistakes and that Hannah would never have to worry about being loved. Or cared for. In addition to his still-active rodeo career, Dallas had recently bought a share in the McMann spread. He, Hadley and Clara planned to further expand the ranch.

After the service, people gathered in small clusters outside the church to converse. Cody stood apart from Willow, wanting to ease this new awkwardness between them, but he couldn't think what to say. Besides, she'd said it all. Or had she?

"Cody." Willow suddenly spoke. "I know you didn't want me to but, um, I spoke to Thad."

His pulse jerked. "You what? I should never have told you about that, Willow." Yet he'd thought she should know the kind of man she was about to marry. "Why in—heck did you do that?"

"Because… I didn't act like it, but I had my suspicions, too. You were right."

Cody ran a hand through his hair. There was no telling what Thad might do next. Maybe he'd move on from the horse to Cody himself, as he'd feared, to some trumped-up reason to wipe out any gains he'd made in his life since Navarro. Or what if Thad harmed Willow?

Her uncertain gaze held his. "Did I really do the wrong thing?"

"Not only for me—"

He didn't finish. Lizzie had come over to them, carrying the baby. Dallas hovered at her shoulder, grinning. "Thank you both," she told Cody and Willow. "I know that was short notice, but I'm glad you were able to come today. We're having everyone over to the house now. See you there?"

Cody shifted. "I appreciate the invite, but I have chores to finish."

"Hold on. Not before we take some photos," Dallas insisted. "You need help later, I'll pitch in."

Dallas had kept his promise to share the work earlier that morning. He must know the chores were already done.

"Spend today with your family instead," Cody told him. Dallas's parents had made the trip from Denver for the special occasion. Last year his mother's health had declined, but she'd gotten quite a bit better, and she seemed super excited to be able to dote on her first biological grandchild. She'd already taken to heart Lizzie's other three kids.

But Dallas pressured Cody again to stay. "You'll be on your own after next week when I'm off to the circuit again, so you and Hadley will be holding down the fort at Clara's. Might as well party while you have the chance."

Without really saying yes or no, Cody walked off into the hot summer sun, leaving Willow behind. That didn't work either. She joined him with the others and the photographer, everyone passing the baby around for another picture and yet another until, finally, little Hannah Maguire was thrust into Cody's arms. "You and Willow with her now," someone said, and the cameras and phones documented the event for posterity. Willow even stood in Cody's light embrace, a hand on Hannah's head as if they were their own family of three.

Cody's heart actually hurt. And he was angry with Willow for butting in on his behalf with Thad, risking herself, too. Obviously, she didn't get how much Thad disliked him—and not because he'd set fire to a barn then gone to prison. Cody gave Hannah back to her mother. Loosening his tie, he said to no one in particular, "I need to get out of here," but folks were drifting across the parking lot to their cars and Cody got swept along with them.

Lizzie and Dallas, the pastor, Clara, Dallas's parents and half a dozen other people Cody didn't know were in their cars as he reached his truck. Willow had stayed behind. "Cody, after you told me, I couldn't keep from calling Thad out. I was astonished by his behavior, but I didn't mean to make things tougher for you."

"Never mind me. What about you? He can't be happy with you for calling him out. And isn't your engagement party next week?" He paused, making the decision on the spot. "By the way. I'll be at Olivia's on Monday, Wednesday and Friday, noon to one o'clock." His lunch hour. "You should plan your training sessions for whenever I'm not there."

"Cody," she said again, but he hopped into his truck and gunned the engine.

He didn't move from his spot, though, until Willow had started her car. By now they were the only two remaining in the lot, and he wouldn't leave her there alone. A minute later, still debating with himself, he watched her drive off. If he didn't show up at Lizzie and Dallas's home on Tumbleweed Street, they'd wonder why he was so all-fired eager to go back to work when there was no work to be done. Or maybe they'd ask, as Dallas had, about him and Willow again. Neither of them needed to become the town's latest topic of interest, especially when she was so determined to marry Thad. Cody could feel his still-aching heart break all over again.

CHAPTER SIXTEEN

"I can't blame Cody for setting a new boundary," Cass told Willow.

"That would probably please Thad—if he knew. I didn't tell him."

The day before the engagement party, she and Cass had gone into town to get their hair done. This was not Willow's normal routine. She rarely even had her hair trimmed, but getting several inches chopped off felt freeing today, and Willow left the salon with her mood lighter. Last weekend's christening with Cody had shaken her.

So had her talk with Thad about Diva.

Cass, who'd had highlights added to her hair today, glanced over as they walked toward the café. "I hope you know what you're doing, Willow."

She must not mean about Cody alone. Willow couldn't pretend to misunderstand. "This, from the person who questioned my relationship with Thad from the start—then stabbed me in the back by standing up for him because you don't want Zach to think badly of you."

Cass winced. "You mean think worse of me than he already does?" With a scoffing sound, she waited for a car to pass before they crossed the street. "I don't blame *him* for supporting his best friend, his best man now," she added. "You have to admit, Thad had every right to be upset with you. So, for that matter, did Cody. One man who meddled, you *think*—"

"I know."

"—another who didn't appreciate your interference. And you keep saying you don't have a thing for Cody." Cass strode to the café's door and yanked it open. The place was filled with noontime lunch customers. "Willow, I may have urged you to break up with him once, largely because of what that relationship was doing to your family, but I could always see that chemistry between you," she murmured, "even then."

They went inside the restaurant, but Willow no longer had much of an appetite. Tension always soured her stomach.

"From what you've told me," Cass added, "I can imagine that spark is still there."

Willow pulled Cass around to face her. She'd had enough. "You and I have been friends since we were in Barren Middle School, but you just stepped over *my* boundary. Maybe you should give some thought to your own problems rather than mine." Willow knew she shouldn't go on or it would seem like tit for tat, and childish, yet this also seemed to be her week for confrontations. "What kind of relationship could you and Zach ever have—as much as I'd like to see you together—when all you do is kowtow to whatever you think he must want? I told you, you need to figure this out, which first means doing something about Wanda."

Cass stared at her in shock. Other people in the café were beginning to notice them, but Willow couldn't stop. "She's not a bad person. I was there, too, when you were a girl, and even I know that controlling your dad wasn't possible. Wanda may have protected you then in the only way she could by agreeing with him, placating him, trying to defuse any volatile situation. Why not give her another chance to defend herself? Or are you going to dine out on your resentment of her forever?"

"How dare you. Look at yourself, Willow."

"Oh. So you can accuse me about Cody, but I'm not supposed to mention your mother? And, of course, I shouldn't bring up my own brother? Maybe I shouldn't because you'd only stonewall me again anyway."

People in all the booths and tables were definitely looking at them, glancing away then back again as if they were at the scene of an accident.

One of the waitstaff bustled up to them, carrying a tray of entrées. "Table for two?"

"I can't stay." This felt too uncomfortable and Willow turned away from Cass. "I forgot Mom needs me at home. As you might imagine, she's beside herself about the party tomorrow."

"Jean's probably in a swoon by now," Cass agreed, following her outside and leaving the curious gazes behind. "I'll come with you."

"I'd rather go alone." Unfortunately, they'd driven together from the ranch. After all, Cass was their event planner, and she had told Willow this morning that she also had a dozen details yet to see to at the WB.

In silence they marched toward Willow's car. Although she regretted speaking so bluntly and hadn't meant to hurt Cass, this new gulf between them wouldn't get closed today.

Willow had a sinking feeling that Cass had been right—maybe she'd responded with anger because she couldn't face her own dilemma.

What was she going to do about Thad?

CASS USED TO dream about kissing Zach Bodine. Then one day her fantasy had come true, and she hadn't been the same since. In California, she'd ended up making a fool of herself again, and here she was, back "home," getting this party ready to fly.

After her quarrel with Willow in town, at the ranch Cass had taken care of those few last-minute party glitches, then decided a short ride might improve her mood. But as Cass walked into the barn, she saw Zach in the aisle. Too bad she hadn't checked the area first. She was usually better at avoiding him, but today she'd been distracted. He gave her a quick look, then went back to coiling a rope. So, fine. He'd ignore her, too. Cass spoke anyway.

"Willow said it was okay for me to borrow a horse."

"Take your pick." He headed for the tack room, but Cass stopped him.

She'd already made a mess of her friendship with Willow. Might as well keep going. "Zach, I know you didn't want me here in the first place, but I've tried to do a good job for your mother and Willow, to make her party even more than they asked for. Isn't it time you and I straightened things out? Before tonight?"

His beautiful hazel eyes held hers. "Should I pretend I don't know what you mean?" He glanced behind her at the ladder to the barn loft. Cass wondered if its second-from-the-bottom rung still creaked, as it had that long-ago day. "We're talking, right, about that summer afternoon when I caught you up there, hiding from your father."

Cass had been hired when school let out that June following her junior year to help Jean in the kitchen. The day had been hot, hazy, the air filled with the scents and sounds of the Herefords from the nearby pasture.

Heart pounding, Cass had lain there on her stomach in the hay, looking down through the loft's small window at the WB drive where her father's rattletrap truck had pulled up with a screech of brakes moments ago. She'd had just time enough to run.

What had she done wrong this time?

"He was talking to my mother," Zach remembered.

Alone in the loft, Cass had seen her dad gesticulating and raising his voice to shatter the lazy afternoon. When she'd first heard steps in the barn, then at the base of the ladder, she'd frozen. Had she missed seeing him cross the yard? For one thing, he hadn't liked the idea of her working for Jean Bodine—he'd called her "uppity," and claimed Cass shouldn't take what amounted to charity, which shamed him. A man took care of his own, he'd said.

It wasn't the first time her wastrel father had come looking for her. She supposed he'd drag her home, punish her somehow, take away the few privileges she had. Then the name-calling would begin...

But it wasn't her father in the barn with Cass. To her relief, instead Zach had climbed the ladder. "Is he still here?" she'd asked, tears leaking from her eyes.

Now, years later, Zach caught her gaze again. "Things were bad that day," he said. She could tell he was back there with her, recalling everything when she'd still been called Cherry rather than Cass. "I only came out here to help you then. I didn't expect to..."

She knew what he meant. For years, she'd been his little sister's friend, a fairly constant presence in the WB's kitchen, a frequent overnight guest, the girl from the wrong side of the tracks who went riding with Willow on a borrowed horse. He'd mostly ignored her except to tease her now and then, as he had his sister. Then Cass— Cherry's—thin frame had begun to fill out, her auburn hair had a new gloss and her body seemed to change every day. Boys at school began to notice her. But until that day, Zach never had.

He'd handed her a handkerchief. His mouth looked tight, but he wasn't angry with her. He swore under his breath, using her father's name, and said, "Wipe your eyes, baby." He meant it in a kind way, but she used the cheeky tone she always did when she felt uneasy.

"Don't call me a baby." This was clearly a new situation, though, and to her surprise he didn't call her out as he normally would. He hunkered down in front of her to trace a faint line down her cheek with one finger, and she felt his touch from the roots of her hair to her bare toes. "You wait here," he said, "until he's gone. Mom will take care of him. I'll stay with you. I won't let him find you."

Outside, below the barn loft, she finally heard the truck door slam. A second later, her father tore off down the drive, his loose tailpipe rattling. She didn't move until she was certain he'd turned onto the road. He'd be even madder—whatever his reason—by the time she got home. She wished she never had to leave this ranch. She'd never talked like this with Zach before. Just worshipped him from afar. Did he know she had a wild crush on him? A stalk of hay had caught in his sun-gold hair, and those hazel eyes held hers. Looking as if he cared about her.

Without thinking, she reached up to remove the hay, and Zach went very still.

"Don't," he said. "Not a good idea."

"What?" She was holding the piece in her hand. Zach covered her fingers with his.

"Touching," he muttered. "Neither of us needs that kind of trouble. You should go before I—" He didn't say the rest. He must have read in her gaze that she'd been in love with him since she'd turned fourteen. For three years, she'd followed him around like a puppy, hung on his every word, imagined that one day he'd really see her, hoped he would feel then as she did.

Without stopping to consider her decision, she rose up to meet him halfway. She kissed him first, and for that one moment she no longer believed her father might be right about her, that she wasn't the sort of girl a man took home to his parents. That she could never belong on the WB. "Zach," she whispered against his lips, and he'd deepened the kiss. For a long time they'd held each other close.

The memory of him talking softly to her that day would never leave Cass. And when he'd framed her face in his hands and looked so deeply into her eyes?

Now she gazed at Zach in the barn aisle, the hayloft above them, the remembrance carved, apparently, in both their minds. And on Cass's heart. She'd never even told Willow.

"What started out that day with me feeling

bad about your father ranting and raving at the house," he said, "ended up being something very different. My fault," he added.

Cass tried not to react but failed. "I can't disagree. The very next day you turned your back on me, treated me like some pariah." He'd avoided her from then on. "I don't think we ever spoke five words to each other after that."

"I'm sorry, Cass. I made you feel worse than he did."

"Yeah," she said.

"What's my excuse? There's not one except I was a twenty-one-year-old kid," Zach said. "You were going into your senior year of high school. I already had my life laid out in front of me, trying to show my dad he could trust me with the WB. I handled that badly, didn't I?"

"I guess you did." She paused. "Maybe so did I."

And to her amazement, he gave her that same look he had ten years ago. Maybe Willow was right, and Zach didn't dislike Cass as she'd thought… Or as he'd wanted her to believe. She'd seen a glimmer of that the night she came to stay after seeing Wanda. What if he still felt the same tug and pull between them that Willow must feel with Cody? For an instant she wondered if Zach would kiss her again now, too. He didn't, though.

"I'd better take my ride," she finally said. "Jean will need me again soon." But maybe Zach felt guilty. Or maybe he really did care.

"I'll go with you," he said, the biggest surprise of all.

Cody, sorry to tell you this but wanted to prepare you for the bad news. Your application has been denied.

AT ONE O'CLOCK, the text from Darryl Williams reached Cody at the Circle H. Leaning on the rail at the arena after his session with Olivia, he stared at it for a long moment. She had gone into the barn to put Prancer away. They'd had their hands full today with the gelding for half of the training hour before he settled down to follow Cody's cues, and Olivia wasn't in the best mood either. Her trip to Tulsa had been a bust. The horse she and Sawyer had looked at there, she'd told Cody, had serious aggression issues she didn't care to address.

"Are you okay?" she asked now, stepping out of the barn. She must have seen the expression he wore. He hardly had the strength to tell her, and his wrist had begun to throb like a sore tooth. The horse had caught him in a weak moment earlier and taken a piece out of him. But he wasn't thinking about Prancer. "I lost Diva."

He was about to show her Darryl's message when his email notification pinged. That only confirmed what he already knew. The state of Kansas was also letting him know he was out of luck, out of business. At least he'd been warned. "Official version," he said with a shrug, letting Olivia read the letter filled with legalese. "Diva's going to someone else."

After scanning it, she laid a hand on his shoulder. "Not the result you wanted. That's a low blow, Cody. You're such a good trainer. You would have done a great job with her—" she paused "—but at least you gave her a start."

Cody couldn't find that silver lining in his cloud. "I hope so," he said, resenting the person who would be giving Diva a home instead. Treating her right, if she was lucky. Not every mustang was. Some ended up in bad places with people who'd thought they were getting a bargain for a hundred and twenty-five bucks only to discover they had no idea how to gentle a wild horse or gain its trust. Others—he didn't like to think of this either—ended up at a slaughterhouse, getting turned into dog food. His stomach flip-flopped. He feared he was going to be sick. "Gotta go," he said.

"Wait. We need to clean that wound on your arm."

"I'll do it later." He peeled away from the fence. "Good lesson today, mostly…"

"Cody, you'll make it. Once you come to terms with this nasty outcome, you'll find another horse. Start your business. That's probably hard to hear right now, but I'll help if I can."

"Thanks." He didn't believe her about Diva's replacement. For Cody there was none. The mustang mare was the only one he'd wanted. He strode toward his truck, his head full of cotton, feeling as if his boots weren't quite hitting the ground beneath his feet. He shouldn't have gotten his hopes up.

Cody had no doubt Thad was behind this. Just as he'd threatened.

WILLOW KNOCKED THAT night at Cody's bunkhouse door. When he didn't answer, she rapped again and called his name, hoping she wouldn't rouse everyone else on the McMann ranch. Finally, Cody appeared in the doorway. Even in the light from inside, his face looked gray and there were dark shadows under his eyes. "What do you want, Willow?" he asked.

She resisted the urge to touch him. He wouldn't want her comfort, yet she'd been unable to stay home when she knew he must be hurting. "Olivia told me. I worked with her this afternoon—you'd left by then—putting her horse Blue through a kind of training tune-up..." She ran out of words.

He gazed at her another moment. "I'm not up for company," he said, turning back into the bunkhouse. He hadn't closed the door, so Willow followed him inside. Cody sank onto the sofa in front of the cold woodstove, arms crossed over his chest like a barrier. He didn't invite her to sit. "Didn't you hear what I said?"

"I know you're angry with me."

"I'm not angry."

"Yes, you are." And hurt. "You ignored me at Lizzie and Dallas's place, the same way you did during the christening." She'd tried to talk to him, but Cody had walked away from her then, too. She hated this new distance between them just as she regretted being on the outs with Cass. "Cody, talk to me. If you think I made the adoption more difficult because I spoke to Thad—"

"Doesn't matter. The thing was probably done by then anyway." He glanced at her ring, then at her new haircut. And she saw that his feelings went deeper than anger. "Why aren't you home getting ready for that big party tomorrow?"

His defensive attitude, his steely expression, wouldn't deter her. After her argument with Cass, Willow had left her at the WB, calmed her mother, then finally driven to Olivia's, where she'd learned about Diva. "Cody, I know you're upset—how could you not be? I came because I wanted to tell you in person how sorry I am about... Diva."

"You seem to have a lot to feel sorry about. That horse, Thad, me..."

"Don't leave Cass out," she said. "We had a quarrel, too, partly about you."

"Yeah?" He shot to his feet, about to usher her to the door. "Willow, I'm not going to spend another minute of my life wondering why you picked him, because I already know—he's your comfort zone—and I was right from the beginning. What would you want with a guy like me? Still, I've always been a slow learner—at first after I got out of Navarro, I told myself I should try to save you from making a huge mistake with him. As if I were the bigger prize... But I'm done now."

"You weren't wrong. I have seen his darker side, Cody. Several times."

He studied her, as if trying to see into her mind. "But you're still with him. Watch yourself and I mean that."

"Thad would never hurt me."

"Don't be too sure. My mom never did realize what she'd gotten herself into until it was way too late. And how did I ever dream you and I could be together? With Thad and Zach in the way, your father before that, I never had a chance."

"That's not true," she said on the verge of tears. "Years ago—"

"No wonder they didn't want you anywhere near me. You took a chance with a guy— me—whose father *murdered* my mother."

"That was dreadful, and I know you still

have nightmares—who wouldn't?—but that's not *you*. Is that what you think?"

"I'm not going there." He tried to change the subject. "I do feel sorry for Cass. She'll never wind up with your brother—she should salvage her pride, too."

The boulder lodged in Willow's throat, the guilt, kept her silent. She looked at Cody's hand, a bandage with gauze and tape around his wrist.

He glanced down as if he'd suddenly noticed the wound. "I got careless with Prancer. My turn, I guess. He took a chunk out of me. Olivia didn't tell you that, too?"

"No," Willow said. "And *I'm* sorry—"

"For what this time?"

Her mouth quivered. "Everything. I don't know what else to say. I don't know what you want right now."

"What I want is for you to leave this cabin," he muttered. "Go back to Thad and the cushy life you'll keep leading together. That shiny new Tesla of his is only the beginning. He's going to drive you straight to the governor's mansion one of these days. You'll become the state's first lady, and I'll probably still be mucking stalls somewhere, feeding horses that aren't mine."

"Stop," she said. "You have a right to your bad mood tonight—even to feel sorry for yourself—because today wasn't your best ever—" she eyed his bandaged wrist "—and I hate being partly to blame, but, Cody, I'm not that shallow. That isn't why I'm marrying Thad."

He stood, legs braced, in front of her, his eyes cold. "Then why are you?"

Willow took a breath. She should tell him she loved Thad, but her fears had come true. He'd seen to it that Cody lost Diva. She still needed to deal with that. "Thad's been good to me," she said at last, "and overall, it's true, we fit into each other's lives. Part of that is obviously due to my background and his." Another deep breath. "But we're not talking here about just me. You once told me I blame myself for my father's death when I shouldn't. But I'm not alone. You're still in that living room with your parents shouting at each other for the thousandth time, your dad pulling a gun—"

"Didn't you hear me before? He murdered my *mother*. And then killed himself." He looked at the floor, but Willow could tell he was no longer here. His words were strangled yet the dam holding back his emotions had burst. "Know what I did after it happened? I dropped onto our couch, numb all over. There was so much blood," he said in a barely audible voice. "Then, all at once I was screaming my head off. I…kicked the pistol away from my dad, kicked it clear across that room into the wall. It was a wonder the gun didn't go off again, kill me, too. I didn't stop screaming till the cops arrived."

"That was terrible, Cody, horrendous." Yet she was glad he'd finally dredged that up from the deep well of his grief. "But you can't let that tragedy consume you."

"That's sure the pot calling the kettle black."

"Maybe so." Willow blinked a couple of times as his image wavered before her eyes. "And I can't deny that, before my dad died, I was given every advantage you never had. I haven't experienced anything like the horror you did then. When you were twelve years old, a witness to that, where was I? Having sleepovers with Cass, giggling about boys.

But my privileged life at the WB never kept me from—"

"Taking up with a bad boy to peeve your daddy? His anger wasn't your fault either. His own arrogance was his downfall, all that power he held over other people till his blood pressure hit the roof—"

"You're not a bad boy now," she said. "You're not. Don't be like Cass and see yourself in the wrong way."

"No? What if I am just like my father? Huh? What if we were still together and one night I snapped just like he did?"

Her blood chilled. "Cody, that would never happen. You aren't like him. Yes, we both have issues, and you and I didn't work out, but I wasn't lying when I said I've always cared about you. I still do," she admitted. "I'd trust you with my life." Her voice broke. "Can you forget that day after the festival? I can't."

His stare only hardened. "I'm trying."

She reached out blindly to grasp his forearm just above the bandage. "Please, forgive me. I never meant to hurt you. I missed you in the arena today, and when Olivia told me you'd lost Diva—"

"You had to come rub it in," he said.

Willow refused to let him push her away. He hadn't yet shrugged off her hand. "I only wanted to help."

"You mean, like talk to Thad again?" He shook his head and Willow knew he had a point. Like Thad, she had interfered. She still had to straighten out her feelings for the man she was supposed to marry, but she wasn't doing much good right now either with Cody who was shattering her heart. "Why didn't you just stay home?" he said, sounding as tortured as she was.

"Because I had to see you." The tears welled in her eyes.

He didn't appear to hear her. "You would have been nice and safe where you belong, instead of driving all the way out here." Then his hard gaze faltered. "Alone on those dark roads..."

A tear rolled down Willow's cheek. Even when he was rejecting her, or rather what they'd once had, he cared enough to worry about her. He looked down at his wrist, the bandage, until she dropped her hand. His voice turned husky. "What kind of game are we playing, Willow?" and, hearing the fresh hurt in his tone, she stepped closer to him. *What are we doing?* she'd asked him once.

"No game," she said, barely above a whisper.

"You're dancing around here, back and forth, like Prancer." Again, his gaze almost softened before he glanced away. "Just go," he grated the words. "Go right now before I—"

It was too late. Cody reached for her, and at the same time she threw her arms around his neck. His mouth came down on hers, and he groaned aloud, as if he couldn't keep from kissing her yet knew he shouldn't. Her engagement ring pressed into her skin, a reminder she didn't heed. She knew he felt desperate without Diva, without whatever he and Willow had once had, what he'd still wanted with her, no matter what he'd said, but for selfish reasons she hadn't been fair. She couldn't keep doing this to Thad, but she hadn't been able to give Cody up completely. "If you don't want this—" he started to say.

"I do," she whispered against his mouth,

With another moan, he deepened the kiss, taking her under, into the private world they'd shared before, his arms warm and tight around her, his lips on hers reminding her of all those days and nights together. Only now their connection seemed even more intense, all-consuming as if he would draw her into himself and never let her go. No matter what he'd said, he did still care.

So did Willow. She loved him.

Where could they go from here?

Yet this kiss was different from any they'd shared in all the time she'd known him. Cody was the first to ease back, his lips leaving hers a little at a time until they were a mere brush of air against her mouth, then no longer touching at all. He unwound her arms from around his neck. "No more," he said.

And she knew. He'd been kissing her good-bye.

CHAPTER SEVENTEEN

WILLOW STOPPED HER car short of the WB's front porch. For a long moment she sat there in the dark, remembering Cody's kisses, knowing that although she hadn't been able to let him go, he'd finally given up on her. And why not? What kind of person was she to keep letting him hope they could be together when, as he'd pointed out, her engagement party would begin less than twenty-four hours from now? She could see her mother through the windows, moving about in the well-lit house.

Cass was there, too, following after Jean. Had she told Willow's mother about their quarrel? At least overseeing this event and Cass's efforts with the planning had reenergized Jean, blunting the loss of Willow's dad less than a year ago. Reminding Willow of her obligations to her family.

She got out of her car, then ran up the steps.

"Mom, I'm home." She swept through the front door. Even after seeing Cody, there was no way she could not go through with this party when most of Barren would be there, all of Thad's friends and contacts, the state's attorney general—his *father*—and her own family. She'd gotten in too deep to even think of backing out now.

And Cody no longer wanted her.

Good job, Willow, you really know how to break a man's heart. But he'd also broken hers, and she couldn't have it both ways. *What kind of game are we playing here?*

With Cass at her heels, Jean rushed toward Willow. "I was getting worried. Why did you disappear tonight of all nights?" She tugged Willow into the kitchen, then indicated the array of appetizers on the counter for the cocktail hour. "What do you think?"

"Those are bacon-wrapped scallops," Cass said behind her. She hadn't looked at Willow. Obviously, their earlier quarrel still troubled her, too.

"They look fine to me," Willow told her mother. "It's fresh seafood, I hope."

"Flown in this morning from San Francisco," Cass murmured, then started toward the door. "I'll call the Bon Appetit to be sure they were sourced as we wanted. I need to ask about the cake anyway." She vanished around the corner into the hallway. Willow heard her say something to Zach, and his brief reply, before Cass's footsteps headed toward the ranch office.

Jean called after her. "We ordered a gluten-free cake, as well."

Willow doubted Jack would need the reminder. She could also guess Cass, because of her estranged mother, didn't want to talk to him. Willow had noticed she didn't use his name. "Mom, relax." Jean was still fussing with the food on the counter. "The guests will be too busy talking, drinking, eating whatever's on the tables tomorrow night to even care what we serve."

"I care," her mom insisted. "I want perfection."

Willow hugged her. "You always do, but haven't you heard? Perfection isn't attainable. Daddy wouldn't want to see you like this, would he?"

"No," Jean admitted, taking a deep breath, "but, Willow, we don't have much time.

Where were you all evening?" she asked again.

"I went to see Cody. He got some bad news today."

"That boy," Jean murmured. "I don't even want to know, or I'll lie awake all night."

Unlike Willow's dad or Zach, her mother had never actually disliked Cody. She'd heard about his parents' tragic deaths when he was a boy, and empathized, though she didn't feel he was the man for her daughter to marry. Perhaps her own loss of her husband made her feel for Cody now, or maybe it was simply her loving nature, as if all children were her family.

Willow did tell her about Diva's adoption. "Not to raise an issue when you're focused on the party, but I'm not pleased with Thad."

"What could he possibly have had to do with that?"

"He made sure Cody would never get that horse."

"Please, Willow. You aren't engaged to Cody," she pointed out needlessly. "I'm sure Thad thought he was doing the right thing. Whatever that was."

"Like buying me that red dress?" Willow hesitated. Failing to support her training hopes? Even picking out potential houses without any discussion? That was a smaller matter, and still undecided, but… "Sorry. I don't mean to upset you."

"Then why have you?" Zach walked into the kitchen. "Mom, why don't you go up to bed? Willow can handle anything else down here, and if she needs help, I'm not going anywhere."

Their mother didn't argue. Clearly exhausted, she kissed him, then Willow on the cheek. "I know when I'm beaten," she said, heading toward the stairs. Willow could hear Cass's voice on the phone down the hall.

"Good night, Mom," Willow called out, but Jean didn't answer.

"Nice work," Zach muttered, taking a beer from the refrigerator. "The night before your party, you spend most of it with Cody Jones."

She tried a light tone. "Just saying goodbye." But she'd choked on the words.

She heard Cass's footsteps on the stairs. Her call had ended, and she was going to bed, too. Cass was staying overnight before the party.

"Quit worrying about me. Please. Whatever will you do, Zach, after Thad and I are married? I can't imagine what you'll do with your time."

"Keep this ranch going," he said, as he always did, then took a long swallow of his beer.

Willow wasn't in the mood to be charitable. "The responsibility weighs heavily on those broad shoulders, doesn't it?"

He sighed. "You seem determined to annoy everybody in this house tonight. I hope you're not going to screw things up with Thad because you're obsessed with another guy."

"I'm not obsessed."

"Then what business was it of yours if Jones didn't get a horse he wanted? If he stays in Barren or if you never see him again?" He held Willow's gaze as if to gauge her reaction. "I don't want to miss anything here, but you have obligations. That means Thad—and not putting Mom through any more than she's already suffered. Not that you would know, being over at the McMann's spread the night before this party. With him."

She could hardly tell her brother she loved Cody, much less that he'd rejected her. She wouldn't mention her unhappiness about

Thad, her growing doubts. "I know my place, Zach." She flashed her ring at him. "I didn't want this party—I think it's way over-the-top for an engagement—but I'll be there. And at Christmas I'll be walking down the aisle on your arm. Is that good enough for you?"

He set down his bottle. "I'm not sure it is. Ever since Thad proposed, I've hoped you wouldn't let your old feelings for Jones surface and carry you off again into a life you were not born for—"

A surge of loss made her voice tremble. "That will never happen."

Zach's demeanor softened. "Good." He kissed Willow's forehead, then seemed to make a decision. "Now, tell me. What happened with Cass today? She told Mom you had a fight."

Willow sighed. "If you have to know, we argued about her mother—and you. Honest, you make me so frustrated. Zach, if you can multitask with the WB, there's room to have a personal life, too. Why can't you see that? Cass is still here, but she won't stick around forever. Don't lose your chance."

"Cass has a lot of baggage." But his gaze had left Willow's.

"Don't we all?" Willow drew back to see his face. Why not leave her own issues for now? And try to help her friend? "Come on, big brother. Stop thinking about cattle for a minute and start thinking about what else could be possible."

Zach's mouth twitched. "I'm counting the hours until that party's over. I hope Cass enjoys her last night sleeping on the WB."

Willow gaped at him. "Seriously? You can't be that dense. You two make the cutest couple—I mean that—" she'd seen the start of an eye roll "—and she adores you. She has for a long time."

He cleared his throat. "Doesn't mean I need to adore her."

Willow flung out a hand. "You're impossible."

"Yeah," he said. "And tomorrow morning, as soon as I finish feeding stock, I'll carry her bags to the car myself and wave her off down the road."

Willow blinked once, then again. She'd had too many goodbyes for one day. Her life seemed to be rushing toward a future that, perhaps, she shouldn't have chosen. If only her brother would come to his senses, if she could help Cass, make up to her for their rift.

Then, suddenly, she realized Zach was grinning. The way he often had when they were kids and he'd wanted to get her goat. "Gotcha," he said, his eyes glinting with mischief.

Her big brother hadn't been serious after all. So what *was* going on?

"Cass and I had a talk not long ago. I guess we'll be having another," he admitted.

Willow's smile must have taken over her whole face. She had always hoped they would work things out—which only made her wonder again about the ring on her own hand.

"WHY SO GLUM?" Hadley asked Cody.

"No horse," he answered, applying more brass polish to his bridle in the tack room. They planned to move cattle this afternoon, but the way his luck was going this morning, he expected to get thrown off Thunder and break his neck. He told Hadley about Diva and his certainty that Thad Nesbitt had pulled strings to see that Cody was shut out of the process, but he tried to sound upbeat.

He'd wallowed enough in his misfortune

with Willow last night. "I'll have to save some more money, buy myself another h—maybe not a mustang." Financially, he was doing okay. He'd managed to pay off the saddle Earl had sold him, and he'd reimbursed Dallas, too. Cody had bills to pay, a truck loan. Like any solid, responsible citizen. He even had a few extra bucks now.

Hadley sat beside Cody on the tack trunk. He spread his legs, rested his hands on his knees. "I know you were counting on the mare."

"I hope she wasn't counting on me." He had spent the rest of last evening and breakfast today studying the picture he had of Diva from the website. Feeling his heart crack open wider.

Then there was Willow... *Don't think about her*. Last night had been the end of them, too, or rather him. He shouldn't have kissed her again, yet he'd known he wouldn't be able to let her go without that.

Had he been right to fear he was like his father? Maybe that had always been in the back of his mind and only came out in that moment of desperation. But to think he might ever hurt her—he had a bad history. What if his trying to reform turned out to be a cover-up, and in the end temporary? What if he had that capacity to turn violent? She was better off without him.

Her engagement party was tonight—soon there'd be no more hours left, and according to the weather report, she'd have a wet one. He needed to focus on his job.

"Things don't always work out, Hadley. What time you want to ride?"

"After lunch. There's nothing more you can do about the adoption?"

"Not unless I want to find myself back at Navarro on the other side of those bars." Cody's parole officer had advised him not to make waves. Had Thad spoken to him, too? He glanced at Hadley, who was studying his face. "What?"

"I don't know Thad Nesbitt well," Hadley said, "but I hear he tried his best to get you the maximum sentence last fall. Are you gonna let him win now?"

"Who's taking bets? On what?" Dallas asked from the nearby aisle of the barn. Wearing his now-familiar cocky face, he strolled into the tack room, assessed their more serious expressions, then leaned against the wall, one booted foot crossed over the other. "My money's on Cody." They'd had a good talk at the house after the christening, even better than the one in the ranch office. "You work with a man every day, you get to know him. I've seen you with the horses, and Lizzie tells me Olivia thinks highly of you as a trainer."

"I'm also the guy who ripped you off for five hundred bucks."

"And paid back every dime." He paused. "You're pulling your weight here, Cody, and day by day I've watched you turn your life around. That's good enough for me."

At least his atonement with Dallas was complete.

Hadley stood up. "This little lovefest is fine, but talk isn't going to get Cody that horse."

"I don't know what else I could do," he admitted.

Hadley gazed at him as if to judge his commitment. "First, we need a plan."

LATER THAT AFTERNOON, when they'd finished moving cattle to another pasture and the clouds had moved in, Cody drove over to Navarro. In his opinion, their discussion in the barn had produced no workable solution but they'd tried. He had Hadley's and Dallas's support, but there didn't seem to be anything else he could do. Except this… Cody hadn't been to the prison since his release, but he had a mission now that made his heart slam against his ribs as he pulled into a visitors' parking space near the administration building. He got out, pulling a deep breath of fresh air into his lungs, remembering the day he'd left here and found Derek waiting for him in his truck.

Cody was glad he and Calvin were his friends again. Together, the three of them could keep each other on the right path.

No one was waiting today. Hadley and Dallas didn't know what he was about to do. Already he'd lost Diva and had no further chance with Willow.

Wise or not, Cody meant to at least see Diva—one last time.

His hat pulled down in case the dark clouds overhead let loose with all the rain that had been predicted, he walked along the fence line. Darryl had said he'd try to bring the mare to this pasture near the road as far from any prying eyes inside as possible. And, yeah—his heart rate soared—there she was. The horse lifted her head, sniffed the air, then nickered. Ears pricked, her warm brown gaze homing in on Cody, she pulled at the lead in Darryl's hand and, with a laugh, he let her go. Diva broke into a snappy trot, shaking her head as if to say *I can't believe you're here*, and came right up to him at the fence. She hadn't forgotten Cody.

"Hey, gorgeous." He reached out a hand for her to smell. She whinnied, as if in sheer pleasure, and Cody's throat tightened. "Darryl," he tried, "I can't tell you what this means—"

"To her, too."

His heartbeat settled into its normal rhythm, but he felt the sudden sting of tears in his eyes and looked away. "I know you're taking a risk. I don't want to make trouble for you," he said.

Darryl shrugged, but the move wasn't convincing. "It's after hours. Few people around the barn. Still, pretty soon some guard will patrol, and the cameras will swivel our way. Maybe they'll think you're some curious tourist, but I wouldn't bet on that."

"I understand." He laid a hand on the mare's neck, then ran his touch over as much of her as he could reach through the fence, felt the warm flow of blood in her veins just under her brown-and-white hide, the same connection between them that he'd known in prison. He tugged at her snowy forelock, teasing her as he used to do, and Diva pushed her face into his hand.

"You know who's taking her?" he asked Darryl. He'd told Cody the horse would leave by tomorrow for her new home, the one Cody hoped—prayed—would be good.

"I don't," Darryl said, looking downcast.

He shook his old supervisor's hand. "I really appreciate this. If I could have done more for her, I would."

"I know. The process took over, that's all, maybe with some help." Did he mean Thad? Finally, Darryl said, "You better go."

"Thanks," Cody said, letting his hand trail from Diva's forelock back to his side, his hands turning into fists, then he stepped back from the fence. He'd kept his hat low over his eyes, but you never really knew who was watching. The thought of being behind those bars again made him twitch. He still wouldn't have Diva then.

"You have my cell number," Darryl said. "You need anything, let me know."

"You just gave me what I needed. I got to see her once more." Yet on his way to his truck, looking over his shoulder every step of the way for one last glimpse of Darryl leading Diva toward the barn, Cody knew that wasn't all. The image of Willow crying last night, then in his arms with Cody kissing her for all he was worth, refused to leave him either.

They'd said things they couldn't take back—most of them true. He'd tried to tell her she wasn't to blame for her father's death. She didn't need to atone for that with anyone, including her family. Jean wasn't that fragile, and as for Zach…maybe he was too stubborn to change.

She'd been right about him, as well. At times, he was still back in that living room pleading with his mom to run, begging his dad to put away the gun.

Willow was the only person he'd ever told that to except the police.

Now, in spite of the dead-end discussion he'd had with Hadley and Dallas about the mustang, his thoughts of Willow and seeing Diva, he didn't have a plan. He hadn't been able to save his mother. He hadn't saved Willow—yet somehow, he had to find a way to save Diva.

For starters, that horse wasn't going anywhere except to Clara's ranch.

CHAPTER EIGHTEEN

IT HAD RAINED since late afternoon into the evening. By the time people began to arrive at the WB, the white tents on the lawn were sodden and Willow's mother feared they might collapse under the weight of so much water. With the creek nearby threatening to overflow, Jean had made the decision to bring the whole party into the main ranch house, and the first-floor rooms were now at full capacity.

Willow saw Hadley with Jenna, who was glowing, then Dallas with Lizzie. Many more of her friends, including Becca and Calvin, and every rancher in the area had come. Olivia waved at Willow, her free hand tucked into the bend of Sawyer's arm.

"Welcome, glad you could come," Willow told nosy Bernice Caldwell, who'd probably grabbed at the invitation so she could report every happening to the whole town tomorrow.

That "scoop" shouldn't matter. A considerable segment of Barren's population seemed to be here as firsthand witnesses, which would steal Bernice's thunder. "Thank you," Willow said to someone else who'd asked to see her ring and congratulated her on her engagement "to such a handsome young man."

She circulated among her guests, greeting friends she'd known all her life and gone to school with, people she'd met with Thad once or twice, and, of course, the political entourage his father had brought with him, making a grand entrance as if Grant Nesbitt were the US president instead of the state's attorney general. Across the living room she could see the governor himself standing with a drink in his hand, talking to constituents and probably courting votes for his next election.

The party's atmosphere didn't feel very romantic to Willow, who would have preferred a smaller gathering of close friends and family. Instead of the filmy, seafoam-green gown that floated around her ankles, she wished she'd worn her trusty royal blue. She was still so angry with Thad about Cody's horse that it would give her pleasure to see his face turn as red as that satin dress he'd bought her. For the hour since he'd stepped into the house, Willow had largely avoided him—his increasingly wounded expression. She shouldn't have lied to him about Cody in the first place, but she'd had reason, and been proven right. Twice over. Thad was hardly innocent himself, but for her mother's sake if not her own, tonight she didn't want to make a scene.

But what *did* she want? She was running out of time. She wished now that she hadn't gone to see Cody. If she'd had doubts before, his goodbye kiss had only made them worse. Made her sad.

Surely, he didn't really believe he was capable of hurting her? *I'd trust you with my life*, she'd said.

Willow moved through the crowd in the living room, hearing the clink of glassware, smelling the aroma of bacon-wrapped scallops, shrimp scampi and grilled mushroom caps.

All of a sudden, Cass rushed up to her, appearing panicked enough to overlook yesterday's argument. "We're already out of those tiny quiches."

"I think there were more in the extra freezer. Did you look?"

She quickly glanced away from Willow, as if she'd just realized they weren't speaking to each other. "No, I haven't. Thanks. I'll try that."

"Cass." Willow caught her arm. "Can we talk?"

"Not now," she said, taking a step toward the kitchen and the enclosed rear porch. *Maybe not ever*, Willow could imagine her saying.

Thad chose that moment to beckon her from where he stood in the other room with three of his colleagues. Willow had met them at the bar association dinner/dance, but she couldn't speak to them now. "Please, Cass. I'll help you while we discuss this."

And Willow could briefly escape—before she said something she might regret to Thad. She hadn't missed seeing his frown when she turned her back on him. With a shrug, Cass went through the kitchen with Willow behind her.

Cass rummaged through the huge chest freezer on the porch. "Wouldn't the quiches be on top? Jack brought everything over this afternoon."

Willow dug through her side of the freezer

until she came up with a package of the little pastries, which Jack had prepared, then frozen for them. She held up the box. "Will this do?"

"I should have seen it." Cass took the container without meeting her gaze.

"Our deal was for me to help and you to listen," Willow said.

"I think we said everything yesterday. Why don't you enjoy your party while I pop these in the oven before the cocktail hour is over? It's my job to serve, yours to—"

Willow bent to catch her gaze. "Jack does know how to cater an event, too." He and his staff were out among the guests with trays full of drinks and appetizers, yet Cass seemed as edgy as Jean tonight. "Cass, we've never had an argument like that before. Why won't you talk to me?"

"Why? Look at you." She waved a hand at Willow's gown, then at her own black dress with a white apron over it. "This is the very essence of our friendship— It's not about me pining after Zach or not talking to Wanda. I'm the one who goes to parties like this to pass around canapés."

"You're not the waitstaff—you're our event

planner. Give those quiches to someone else and take off the apron. Your dress is far too pretty to cover up."

Cass's gaze faltered. "Don't you get it? There's a line, Willow, and I—one of the worthless Morans—can never cross it."

Willow was stunned. "I've never thought of you like that."

Cass's eyes filled. "You didn't have to. You weren't the one on the outside looking in, and everything I do ends up confirming that. It all started on that old farm, then happened again in LA. Now I'm here on the WB, where your mother so graciously took me in, yet I've always known I never really belong." The tears in her eyes spilled over. "That's who I am, Willow. I wish you all the best with Thad but I'm not going to try any longer to be part of your perfect life."

"It's not perfect! Far from it." Why couldn't she see that?

Cass went on as if she hadn't heard. "And about your wedding…"

Willow almost strangled on the words. "Please don't say you won't be my maid of honor." She couldn't bear that.

Cass shifted the box of quiches. "My

hands are freezing. I need to get these hors d'oeuvres in the oven."

"Not until we fix this," Willow insisted.

"There's nothing to fix. I've smiled my way through a dozen events like this—for you alone—but this is the last one. And, oh," she said, her gaze faltering, "try to smile. Frankly, you look miserable, and people have noticed. If that's about Cody—"

Willow knew that was truly over now. "No, it's about Thad. I don't know what to say to him."

"Well, you'll think of something, I'm sure. After tonight, you have the rest of your life to figure it out. I'm sorry, Willow, but I'm leaving as soon as this party is over."

Willow couldn't let it go at that. She dogged Cass's trail back into the kitchen, Willow's heels clicking on the tile floor. Cass had worn more practical flats tonight. As soon as she slipped the quiches into the oven, Willow gently approached her again. "We're not ending this friendship. We've been best friends since we were girls, and I never once thought of you as my inferior. Do you hear me?"

"I heard you." Cass's eyes watered again.

"I love you," Willow said. "Please don't

leave. We haven't talked about your conversation with Zach either."

"What talk?"

She'd been stonewalled again. "He told me you did. If you never want me to mention him again, that's okay. If you don't want to speak to Wanda—by the way, she walked in the door just before you asked me about the quiches—I'm okay with that, too. I never should have pressed you about either one of them. But, please, don't shut *me* out of your life. I can't lose you, Cass."

More tears ran—Willow's, too, now—but Cass half smiled through them.

"You really care that much?"

"We're two women now, not girls. All that matters to me here is our friendship." And she drew Cass to her.

"Wow," Cass murmured. For a long moment they held each other, their foreheads pressed together until one of the waitstaff bustled through the kitchen door with an empty tray. "I guess I can't argue with that."

WILLOW DRIFTED THROUGH the rest of the party on autopilot. Almost losing Cass's friendship had badly shaken her—she'd rarely begged anyone before. Part of the problem, perhaps, because from birth she'd been put on a pedestal on this ranch, not realizing that Cass had felt as if she were Willow's inferior. Which she definitely wasn't. Grateful that Cass had promised to stay in her life, Willow tried not to worry about her with Zach—hands off, she'd promised even when a part of her hoped they'd find a way to be together.

With Jack's help, dinner was served in the house, one of the tents on the lawn having indeed collapsed from so much rain. The tables and chairs had been moved indoors, the floral centerpieces, too, and despite the cramped quarters in all the rooms, even in such a large house, everyone seemed to be having a good time until—

"Willow, may I see you?" Her mother rose from her seat at the head table and waited for Willow to do the same before they crossed the crowded room together. Willow felt Thad's perplexed expression on them. He'd been seated next to her, of course, but still she'd barely spoken to him. In the hall Jean led the way to the ranch office. She closed the door behind them. "What is going on with you and Thad?"

"Nothing," she began, but Jean had propped both hands on her hips, a sign from Willow's childhood like raised eyebrows that she must be in trouble. The motion had wrinkled her mom's periwinkle blue dress, which Jean, who was always impeccably dressed, didn't seem to notice.

"You have avoided Thad all evening."

"I sat with him at dinner," she said, "but, yes, there's something we need to discuss."

"You must mean that horse—and Cody. Willow, really…"

"There's another reason, Mom. With the *governor* here, his people and Grant Nesbitt's, I feel like I'm at a political rally rather than my own engagement party." The official announcement would be made by Zach, who was supposed to do the honors with a toast. Any minute now.

"You know what Thad's life is like. That will be your life, too, after the wedding. After tonight, really. I'll remind you that you had a preview of that at the bar association event. Now you're having second thoughts? You are, aren't you? Willow, if you don't think you can support the man you've agreed to marry—"

The words burst from Willow like a river

overflowing its banks. "Mom, I don't want to let you and Zach down."

Jean stared at her. "Surely you aren't marrying Thad to please *us*."

Willow studied the floor. "I made a bad error in judgment once before. My relationship with Cody then hurt Daddy, destroyed his health, and because of me he's not with us—with you—any longer. How am I supposed to live with that?" she asked, even though Jean and Cody had claimed she wasn't to blame. "I'll be making up for what I did for the rest of my life. I love you all so much, even if Zach has been clueless about Cass." After what he'd said to Willow, she did have hope for them, but…

"That is for Cass and Zach to manage. We're talking about you." Jean tilted Willow's chin up with one finger. "Honey, you can't make a lifetime decision for anyone else. I'm surprised, frankly. You've always been strong, certain of what you want. I admire you for working as hard as you have toward becoming a professional trainer. But you—and Thad—deserve to have the kind of love your father and I shared. Goodness, I never realized you felt so guilty. Your daddy passing *wasn't* your fault. He didn't take good care of himself."

"Cody said that, too, but I was there the day Daddy died. Cody wasn't. Dad and I quarreled about him before he just...fell."

"Then you must remember he did his share of shouting, too. Willow, I can't tell you how many times I tried to get your father to change his habits, but that temper of his, the arrogance at times, and of course the way he chose to eat for more than fifty years is what killed him. I'm still angry with him because he could have made better choices—he didn't *have* to leave us—but I couldn't change him. Neither could you."

"Mom." Willow hugged her tight. She didn't want to cry again, as she had with Cass.

"If I were you, I'd take Thad aside as soon as possible to talk. For both of your sakes. This is partly my doing, and probably Zach's, too," her mom said. "As soon as Thad proposed to you, I was all over that ring, wasn't I? Off to the races about this party—already making wedding plans. If you're this unsure, please at least postpone everything until you and Thad have reached some decision together."

That made sense.

"But I hate to—"

"*Disappoint?* Is that what you think?" Her eyes overly bright, Jean brushed a stray hair from Willow's cheek. "You've always been the best daughter, honey, but this isn't about our family," she said. "Heavens, you must have felt like I was pushing every step of the way when all I really wanted..." Her voice thick, she couldn't finish.

"It's okay. I understand. I love you, Mom."

"Yes, I know you do, and I love you. More than I can say." She took a breath. "Forgive me, Willow." Her voice quavered. "I just wanted all of us to be...happy again. Especially you."

"WHAT WAS THAT ABOUT?" Thad had intercepted Willow on the threshold of the living room. "Your mother hasn't settled down once this evening. I hope she's not getting ill."

"Well, no, but she did work herself into a frenzy over this," Willow told him, gesturing at the overflowing room around them. Perfect opportunity or not, after speaking with her mother, she and Thad had to talk. Now. Before her brother rapped a fork on his glass for attention, made his toast, and there'd be no going back. "Let's go into the hall where it's quieter," she said, eyeing the crowd.

Curious glances followed them before people turned away to continue their conversations. "Why is your mom so worried? The party's a great success," Thad said, sitting down on the carpeted bottom step to the second floor. "My father's people are impressed." The hallway's soft lighting dipped beneath his sharp cheekbones to carve shadows there. "I hope my dad or one of his minions didn't say the wrong thing."

"Mom's actually fine. I'm not, Thad."

"Are you still mad at me? Over that horse business?" His tone sounded dismissive, as if he'd flicked off a pesky fly, yet she heard an undercurrent of—was that guilt? "Why should any of us worry about that?" *About him*, meaning Cody, which went unspoken. He gently pulled her down beside him on the stairs, and Willow hoped he wouldn't feel how cold she was. Her hands felt like ice. "Come on, sweetheart. This is *our* night. Let's not spoil it over someone who doesn't matter." He took her hand in his warmer one, then kissed her temple. "You look beautiful— did I tell you?"

"About ten times, yes," she murmured but couldn't smile. She clung to his hand.

He bent his head to meet her eyes, his tone teasing. "This is where you're supposed to say how good I look in this tuxedo."

"You look very handsome. You always do."

He stroked her palm with his thumb, but Willow felt numb inside. "In another few minutes we'll be in the center of that room—" he motioned at the living area, where a round of laughter had risen on the now-stuffy air "—as Zach gives his toast."

"Not that anyone will be surprised," she said. "The whole town and probably the rest of the state already knows."

"But they don't know which date we've picked. We'll tell them as I suggested. Together. How does that sound?"

Willow didn't know how else to say this, except plainly. "Thad. About this party, the wedding and our engagement… I'm not sure," she said, "that this is…right."

He glanced at her ring. "You mean us?"

"Yes."

"I'm shocked." He was frowning, his eyes

clouded. "Willow, I've loved you from the first day we met—you must have been about twelve when Zach and I came home for a weekend from that boarding school our fathers sent us to back East."

She'd been the same age then as Cody when he witnessed his mother's murder.

Thad said, "I went head over heels, charmed on the spot, years before I could even think of asking you out. Before you were old enough and I was in a position to support you—in every way."

"Zach hated that school," she said. "He always told me the only good thing there was your friendship." Like hers with Cass. She thought of Thad's boyhood, his powerful yet neglectful father. The insecurity she'd seen more recently in Thad, his jealousy, overriding his outward confidence. That had come at first as a surprise, but, considering his background, maybe she should have expected that. The knowledge almost made her change her mind now.

"Zach's friendship means the world to me, but nothing," he said, "will make me happier than to spend my life with you as my wife."

Willow couldn't meet his eyes. She didn't

respond. She hated doing this to him. The memories they'd just shared reminded her of how much they had in common. Thad did offer her everything a girl could ever dream of, or at least everything Willow had known all her life. He fitted perfectly into her family, and they loved him, too. And yet her mother had said, *I just wanted all of us to be happy again. Especially you...*

"What have I done wrong?" Thad asked, sounding desperate. He released her hand and sat back, elbows resting behind him on the step above. "I know how sensitive you can be, so... Wait. Is this because I bought that red dress for you?" His tuxedo jacket brushed against the gauzy fabric of the seafoam gown she'd worn tonight.

"No," she murmured.

He looked skeptical. "Or because I proposed in a restaurant filled with other diners?"

"You knew I wouldn't be able to say no," she agreed, feeling the sting of tears. "You must have known how uncomfortable I would feel, but that's not why. Neither is the dress."

His gaze narrowed. "Ah, then you really are still upset about that horse from Navarro?

Because I saw that it went to someone more deserving than Jones? Willow, where exactly does your loyalty lie? With me or him?"

Willow froze. Thad had just admitted the truth. He'd done that to Cody, interfered with his application then made certain another person got Diva, as she'd suspected. His question was a good one.

"It's not about loyalty." Or Cody, now.

Thad's mouth set. "Well, I guess I should cancel those first-class tickets to Bora Bora and our reservations at the five-star resort I've booked for our honeymoon. Is that what you're saying?"

"Thad, that was solely your doing. We've never even discussed a honeymoon. And we're not going to." She rose from the step, her skirts rustling. Before she could move any farther, he shot up from his seat.

"You'd break up with me because I tried to please you? Are you kidding me? I'm sorry you're having a few doubts, but every bride must feel that way—lots of grooms, too, I'm sure. I've been part of enough weddings for my friends to know how true that is, but they aren't *us*, Willow."

"You broke my trust in you, Thad. More

than once." She swallowed. "And yes, I did break yours, too. Cody and I…" She didn't get to say the rest before Thad stopped her.

"Whatever you did with him—"

"Is over now. But it did happen."

And she had betrayed him. She was equally to blame. Could this get any worse?

The answer was yes. Instead of letting go, Thad tried to draw her close. "Then we've both made mistakes. But, Willow, we're meant to be together. One day I'll be sitting in the governor's mansion and you'll be there beside me." He said it as if that would be a lure, his closing argument, rather than something for Willow to avoid. Her fault for not making herself clear sooner.

Those were things Thad wanted for himself when what she wanted most was to be her own person, to train horses without someone standing in her way. Her plans, shared this summer with Cody, were simpler, plainer, and in that moment Willow's inner vision cleared.

She'd accepted Thad's proposal because she did care about him and it was what she'd thought her family wanted for her, what she owed them then. Willow had been drowning in her own guilt over her old rebellion with

Cody and her father's death last year. But no one else blamed her. It was, after all, Willow who hadn't been able to forgive herself.

Right now, Thad was fighting for the survival of their relationship, but, sadly, she knew they could never make each other happy.

Her trust, and her heart, lay elsewhere.

She did still love Thad, she always would, but not in the same way she loved Cody. Even if they never reconciled.

"I don't want to be first lady," she murmured, not wanting to hurt Thad. "We aren't as similar as you like to think we are. I don't feel we could ever have the kind of marriage I need, in which my wishes are equally important. Thad, I'm terribly sorry." With tears in her eyes, she tugged at the ring on her left hand. She'd rarely been able to leave it alone, and now she knew her fidgeting hadn't been only a bad habit.

The diamond didn't belong there.

"You need someone who will love you, Thad, just as you should be loved. We'd be making a serious mistake."

"I wouldn't," he said, reaching for her hand again, but Willow slipped the ring into his palm. For a long moment he stared down at it. "All this," he said, his expression becoming resigned at last, "was too good to be true, wasn't it?"

"Maybe so."

"Or maybe it was just me, envying Zach at first, then you, the kind of family I never had." He shrugged, the pain clear in his voice. "My dad was rarely there—to be honest, he's still not unless he needs me for something or wants someone to know his dynasty won't end with him. Most of the time, I'm mainly his shadow."

"I saw that at the bar association that night. I felt bad for you." And she did now.

"No, it is what it is with him. As for my mom, for a long time she was, let's say, lost in her martini glass." He tried a weak smile. "And, hey, you said it yourself—having Jean for a mother-in-law must be every man's dream. I know it was mine."

"Oh, Thad."

"It's okay. I understand. We both made choices we might have come to regret, but…" With the ring in one hand, he gestured with the other toward the living room, where party guests were shifting their chairs and Zach was calling Thad's name then Willow's. "What am I supposed to say in there?"

Willow's throat had closed.

Before she could recover or think what to tell him, she heard quick footsteps on the porch. The front door swung open and, to her astonishment, at the worst moment Cody walked in, his expression stony.

Thad turned, presumably to call for help from the security men who were coming up the porch steps.

"I'm not here to crash your party, Nesbitt," Cody said. "You won't need the guards. I wouldn't have come, but you're the only person who can tell me where my mare is going. Then I'll leave you to your celebration."

In the other room people had begun to buzz among themselves, and Willow spied Zach coming toward the hall to see what the delay was about. Cody ignored him.

"Who did you bribe to take Diva?"

Zach came to a stop in the doorway. He looked at Thad then Willow and, finally, Cody, but he didn't move.

"The horse will be with whoever I decided she should be," Thad told Cody, but his gaze flickered. And Willow knew without any doubt that *she'd* made the right decision to return his ring. Now she had to make another choice.

Her best course was to get Cody out of here before he wound up in a holding cell at the county jail.

Willow laid her hand on his shoulder. "Cody. Let's go."

Zach finally spoke. "Willow…"

"I know what I'm doing." She also knew what the risks might be, but for years she had bent over backward to please everyone except herself. For one more instant she held Thad's gaze. "I'm really sorry."

Then, with her skirts trailing and Cody's booted footsteps echoing on the entryway floor, they went out the front door and down the stairs. She was leaving the WB.

To find Diva. After that, she didn't know what to expect with Cody.

CHAPTER NINETEEN

CODY LED WILLOW across the driveway toward his truck. Because of tonight's bash he'd had to park halfway to the road. With Willow wearing heels, he slowed up. Why had she left with him? *Just go*, he'd said before. Then tonight he'd charged into her party like Dustin Hoffman as Benjamin in the old film *The Graduate*, determined to rescue Elaine at the church altar.

Which wasn't why he was here now.

"Sir," someone called after them. "I'll get your car."

Cody ignored the parking valet. Thad had deliberately been no help with the name he needed. "I didn't mean to barge in like that," he told Willow, "but there's no time left. It's tonight or never before Diva disappears down some hole and I never see her again. The question is how to find her."

"Someone else must be able to help. What about your friend at Navarro?"

"He didn't know who won the adoption."

Willow hopped up into the passenger side of his truck, almost shutting the hem of her gown in the door. "Then what are we going to do?"

Cody punched the ignition button. "We?" he asked with a sideways glance.

Willow simply raised her left hand to show the faint white line around her fourth finger. Bare.

"You gave it back?" Cody couldn't quite believe that. "You're not— I mean, you aren't going to—"

"Marry Thad? No," she murmured, holding his gaze. "I realized he—our engagement— was that mistake you warned me about."

Cody had started the evening knowing he'd lost her, this time for good. "Willow…"

"We're wasting time. We can talk later— once we have Diva."

"But I—but you, we—"

"Would you put some pedal to the metal here? Go."

Cody slipped the truck into gear, hit the accelerator, and dust and gravel flew out from the wheels like gunshot. BBs, anyway. For obvious reasons, Cody had never owned a weapon. He let a slow smile creep across his face. There was no telling where he and Willow might end up, but for now she was on his side. And she wasn't wearing Thad's ring. He couldn't wait to hear that story.

In the meantime… "First stop, Hadley and Jenna's place. You can't be my willing accomplice wearing that. We need to borrow some clothes for you." Cody paused. "By the way, the dress is amazing."

Willow grinned. "Just drive," she said as the truck picked up speed and the night wind blew through her hair.

BY THE TIME Willow had driven off with Cody, Cass was a wreck. Her apron hadn't quite protected her new black dress, her hair was dusted with flour and her back ached. Still, the night had been a success—until that commotion in the entry hall. Those few people who had lingered afterward were still talking about the scene as they finally left. Cass couldn't believe Willow had broken her engagement!

"Cher—Cass?" The familiar voice stiffened her spine. She should have known. Wanda was coming along the hall with Jack, who still wore his chef's toque. Cass was off duty now, discharged from her responsibilities to Willow and Jean. Tomorrow, she'd be free to make a decision about her next move. Literally. Maybe she'd fly East...

"I was on my way out," she said, taking another step toward the front door.

Jack had his arm around Wanda, and Cass saw him nudge her a bit. "Go ahead," he urged her. "Cass, you need to listen."

Well. So much for her earlier camaraderie with Jack in the kitchen, the jokes they'd tried on each other and the easy way he had solved every little food crisis. The quiches had been more than adequate, and people had raved about the meal. After Willow's departure, the cake had never been served yet Cass should feel proud. She'd done a great job tonight—with Jack's help. She did like him after all.

"I'll be in the car, Wanda. Take your time," he said.

Wanda gazed after him. "He's a keeper."

Cass nodded but said, "I never thought I'd see you married again. After Daddy, how on earth did you ever trust another man?"

"Cass, I know you're still hurting. Please tell me about your daddy. What happened with him?"

Cass's eyes watered. The years seemed to slide away, back to that old farmhouse, to the room she'd slept in by herself after Jenna was gone. Shadow had left by that point, too, and Tanya was away at college—she'd had to work hard for a full scholarship because, certainly, *Daddy* would never have found the money to send her. Any cash he had, he spent on himself.

Cass was shaking. "You want to know what happened? Over and over he told me I was no good, that I was ugly. He made me feel like *nothing*. He said I'd never amount to any-thing and I should marry the first guy who'd have me—if anyone would—get out of his house and start having babies because that's all I was good for. He called me a tramp, but I wasn't."

"Oh, sugar…" Wanda's face crumpled.

Cass had to keep going now. "And you—you never said a word to stop him."

"I should have. I know that now but keep-ing the peace seemed more important to me then than protecting you—I was wrong."

"And you left me *alone*. You let him destroy me from the inside out. He sure did a good job, *Wanda*, and so did you."

Her voice shook. "Cass, you weren't alone. He said those things to me, too. He told me I could never leave him because without him I was nothing."

Stunned, Cass couldn't speak for a moment. "You married him. You had six babies with him. Why?"

"I did, and I wasn't a very good mother to any of you then, was I? This will sound bad, but I did love him. By the time I realized what I'd let myself in for, I couldn't think what else to do except to go on trying to…please him. I had nowhere to go, baby, no other family, no money and no skills. How was I supposed to keep a roof over our heads and food in our bellies?"

"He didn't do a good job of that himself," Cass pointed out. And Wanda had been trapped in that old house, too.

"No, he was an angry, bitter man—not half the man my Jack is, but I worry about you now, Cass. You tell me you've chosen the wrong men—and maybe you have a few times. Who hasn't? There's a better one right nearby, yet all you do is try to sass your way out of any meaningful conversation. Does that keep you from getting hurt again?"

Cass's heart skipped a beat.

"You've been in love with Zach for years. Do you think I didn't wish he would be your future? That you'd leave the farm to marry him? Have a better life than I did? Isn't it time you stopped pushing him away, letting him push you? I wish you could stop seeing yourself as that powerless little girl."

Feeling the past weave itself around them, through them like a tattered sweater that might be mended after all, Cass saw that they were two women—like her and Willow—but whose self-esteem could use a pick-me-up. They were, after all, kindred spirits.

"I like Jack a lot. I'm glad you're happy with him, safe," she said, and she was.

Wanda smiled. "We're good for each other. That's the way it should be. Find out where that might lead with Zach when you're not both determined to avoid your feelings."

And *that* was her mother talking. Advising, as she rarely had before.

"Talk to him, sugar."

Cass pulled Wanda close, and they let their

tears fall. Cass wasn't the only one who had suffered. She said, "I think I will, Mama."

This time the name didn't come from anger but from love.

WHEN WILLOW ARRIVED with Cody at the Mc-Mann ranch, Jenna and Hadley had just come downstairs after putting the twins to bed. They'd left the party early to relieve Clara, who'd babysat tonight. Jenna was rubbing her lower back.

"You sure you're okay?" Hadley asked. "Don't keep anything from me. We have to stay on top of this."

Jenna sent Willow and Cody an indulgent smile. But it wasn't for them. "This man," she said, looking serene and adorable in stylish dark leggings and a tunic, "has become a terrible worrywart. I'm fine, Hadley. That rest Sawyer had me take worked wonders and he says this is a textbook pregnancy—a miracle, I know—but everything is completely normal and, really, you have to stop hovering."

"I'm a helicopter husband," he told her with a grin. He glanced at Willow, his gaze taking her in from head to foot. "This may be the first time I've seen a woman in fancy dress on this ranch. What's the deal? And I thought you were in the bunkhouse for the night, Cody."

Jenna focused on Willow's bare hand. "You're not wearing your ring."

"After you and Hadley went home, I took it off." Her voice quavered. "Thad and I are no longer engaged. I'm afraid I ruined the end of the party."

She'd also hurt Thad, even when he'd said he understood, and she wasn't sure where she stood now with Cody.

He'd scarcely spoken on the drive from town, and Willow watched him jingle some coins in his jeans pocket. "Diva's being moved soon—maybe she already has been. I still don't know where or who adopted her."

They had to hurry, but Willow first had to change her clothes. "Obviously, this dress isn't the best outfit to go horse hunting. Jenna, do you have something I could borrow?"

WHILE WILLOW WAS upstairs changing, Cody paced the living room, the coins jangling. "I don't even know where to begin looking," he told Hadley. "You wouldn't have any new ideas, would you?"

"Not unless you can lean on Darryl Williams again."

"I hate to put him on the spot."

But Cody went outside to phone his friend and ex-supervisor. By the time Willow came down the steps in her borrowed T-shirt, jeans and boots, he was back in the living room.

"She's gone," he reported. "Somebody trailered her around dusk. Darryl's not on duty so that's what his coworker told him. The guy didn't get a name. I never met him but Darryl says he's not the most attentive man in their group—he just looked over the paperwork, signed off and let her go." He ran a hand through his hair. "She could be halfway to California or anywhere else by now. No use in us driving around aimlessly all night."

"Cody, there must be some way—" Willow broke off. "Wait. I may know something I didn't realize I knew. When Thad and I talked about the adoption a while ago, and that other applicant, he almost said the name before he caught himself. All I heard was part of it, but the first letter is *M* for sure."

"That's not enough to go on."

"After that, I think there was something like *i-l*. Mills, maybe?"

Hadley spoke up. "What if Diva is still in the area? Close by, I mean."

"Fred Miller?" Cody's spirits had brightened, then dimmed again. "That doesn't make sense. He's been liquidating his herd."

"And I've been buying some, including that Angus bull. You know the one, always looking for love out in our far pasture?"

"That still doesn't fit. Why would Miller want a horse? His family's grown, left home years ago, and I doubt he'd ride at his age. He's planning to move south, isn't he?"

"Selling out, yeah, when he finds a buyer, but that doesn't mean he wouldn't snap up a quick bargain to benefit himself."

"You mean sell the mare for an inflated price to make a nice profit?"

"Thanks to the training you put into her," Hadley said. "Let's find out. I'll go with you. We can use Clara's and my rig."

In that big four-horse trailer, Miller would see them coming from far off, and Cody wanted to check out the situation first. What if they weren't right? "No," he said, "you stay with Jenna and the kids." He held out his hand to Willow. "I'm glad you've got a good memory, angel. Let's see if Miller is the one—or if we're on another wild-goose chase."

CHAPTER TWENTY

"GET OFF MY PROPERTY," Fred Miller said, cradling a shotgun. The longtime owner of the Bar B&J ranch was not the most amiable person Cody had ever met. In fact, tonight Miller more than lived up to his crusty reputation.

He glared at Cody and Willow. "You know what time it is? When you pulled up to this gate, my wife and I were in bed asleep." Miller took a closer look at him. "Cody Jones," he said.

He and Miller had a history. After Cody and his pals had rustled the Wilsons' cattle, Miller, who was Calvin's uncle, had hidden those steers on this property.

The gun made Cody uneasy. He shifted to shield Willow. "This won't take long, Fred. I'm wondering if you just bought yourself a horse. Nice brown-and-white mustang mare from Navarro."

"What business is that of yours?"

"I'm the guy who trained her." He told Miller about his application to adopt. "I got turned down. Somebody made that happen and I'm guessing you got her instead."

Miller's gaze darkened. "You guessed wrong."

Cody didn't believe him. Near the barn he saw the same trailer rig that had transported the stolen cattle and he felt sure he'd seen fear, laced with guilt, in the man's eyes. Diva had to be here. "I'll buy her from you." He reached for his wallet, but the shotgun leveled at his chest. Miller must have interpreted the move as a threat, as if Cody could be carrying concealed. If he only knew... Cody was afraid of firearms, and the sight of Miller's shotgun carried him right back into his past, to the living room where he'd watched his parents die.

Miller looked toward the barn, too, which would have been another tell if they were playing poker. "No horse for sale here. At any price."

"Take that shotgun out of my face." Cody stood his ground. "I'll make this worth your while. Fair and square."

Miller's gaze shifted. "You couldn't pay me enough—*if* I had the horse."

"You haven't heard my offer yet."

"There's not enough money in this world," Miller said, then gave up the pretense of innocence. "The mare's not mine, and she won't be here long. I'm her temporary stopover—kind of like a bed-and-breakfast place." He laughed. "When the meat wagon rolls in a day or two from now, she'll be gone."

"Gone where?" Cody gaped at him. Miller didn't want Diva at all. His ranch was a kind of halfway house. The money Cody offered didn't matter to him. Then *why* had he taken her for a short time? Like he had hidden those cattle? Cody's stomach knotted. "You mean to the slaughterhouse? You'd have her killed?"

"Not me."

Cody took a step, but Willow put a hand on his back in warning and, eyeing the shotgun, he stayed where he was. He hadn't saved his mother, and he wished he was anywhere except here with that gun aimed at his chest. Cody had begun to shake. *Dad... Mom... Nooo.* And he heard that blast again, watched his mother fall. He had to save Diva now.

"Who, then? Who's responsible for taking

a perfectly good horse and—" he forced himself to say the rest "—turning her into dog food?" His thoughts didn't have far to go. "Thad," he said.

Willow had turned pale. She hadn't known that part either.

For another tense few seconds, the shotgun wavered in Miller's grasp. Then he lowered it to his side, as if he couldn't hold its weight, or keep his secret, any longer. The gun was no longer pointed at Cody, but he wouldn't let down his guard. During Cody's trial for arson, Miller had been a witness for the prosecution.

"Thad helped send me to prison," Cody reminded him. "That was the right thing to do—though it had a personal side, as well."

With Miller, too. Thad knew the older man had disliked Cody, who could have gotten Miller into trouble then as an accessory to the cattle rustling.

"I let my nephew talk me into keeping those cattle here."

"And Thad used you now. Didn't he?"

Miller's mouth tightened. "That mare wasn't stolen. Now, I said, get off this ranch—"

"Come on, Willow." Cody turned away. Obviously, Miller wasn't about to sell Diva to him, and there was no telling how soon she would be sent to slaughter. Even the word made his skin crawl. He couldn't allow that to happen.

With Willow's hand in his, he started for his truck. Let Miller think what he would for now. Cody hated to involve Hadley and Dallas. He thought of calling Calvin, who might convince his uncle to give up the horse, but Cody rejected that notion, too. Derek might help yet Cody wouldn't ask him either. None of his friends needed to risk running afoul of the law, because he had another idea. He'd taken another step toward his truck when he heard that soft whicker he knew so well, then a whinny from the barn as if to say *Here I am. Come get me.* But Cody kept going.

Willow tried to stop him, her voice low. "Cody, we can't leave her here." Miller's ear was cocked, too, toward the sound, the shotgun in the crook of his arm.

"We're not."

Miller didn't look away from Cody until he and Willow were in the truck and he'd started the engine. Cody backed out of the short driveway, away from the gate, already envisioning Diva in a stall with fresh bedding at the McMann ranch, where Clara would fuss over her, Hadley would see that she had an extra ration of grain tonight and in the coming days Cody would gentle her enough to ride. "Let Miller think he got the best of us." He drove down the road a way, then pulled over under the cover of some trees. "You'll stay here—while I steal my horse."

"CODY, YOU CAN'T do that." Willow grasped his arm, the muscles rock-hard under his skin. "Take Diva out from under Miller's nose? Do I need to remind you that would be illegal? He's the mare's owner—guardian, whatever, at least for tonight—and they used to hang people for stealing horses. You'd be looking at another stay in prison."

His mouth tightened. "Trading my ex-con status for a longer term in Navarro doesn't matter. Diva does, and I won't leave her here to wait for the 'meat wagon,' as Miller called it." He gazed off into the distance. "You ever taken cattle to market? Seen the whites of their eyes rolling in terror? People don't think animals have emotions, but they do. I won't abandon her now. If there's any chance—"

"I heard Diva, too, and I agree about those emotions. I've seen Silver whenever I'm feeling low, ready to comfort me. I know when she's sick or getting lame or when she's had enough training for one day and her patience is gone. I know every twitch of her ears, every look on her face—she does have expressions—but I won't see you in jail tonight. You're not thinking clearly." She hesitated. "And I won't be charged with aiding and abetting."

"I don't want you to be." He jerked free of her touch. "But don't you understand? I had a split second years ago to keep my dad from murdering my mother—"

"You were a kid! You couldn't have stopped him."

"Maybe not," he agreed, and Willow watched him begin to weigh that truth, as she had her misplaced guilt about her father. "But we're wasting time. Call Zach and have him come get you."

"I've already made my choice, Cody. I chose my own life, not the one Thad or Zach wanted for me. Now, what is your choice going to be?

Because if you go through with this, everything you've done for Diva, with Olivia and Prancer, all your hard work with Hadley, telling people you're sorry for what you did, becoming part of this community and turning your life around will have been for nothing."

CODY DIDN'T WANT to listen. His thoughts were in free fall—one second on Diva, the next on Willow. Her words about the choice she'd made had surprised him. And she'd spoken the truth. He'd spent the past months trying to redeem himself, to wipe out the memories of prison and the far worse ones of his parents. The echo of gunshots, the smell and color of blood, his own screams sounding even louder in that suddenly too-silent room. If Cody became a horse thief now, he'd surely head back to Navarro or some other facility. Most likely, he'd be imprisoned for far longer than the nine months he'd served before.

He had to choose, as Willow had tonight. Try to rescue Diva from her certain fate. Or, because Willow's blue eyes already accused him, lose her forever just when he'd been given a possible second chance. That simple, moral choice between his two loves, as if all of his life could be reduced to this one fork in the road, threatened to break him.

And yet… Cody had feared being just like his father, that someday he might crack—and even hurt Willow. But she'd been right. He was not his father. He could never hurt her.

For a few long moments, he sat there in his truck not far from the gates of Fred Miller's ranch, Willow's gaze steady on his. Then, finally, his shoulders slumped and all the strength in his muscles, his limbs, seemed to desert him as he would have to desert Diva. "Okay, then. All right," he made himself say. "You win."

"No," she said, her voice husky. "You win."

Not feeling that much better for her support, knowing he would now consign Diva to her dreadful fate, he slipped the truck into Drive. Lesson learned. You could want something with every fiber of your being—two things, actually—but that didn't mean you could have both.

That you could always save everything you loved. *Ah, Diva. I'm sorry.*

"Wait, Cody." Willow had her cell phone in her hand. "Maybe we're not finished. This is a gamble…but let me make one call. Then we'll see."

AFTER HER MOTHER left the WB with Jack, and the cleanup crew was finally gone, Cass wandered through the now-empty house, picking up stray cocktail napkins and empty glasses. Everyone had gone by now, except Thad. He'd been closeted in the office with Zach for the longest time. Best friends, like her and Willow. Because of Willow's flight with Cody, tomorrow's *Barren Journal* would be juicy reading. Cass yawned but wasn't ready to sleep. Following an event, no matter how exhausted she really was, she always felt full of unspent energy, and tonight she couldn't forget her mom's words about Zach.

She kept remembering, too, that day with him long ago in the barn loft, and the unexpected horseback ride they'd taken yesterday, chatting about themselves and that other time. Those memories would have to sustain Cass. She felt another twinge of her old envy of Willow, who had obviously chosen her true path. Which direction would *Cass* take now?

"Surprising turn of events tonight, huh?" Zach startled her as she bent to retrieve a bacon-wrapped scallop from the living room floor. "Mom's out like a light. She'll probably sleep until tomorrow night. Why are you still up?"

"If I stop moving, I'll fall over." Cass didn't know what else to say. In spite of their companionable ride together, she expected him to ask now when she would leave the WB. For good this time. Her usefulness had ended when Willow left with Cody and the party fell apart, amid a hum of speculative conversation.

He sank onto an overstuffed sofa. "Cass," he said mildly. "Sit down."

She was too tired to argue. Maybe he was, too. As if she were a marionette and he'd pulled her strings, she dropped onto a wide armchair, letting the deep cushions embrace her. "If I sit too long, I'll wake up stiff and sore tomorrow." She'd say it for him. "I'll be out of your hair first thing in the morning."

Zach studied the dress boots he'd worn with his tuxedo. "You did a great job with the party, Cass. What do you plan to do next? Event-wise. Willow won't need a wedding planner, that's for sure."

Cass folded her legs under her. "Who knows? I may take off for the Big Apple this time. See what New York has to offer."

"Why?" he asked.

She glanced at him. She couldn't believe he'd praised her about the party. "Why not?" she said at last. For too long, in fear of being fired and left jobless again, she'd chosen trying to please Zach over Willow. Cass had betrayed her more than once this summer. Tonight, thank goodness, they'd vowed their friendship meant more than anything else. Including men.

"I keep seeing Thad's face," Zach said. "I admit, I never saw that coming. He has his faults, likes getting his own way but…"

"So do you," she pointed out, then decided not to push it further. Cass wasn't up for a new argument, and he had made a slight, friendly overture. This afterglow in the empty living room—the catering staff had helped move the furniture back into place before they went home—felt like she and Zach were a couple, recapping a party in their own home, as if the WB could ever be hers as well as his.

Zach said, "I never imagined he'd turn Willow off enough that she'd put that ring back in his hand. Among other things, it seems he blocked Jones's adoption of some horse. I'm disappointed in him. What was he thinking?"

He tipped his head toward the hallway. "He's still here, by the way, in the ranch office. I hope he's giving himself a serious talk. I've never liked Cody, and Thad and I are friends, but he went too far."

"Willow let him down as easily as she could," Cass murmured, then by instinct fell back on her old habit of cheekiness as self-defense. "Not like her big brother years ago, who turned his back on me the morning after." When she looked up, his eyes looked hurt. Which hurt Cass, too. "I'm sorry, Zach. My tongue got the best of me again."

"No, you have every right to call me on that. Cass, I'd do anything to make that up to you." Zach studied her for a moment until she squirmed. "Is there any chance that you and I could start over?"

She barely got the words out. "I…guess we could." But what did he really mean?

"Mom keeps telling me I'm on the wrong track here." He didn't go on for a moment. "My sister—the runaway bride—claims I don't see what's right in front of my face."

Her heart banged against her ribs. "And what is that?"

"They're both right. I took my responsibilities for the WB so much to heart that I've forgotten to build my own life. I've spent a lot of time trying to live up to my promises to Dad—his expectations—about Willow and our mother. Even more so since he died. Tonight, when Willow and Thad broke up, I was shocked. But she probably did the right thing."

"Even if that means she winds up with Cody?"

He sighed. "She left with him, didn't she?"

"She did," Cass said with a feeling of pride.

"Besides, and I'm going to eat some crow here, I never saw her look at Thad that way."

"Me either."

"When Cody walked in, her whole face lit up. I couldn't fail to get that message. My baby sister is in love. Would I have picked Cody for her? No," Zach said, "but really, all I've ever wanted is for her to be happy. The choice was Willow's."

"Goodness. Who *are* you? Am I really seeing the new Zach Bodine?" She couldn't stop herself. "Does this mean you're going to sign up on some dating site now? Or spend your Saturday nights at Rowdy's bar looking for some sweet young thing to marry? To have kids with?"

"Cass, cut it out. I'm not going to let you derail this situation. That's what you do, you know." Just as her mama had said.

Zach had refused to take her bait. "I should have said this a long time ago." His voice turned husky, and when his gaze ran over her, Cass didn't see any disapproval in his eyes. "I'd already found who I was looking for."

Cass wouldn't give him the chance to break her heart again. She hadn't trusted him since that day in the loft. He couldn't be saying... "Was that some corny pickup line? It needs work. Goodness, what a night this has been. Willow and Thad, Cody. I even made my peace with Mama."

Zach smiled. He stood up, then slowly drew her from her chair. "I'm glad, but that's everyone else. What will make you happy, Cass?" She opened her mouth, but he spoke again before she got a word out. "I hope—since I'm putting myself on the line here while you're still being the same sassy girl I first met— and I do know why that was... I hope I'm the answer to that question. I'm not naming our kids yet but..."

She didn't dare to believe. She wouldn't let him lead her on then reject her again.

"You always did have the biggest ego, Zach Bodine," she said, sounding breathless.

"Big enough to handle yours." He wrapped his arms around her, strong and warm and… Zach. "That day in the loft," he said, clearing his throat, "you were too young then for anything serious, but you scared me to death, which had nothing to do with my running this ranch. And everything to do with you. I guess for a long time after that, I was afraid I'd get burned."

She smiled into his eyes. Believing, at last. "Maybe you will."

"I'll take my chances," he murmured just before his mouth touched hers, and with his kiss Cass stopped thinking about leaving tomorrow. Leaving at all. What she wanted most was right here, too. He always had been. "My responsibility for the WB and us being together aren't mutually exclusive," he said.

And Cass murmured the words that had been in her heart long before she'd moved to LA to get away from that love—unrequited, she'd thought. She forgot her lost job there, the disgrace, the old farm and her persistent fcar of being less than she could be. Apparently, she was more than enough for him, too. "I love you, Zach."

"Yeah," he said, sounding dazed. "I love you, too."

Just as Willow and Cody did, she and Zach deserved happiness, like her mother with Jack. For so many years Cass had felt unworthy of Zach and envious of Willow. Funny how things changed when she had come to love herself.

Her past, her father's many attempts to destroy her self-esteem, were behind her now. She and Zach were still kissing when his phone rang.

"Don't answer," she said, pulling his head down to hers again.

"It's Willow." Zach turned aside to take the call. She heard his part of the brief conversation. For some reason, it seemed Willow needed help. "I'm on it," he said, then hung up and faced Cass again, his gaze worried. "How'd you like to take another ride with me? Not on horseback."

THIRTY MINUTES AFTER she'd made her call, Willow and Cody were still a quarter mile down the road from the Miller farm, sitting on the open tailgate of his truck with the headlights off. Every second that passed felt like an hour, and Cody seemed even more tense. "What are we waiting for?"

Willow didn't want to tell him who she'd called or Cody might change his mind and take matters into his own hands after all. "He'll be here soon," she said.

She had just spoken when her brother's truck with the WB logo on its side, towing a dark two-horse trailer, braked to a stop behind them. He killed his lights, too.

"You called Zach?" Cody asked in a disbelieving tone as he jumped down onto the road. And then, "What the—?" Even Willow was surprised to see that Thad was with him. So was Cass, who ran toward them and threw her arms around Willow.

Cass lowered her voice. "This may not be the right time, and it's too early yet to be sure, but I think Zach and I are— Willow, just before you called…he said the sweetest things, then kissed me."

Willow bit back a shout of joy. "That's the best news I've heard in a long time—except, of course, it's not news to me."

She looked past Willow. "And Cody? I knew it. That spark's still there."

"I hope so. It is for me."

"This should be fun," Cass said.

Willow laughed. She wasn't sure if Cass meant her not-so-new relationship with Zach or the horse rescue they were about to pull off. Now that she'd made her own choice—Cody—she felt as free as the breeze that was still blowing through her hair. Later, they would see if they were in tune, but she was no longer with Thad, and that was that.

"Hold on here." Standing a few feet away, Cody had flicked a glance at her. "Who asked Nesbitt to come?"

"Willow. Me. We both did," Zach said in a tone that dared Cody to challenge him. "I doubt we could talk Miller into letting you take the horse any better than you did." It was Thad who held sway over the older rancher, who'd used him. "Willow convinced Thad it was in his best interest to help."

Willow said, "Especially since he's the one who created this problem." She held Thad's gaze. "Really, Thad? The adoption business, Fred Miller and, maybe worst of all, sending poor Diva to slaughter?"

"I'm sorry, Willow. I feel awful about what I did, but I didn't want to lose you. That's no excuse, I know, for what's happened, but—"

Zach stepped in. "After you left the house, Willow, Thad was beside himself."

"I thought after our engagement party, once the mustang was gone," Thad said, "Jones here would have no reason to stick around. He'd get permission from his parole officer—with my help, if need be—to leave the county. He'd be out of your life—ours—at last."

"Oh, Thad." So that was why she'd seen a flash of guilt in his eyes earlier. "And you thought that would work?"

"Tonight would have sealed everything for us—only, obviously, it didn't work out that way." He looked into Willow's eyes, then turned his gaze toward Cody. "I'm not here for you. Willow made it clear that I was to fix this somehow, a closing argument plain enough for even me to understand. Not to mention her brother wielded our friendship like a sword. And I knew, even before that, how wrong I was. I won't say the best man won, but I'm here now because I still care about Willow." Thad's voice sounded unsteady. "Maybe I always knew I'd end up in second place."

Willow's gaze softened. It would be a long time before she could forgive Thad, before they could even think of being friends again, if ever. Yet now she felt sorry for him. He'd done something almost as bad as Cody had by burning down that barn, but Cody had atoned for his crimes. Thad would have to do the same about his behavior, one day at a time. And still, although he'd owned up to his mistake tonight, she knew things would never be quite the same again.

Thad waved a hand as if to sweep away his admission. "Now, here's the plan. I doubt Miller's gone back to bed. I'll go to the house, talk to him. You all stay put."

"Miller has a shotgun," Cody said.

"The guy's twitchy, to say the least," Thad agreed. "Add his inborn mean streak and there's no telling what he'll do." Thad paused. "If I don't come out within a reasonable time, he's probably shot me." He started off. "I'll see what I can do."

Ten minutes after she and Cass had begun walking up and down the road in an attempt to cool their growing anxiety, Thad emerged from Fred Miller's home. He gestured to Cody and Zach, who'd been pacing the driveway. The four men, including Miller without his shotgun, entered into another lengthy discussion. Willow saw a lot of arm waving and finger pointing, heard a few outbursts from Miller and the lower rumble of Cody's voice.

And then... Willow was slow to believe her eyes. While Zach moved the truck, Cody strode to the barn, sliding back the big door. Minutes later he emerged leading Diva, her ears pricked at all the commotion, her hindquarters shimmying as she trotted smartly between the barn and the truck then up the ramp into the trailer.

Cass grinned. "I wouldn't have missed this for the world."

"Me either," Willow said.

Cass rode with Thad in Zach's rig, and it might have appeared to anyone else that the night was over by then. Except it wasn't for Willow, for Cody. They had things to say. She waited in the truck until he climbed in and started the engine. When they were out of sight of the Bar B&J, she asked, "Where is Diva going?"

"To Hadley's. I'll have to meet them at the

barn. I want to settle her in, let her know I'll be there in the morning. Wouldn't want her to feel alone tonight. She's had too much excitement already."

Willow agreed, but she couldn't keep silent. She wouldn't let Cody shut down.

"And where are *we* going?" she asked next.

He said, "I can drop you at the WB first. If you want." He focused his gaze on the road. Willow saw a muscle bunch in his jaw. "Maybe you've had second thoughts about Thad. That was some heartrending apology. He does care about you. He loves you, Willow. He proved that tonight even to me."

She had to smile. "He'll probably be Zach's best man at his wedding to Cass."

That got a reaction. "You're kidding. I wondered why she came along tonight."

"I think they may be working on something good together." Which made Willow happier than she could say for her brother and her best friend. That didn't help her with Cody, though. "So," she tried again, "are you offering to send me back to Thad? Have me ask for his ring?"

"I didn't say that."

"You were thinking it," she said.

He glanced at her. "Willow. I came this close tonight—" he held up two fingers "—to committing another crime. With my background—my folks, then cattle rustling, arson…"

She touched his hand on the steering wheel. "Cody. You've risen above all that. Or do you plan to equate yourself with your father and what he did to your mother forever?"

"No, but…"

"You went through so much trauma—but you're not that person now. You were the one who decided not to steal Diva."

"You tried hard enough to sway me."

"I know, but—"

To her surprise Cody abruptly pulled off the country road onto a turnout, then stopped the truck in a slide of gravel. "All right. Let's talk." Willow wondered if he was about to make a different choice from the one she'd made. If he thought he was doing the noble thing and might tell her he no longer cared.

His arms crossed on the steering wheel, Cody sat there a moment, his head turned toward her. His eyes held Willow's and his voice stayed soft. "I remember the night I met you at that roadhouse. I remember flirting, dancing, and how I guessed you'd probably sneaked off from the WB to have some fun. I remember how you smelled—how you always do—of lemon blossoms. I remember your blond hair, those cornflower blue eyes, everything about you that said you were an angel."

"Hardly that," she began.

Cody laid a finger across her lips. "That night and ever since then. I may not deserve you, but I want you, Willow. I promise I'll never step off the straight and narrow again. I know this isn't the most romantic spot, parked along the road, to say this, but I love you more than I thought I could ever love anyone. I want to be with you all my life, marry you, give you children and grow old together. I— no matter how you answer—" He cleared his throat. "I will love you forever."

"Oh, Cody." She'd never imagined getting such a declaration. "Your truck is the perfect place. Only the words matter." And what she saw in his eyes. "I used to think I loved you too much for my own good. I think I knew from the second Thad asked me to marry him that he wasn't right for me. In part, by getting engaged, I tried to please my family, even when that meant losing my own happiness. You were right—I didn't need to feel guilty about my dad."

"Just as I don't need to carry the awful scene with my mother around with me anymore. I have better memories of her." As Cody turned to draw her close, Willow moved into his arms.

He kissed her then, and Willow kissed him back. His embrace tightened, and for what seemed like a long time their kisses went on, sweet and tender at first, then with the growing passion they'd always shared, locked in each other's arms until, finally, Cody drew back. As if to warn her, he said, "I can't give you the kind of life—the things—Thad would have."

"I'm not looking for *things*."

"I'll probably never own a spread like the WB…"

Now it was Willow who laid a finger across his mouth. "I don't care how we live, Cody, or where. I only care that we'll be together. That's all I want."

"It's all I've ever wanted," he told her.

And kissed Willow again.

EPILOGUE

Christmas Day

WILLOW TURNED IN front of the long mirror in the church choir room. The dress she'd chosen—had chosen herself—swished softly with the movement, and her mother stood back with tears in her eyes. "Oh, honey, you look…bridal."

Cass and Becca Carter agreed, straightening her gown and fussing over her. They wore deep ruby-red dresses.

Willow's wedding gown was simple, with a fitted bodice and a neckline that dipped toward her waist, the narrow gap outlined by starlike appliqués—snowflakes—which also adorned its gauzy, floor-length overskirt. She wore her hair loose and straight the way Cody liked it, a complement for the head piece she planned to wear. "Do you think he'll approve?"

Jean laughed. "He'd approve if you walked down that aisle wearing a feed sack. I hope your entrance doesn't knock him flat. We don't need your groom out cold before you reach the altar."

Cody's anticipation couldn't be any greater than her own. Since that summer night at Fred Miller's ranch when they'd saved Diva, she and Cody had become inseparable. At Clara's ranch then, they'd calmed the mare, gradually introducing her over the next weeks to Prancer. They'd begun training together, sometimes with Olivia, and most evenings they'd discussed the ever-changing plans for this special day.

A rap at the door startled Jean, who laid a hand over her heart.

"It's time," Zach called over the preliminary music that was fading to a sweet finish.

For Willow, though, this would be a beginning, and for months she'd looked forward to this day. To her delight, it had snowed all night, transforming the world and her Christmas Day wedding into a wonderland just for her and Cody.

"Willow," her mother prompted, handing her the delicate tiara she'd chosen to wear.

Studded with crystals, it twinkled in the sunlight streaming through the choir room's clerestory windows and on her engagement ring, a shimmering blue opal that Cody had told her in a choked voice "reminds me of your eyes."

She blinked, let Jean smooth her hair, then followed her mother from the room. At the door Cass handed her Willow's bouquet, a cascade of white roses, dark greenery and a few Christmas-red blossoms. Cass's eyes looked suspiciously bright. "Be happy, Willow," she murmured, then she and Becca hurried off to take their places in the processional.

Zach waited in the back of the church, looking more than handsome in his dark tuxedo. "Ready for this?" he whispered in Willow's ear. He had a quieter, more settled presence these days, his hazel eyes quicker to smile, especially whenever Cass was nearby.

Willow told him, "I've been ready since I first met Cody."

Zach refrained from pointing out that their meeting had happened on a night when Willow, just out of college nearly five years ago, had escaped the confines of her life at the

WB, and he didn't say a word against Cody. Not that the two men had become fast friends. That was a work in progress. Instead, he said, "I almost feel sorry for him up there at the altar. I don't plan to be that nervous when I get married."

"Whenever that might be," she murmured.

Zach only smiled before his gaze turned serious. "I'm glad I've opened my mind about you and Cody. I'll be keeping an eye on him, though, so he'd better treat you right."

"He will."

Zach swallowed. "I'm honored to be walking you down this aisle today."

Willow blinked at her big brother. The words caught in her throat. "I love you, Zach. So much."

"I love you, too, kiddo."

Their mother, standing close on Willow's other side, gave Zach a pointed look. She rearranged the skirts of Willow's gown, then said, "Your daddy would be so proud today. I know he could be prickly, even overbearing, with both of you, but he would have been practically bursting his buttons right now. He only wanted the best for you, honey."

"I know." Willow's tears felt close to spilling over. "Don't make me cry or all that eye makeup you girls urged me to wear will run, and I am not going to ruin this dress."

Jean kissed her cheek. Cass and Becca had reached the altar. The wedding march began, the music soaring toward the winter sky, and, flanked by her mother and Zach, Willow started down the aisle.

Cody caught her eye and she actually saw him take a sharp breath. Then his gaze locked onto hers, and with people standing, watching, she felt the force of his love. Willow passed by so many of the people she knew, people she had grown up with and called friends all her life. She was taking her last slow hesitation step when she noticed Hadley and Jenna, cradling her baby bump. Beside them were Shadow and Grey. Her sisters both here. In the front row, too, Wanda sat holding Jack's hand, and openly crying.

Then the music hushed. The minister said a few words, then, "Who gives this woman to be married to this man?" and Zach and Jean at once said, "We do," their voices steady. Together, they placed Willow's hand in Cody's. She looked up into his eyes, and his strength, his sweetness and goodness flowed through her.

"Finally," he said for only her to hear, and within minutes, they'd repeated their vows. And were married. Cody kissed his bride, his lips lingering on hers. By then, Willow knew she must look starry-eyed, as happy as she felt inside.

The minister smiled at them, raising his voice to the congregation. "May I present Mr. and Mrs. Cody Jones."

THEIR RECEPTION WAS held at the WB and catered by Jack, of course, but there were no tents on the lawn in the rain like the night of Willow and Thad's engagement party. On Christmas Day, sun and snow glittered on the lawn, and the inside of the house looked more festive than it ever had.

As Willow moved among her friends and family, her gaze darted around now and then to find Cody, to reassure herself that she hadn't dreamed all this. She smiled when she saw him slip a finger between his neck and the collar of his dress shirt. He felt more comfortable in T-shirts, jeans and boots, as she did, but he also looked amazingly handsome in his tuxedo. Their reception was fun, more relaxed and intimate than the one she might have had with Thad. As grateful as she felt for his help that night in saving Diva and although she was working to forgive what he'd done to Cody, Willow hadn't invited him to her wedding. That would have been awkward, and she'd heard Thad was now dating someone else who, she hoped, would suit him better.

"Hey, you." Cass caught Willow's arm as she turned from a conversation with the minister to look again for Cody. Cass grinned. And wiggled the fingers of her left hand, a ring sparkling in the light. She and Zach had been dating since summer.

"You're engaged?" Willow hugged her, and they both started laughing. In sheer joy.

Cass said, "He claims you two inspired him—once he got past his dislike of Cody." She drew back. "Mama's already planning for at least four grandchildren." She took a step backward. "I need to find that man again, make sure he knew what he was asking." Yet she didn't seem concerned. Cass's engagement to Zach had made Willow's wedding day even more perfect. They would be sisters-in-law, too.

The WB was in good hands with her brother. And so, now, was Cass.

A few moments later Cody slipped up behind Willow. He put his hands on her waist and nestled his chin in the curve of her neck. "How long before we can leave?"

"A girl gets only one chance to enjoy her wedding day." Willow was teasing, yet she couldn't wait to start their honeymoon either. His eagerness to leave the reception matched her own.

She quickly told Cody about Cass and Zach's engagement, but he only responded, "Good for them," before hurriedly adding, "Tell me more later. It's going to snow again soon. We should head for KC." He kissed the side of her neck. "Besides, I've been wearing this tux long enough. I never plan to again until one of our kids gets married."

She and Cody were spending tonight in a hotel then flying to New York tomorrow. After a few days in the city to see the lights and the tree in Rockefeller Center, they'd move on to Miami to board a cruise ship for the Caribbean and warmer weather.

"That might be a while," Willow said. "But we'd better start saving."

They'd made a good start. She and Cody had established their training business. Prancer was now at Finn's place, his permanent home. Diva's training was coming along even better than they'd hoped for, and only last week—in the midst of the prewedding hubbub—she and Cody had met with an architect. Willow couldn't wait to see the plans she came up with for their new home, barn, and indoor and outdoor rings amid the acres carved out of the vast WB. Part of Willow's inheritance ahead of time. It had taken a while before Cody's pride let him accept the family gift, but his tentative new alliance with Zach had certainly helped. She and Cody expected their first clients by spring.

All at once she couldn't wait to be alone with him. She took his hand, leading him from the living room, down the hallway into the office.

After closing the door, she leaned back against it, pulled him to her and kissed him.

"Thank you, Cody."

"For what?"

"Everything. Mostly, for loving me."

"Loving you was always the easy part." Cody grinned. "Today has been amazing, everything I always wanted for us. Even when I didn't have that much to do with this wedding or party—with you and Jean in charge—except to rent this tux, and, oh yeah, put that new ring on your finger." He kissed the platinum band she wore with her blue opal. "You realize what all this means?"

"I'm yours," she whispered against his mouth. "And you're mine," she told him.

"It's a life sentence." Cody drew her deeper into his arms, kissing her for long moments before he finally raised his head. The love in his eyes stole her breath away. But then, the feeling matched Willow's love for him. "Mrs. Jones," he said in a low, shaken tone.

Which sounded just right to Willow. She looked forward—for the rest of her life—to being Cody's forever angel.

* * * * *

THE WESTERN HEARTS COLLECTION!

COWBOYS. RANCHERS. RODEO REBELS.
Here are their charming love stories in one prized Collection:
51 emotional and heart-filled romances that capture the majesty
and rugged beauty of the American West!

Get 4 FREE REWARDS!

We'll send you 2 FREE Books plus 2 FREE Mystery Gifts.

FREE
Value Over
$20

Both the **Romance** and **Suspense** collections feature compelling novels written by many of today's bestselling authors.

YES! Please send me 2 FREE novels from the Essential Romance or Essential Suspense Collection and my 2 FREE gifts (gifts are worth about $10 retail). After receiving them, if I don't wish to receive any more books, I can return the shipping statement marked "cancel." If I don't cancel, I will receive 4 brand-new novels every month and be billed just $7.24 each in the U.S. or $7.49 each in Canada. That's a savings of up to 28% off the cover price. It's quite a bargain! Shipping and handling is just 50¢ per book in the U.S. and $1.25 per book in Canada.* I understand that accepting the 2 free books and gifts places me under no obligation to buy anything. I can always return a shipment and cancel at any time. The free books and gifts are mine to keep no matter what I decide.

Choose one: ☐ **Essential Romance**   ☐ **Essential Suspense**
                              (194/394 MDN GQ6M)   (191/391 MDN GQ6M)

Name (please print)

Address   Apt. #

City   State/Province   Zip/Postal Code

Email: Please check this box ☐ if you would like to receive newsletters and promotional emails from Harlequin Enterprises ULC and its affiliates. You can unsubscribe anytime.

Mail to the **Reader Service:**
IN U.S.A.: P.O. Box 1341, Buffalo, NY 14240-8531
IN CANADA: P.O. Box 603, Fort Erie, Ontario L2A 5X3

Want to try 2 free books from another series! Call 1-800-873-8635 or visit www.ReaderService.com.

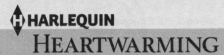
#355 MONTANA WEDDING
The Blackwell Sisters • by Cari Lynn Webb

Luck shines on Georgie Harrison-Blackwell when brand-new acquaintance Zach Evans suggests he be her pretend boyfriend for her sister's Christmas wedding. Once pretend begins to feel real, can Georgie and Zach learn to trust their hearts?

#356 A CHRISTMAS PROPOSAL
Texas Rebels • by Linda Warren

A week in his hometown sounds like a sentence for SWAT leader Bo Goodnight, given his ex Becky Tullous is still in Horseshoe. Could an unexpected second chance turn into the forever they never had?

#357 UNDER A CHRISTMAS MOON
Eclipse Ridge Ranch • by Mary Anne Wilson

Opposites attract for Libby Conner and Jake Bishop, showing them what a holiday romance can offer. Until a fiancé, a snowstorm and transforming a ranch get in their way!

#358 CHRISTMAS ON THE RANCH
Hearts of Big Sky • by Julianna Morris

Alaina Wright isn't interested in romance, but the tall Montana rancher she's met makes her wonder if she's up to the challenge of defeating Gideon Carmichael's bitter heart...and her own.

HWCNM1120

Visit
ReaderService.com
Today!

As a valued member of the Harlequin Reader Service, you'll find these benefits and more at ReaderService.com:

- Try 2 free books from any series
- Access risk-free special offers
- View your account history & manage payments
- Browse the latest Bonus Bucks catalog

Don't miss out!

If you want to stay up-to-date on the latest at the Harlequin Reader Service and enjoy more content, make sure you've signed up for our monthly News & Notes email newsletter. Sign up online at ReaderService.com or by calling Customer Service at 1-800-873-8635.

RS20